# HER HEART'S
# BARGAIN

## CHERYL HARPER

# MILLS & BOON

First Published in Great Britain 2019
by Mills & Boon, an imprint of HarperCollins*Publishers*
1 London Bridge Street, London, SE1 9GF

*Her Heart's Bargain* © 2018 Cheryl Harper

ISBN: 978-0-263-27218-5

0219

**MIX**
Paper from
responsible sources
**FSC˚ C007454**

This one's for my team, the friends who move closer instead of away when life takes a turn.

How lucky I am to have you!

# CHAPTER ONE

THE FIRST TIME a reporter called to ask for an official comment from Ranger Ash Kingfisher, the man in charge of the Otter Lake Ranger Station, Macy Gentry made the mistake of asking for more details. Most of the calls that came in to the station were easy to handle. Directions. Suggestions for hotels. Campground reservations. Questions about the best time to visit to see otters or bears or fall color. Sometimes there was an odd call that got misdirected from one of the state or national parks, but after four years, she'd learned to manage everything like clockwork.

Today, her foolproof system had hit a snag with one simple request for a quote from her boss. She'd stumbled; the reporter had pounced, demanding to know Ash's whereabouts, and she'd hung up the phone.

Since she took pride in her phone skills, that abrupt ending had been enough to rattle Macy.

Very rarely was she pushed to that extreme. Rudeness had no place at the visitor desk of the ranger station. Unfortunately, that rare snowflake had turned into an avalanche of similar calls.

"Sharks, the lot of 'em." As soon as there was one drop of blood in the water, she had a swarm on her hands. After more than an hour of juggling calls, Macy was feeling a bit bloodied and a whole lot frazzled. "What I need is a harpoon, scatter them sharks with one shot."

Irritated with her own overreaction to the problem, she muttered, "Get a grip, Macy. It's easier to turn the ringer off on the phone." The ranger station had protocols for every conceivable emergency.

"*Almost* every emergency." Macy flipped through the binder she'd insisted Ash put together before slapping it back in the labeled slot where it lived. He'd been exasperated by all her "just in case" scenarios. "Looks like I left one off the list—attack of the reporters."

Since she prided herself and intimidated those around her with extreme capability, losing control of the situation was not an option. Macy had a lot of work to do. The ranger station served as the administration building for all the law enforcement rangers and park guides responsible for the educational programs and public outreach at Otter Lake. In this building, everyone had an important job and they all answered to the head ranger, Ash Kingfisher.

Ash made his reports to the chief ranger in Knoxville, along with the fire chief and head rangers of the two other, smaller ranger stations at Awi on the north edge and Lena Prospect on the far southeastern line, but he was the man who kept Otter Lake operational, and she was his right hand. This circus was hampering her ability to mark things off her to-do list.

The man who might explain exactly why there was all this attention on the station was currently AWOL.

With great difficulty, Macy ignored the ringing desk phone to pick up her cell phone and glared hard at the screen. He should have answered her call for help by now.

"In this crazy ol' world, I got you, Ash Kingfisher. Don't you let me down," she muttered and then switched her glare to flashing lights on the ringing desk phone. The second line, the one that only rang when she was absent or too sick to function at an acceptable rate of speed, was lit up. "That devil's selling popsicles today because something has got to be freezing over." Macy took a deep breath and picked up the first line. "Otter Lake Ranger Station. How may I assist you today?" Macy hoped she was the only person picking up on the crack of strain.

"I'm headed in your direction. ETA ten minutes." Brett Hendrix's deep voice was pleasant but not the one she'd been hoping for. As the head of the rangers handling law enforcement at the Smoky Valley Nature Reserve, Brett would be adequate backup, even if she'd much prefer Ash for a situation like this.

Covering her disappointment took a second. "Thanks for the call, hon. I'll put out the welcome mat." Then she hung up. Decoding what it meant that Brett was coming to the rescue instead of Ash would take too much time and brainpower, so she picked up the other line as line one lit up again. "Otter Lake Ranger Station. How may I assist you today?"

"I'd like to speak to Ash Kingfisher. This is Bailey Garcia, from Channel Six News."

Bailey was using her professional reporter's voice, so Macy returned the gesture. "The head ranger is currently out of the office. I'm not sure when he will be returning. May I take a message?" Barely ten o'clock. She had to start closing down this circus, so she could get her day back on track. Where was an empty clown car when she needed it?

"I'll call back, but I was wondering if you might have a comment on the bombshell breaking from the capitol today?" The silence that followed was wide-open.

"I'll need a little more information than that," Macy said. She'd never been known for her ability to keep a secret, so maybe it was a good thing she was in the dark.

Macy Gentry had also never learned to avoid trouble. "What 'bombshell' are you referring to exactly?"

Without some direction, what could she say? That her boss hadn't come in to the station when he was supposed to, and he hadn't called to tell her why?

"Governor Duncan has called a press conference in response to an environmental impact study that shows the lodge the Callaways are pushing through will cause irreparable damage to The Aerie, the highest point in the Reserve." The expectant silence thrummed down the phone line.

"What does that have to do with Ash?" Macy asked. Why weren't the reporters flocking to the Callaways?

"Whit Callaway, Senior, is demanding to know who is responsible for releasing the report and for dragging the Callaways' political opponent into the fray." The pleasure in Bailey Garcia's voice told the real story. All this fuss was about a hot sound bite, ready to lead the nightly news. "His son has been gaining ground in the polls, giving Governor Duncan a serious run for his money. This report may damage those gains and whoever gave it to the governor has made a powerful enemy. Speculation has turned to the most vocal critic of the new lodge."

Since Ash had never learned to hold his tongue about things that mattered, he was the number one opponent to the lodge's construction.

It made sense.

Ash was as predictable as the sunset. His unexplained absence was enough to convince Macy that Ash was in the center of the storm. The fact that she was the last to know? Annoying as all get-out.

If Macy closed her eyes, she could see Bailey Garcia on the television screen, her perfect dark hair in a sleek bob. She smoothed one hand down her ponytail before snatching a pen off her desk.

"I have no comment. All official Reserve press communication is handled by the public affairs officers in Knoxville. If you'd like to leave a message for the head ranger, please don't hesitate to call back." Macy gently set the phone back in the receiver and took a deep breath.

Her cell phone showed no new texts, but the flash of light outside drew her attention to the tall windows that made up one side of the Otter Lake Ranger Station and Visitor Center. On normal days, a peaceful view of a nearly empty parking lot and the forest and mountains beyond was a pretty picture.

Now that view was blocked by a news van that hadn't been there ten minutes ago and what might grow into a full-blown paparazzi pack unless she acted quickly.

Gentrys didn't dither. Gentrys took control. Ash was out of the picture for a minute, but the district office in Knoxville might have answers. She waited for one of the lines to clear and hit the first speed-dial button.

"Smoky Valley Nature Reserve District Office. This is Kayla. How may I direct your call?" Kayla had been the third person to take over reception since Macy had landed the spot at the ranger station. She was probably facing the same barrage of calls Macy had. Her ability to pretend it was just another day explained why she'd outlasted the others.

"Hey, girl, it's Macy. My phone is ringing off the hook with reporters looking for comments from Ash. Is Winter around? If there's an official answer I'm supposed to be giving, I'd love to have it." Winter Kingfisher, Ash's sister, was the public information officer for the Reserve. If anyone had prepared a statement, Winter would have it ready to go.

Kayla answered in a low voice, "Winter isn't in the office. She was here, but she left in a hurry after I put a call through from Whit Callaway." The last two words were whispered.

Macy watched more news vans park in front of the door. "Have you seen Ash?"

Kayla cleared her throat. "Yeah, but he's been in with the chief ranger. My orders are to say nothing but politely. Maybe you can manage the same."

"Good advice. When Ash comes out, could you have him call me?" Macy asked.

"I'll try, but the atmosphere here is tense, you know?" Kayla answered. "The chief just stepped out to take a call from the Callaways, so Ash's meeting may be over soon, anyway."

"Thanks, Kayla." Macy ended the call and straightened as her phone immediately rang again. Reporter? Or Ash?

Macy picked up her phone to text Ash an update. Reporters at the front door. Where are you?

She chewed the tip of her fingernail as she waited. Texting was Ash's preferred mode of communication. Even in person, he spoke as few words as possible.

After what seemed like a lifetime, but must have been all of three seconds, Ash answered. Keep telling them: no comment. Brett is on the way. My orders are to avoid the press and the ranger station for now, but he's close.

Macy considered a few different answers but settled on encouraging. We can handle the reporters. This will blow over.

When he didn't immediately answer, Macy wished she'd erased the last line of the text before she'd hit Send.

Eventually, Ash answered. You can handle anything, Gentry, but I don't want you to have to do it alone.

Macy clasped a hand over her stomach as a weird twist settled there. Ash was confident in her ability as always. His concern for her was sweet, different from his normal stoic self.

Take your time in Knoxville. We'll talk when you get home. Satisfied that she hadn't crossed the line into warm and fuzzy, Macy put her phone down carefully.

Right. Brett's estimated time of arrival… Macy turned to check the oversize clock perched right behind her desk. Two minutes late. "That polecat should be here by now." The crowd outside had grown. Now the reporters had been joined by Sweetwater's mayor, two of the old guys who loitered in the barbershop on Saturday and Macy's landlord. They weren't marching, but the signs they were waving signaled their protest.

"Save Sweetwater jobs. More tourists equal more tax dollars equal more school spending. Callaway for Tennessee." Macy read the signs and had to admit they deserved extra points for preparation. The one with the equal signs and the dollar signs replacing every S was painted in neon orange. If four picketers had shown up this quickly after the story broke, how large could the crowd grow? The people milling around on the sidewalk appeared to be waiting for someone, but eventually, they would come inside.

Unless she locked the door.

Could she do that?

She *could* do it, but should she? Her finger hovered over the panic button Ash had insisted be installed the previous summer when one of the national park rangers had come under fire. If she pushed it, the doors locked and an emergency alert went out to all the law enforcement rangers. Macy had argued then that it was the rangers who needed better protection, not office managers, but today she was wondering if she was going to have to tell Ash he'd been right after all.

That panic button would remain unpushed until Macy drew her last breath. Ash couldn't be right. The man was right too often for her peace of mind as it was.

Then Brett Hendrix's SUV rolled in and it was almost as if she could hear the cavalry bugles playing in the distance. He was only a man, but Brett had the training, the badge and Ash's respect to back him up.

The way all the reporters immediately swarmed him, microphones out and cameras flashing, convinced Macy that no matter what was going on, Ash had made a couple of good decisions already.

Being scarce at this point was his best defense.

Macy stood and did her best to smooth any wrinkles out of her pants before straightening her navy blue Reserve shirt. Ash insisted every staff member wear the uniform and treat it with respect.

When the television cameras turned to her, she figured she'd better look the part.

As she opened the front door, Macy heard Brett say, "I have no new information on the status of the lodge project."

"But is the governor's insistence that there be an investigation a political maneuver?" a tall, thin man at the back of the pack shouted.

Brett held up both hands signaling he had no way of knowing. Macy was certain that was the only possible answer. How were they to know what the governor had intended by seizing this environmental impact study and taking a stand? Common sense said it was about causing trouble for his political opponent, but how much further would he go than stirring up the news media?

Macy had met the guy once. Richard Duncan had run

on a platform of "Tennessee First" and had taped one of his campaign commercials on Otter Lake. He'd been surrounded by an entourage at least four people deep. A hurried handshake was the best he could manage.

"Why isn't the Reserve's public information officer, Winter Kingfisher, here answering these questions?" Bailey Garcia shouted from her spot in the front row. "Surely, she'd have good information, Ranger Hendrix, being so close to all involved. She's employed by the Callaways, engaged to the governor's rival and the sister of Ash Kingfisher."

Brett propped his hands on his hips. "Great suggestion. As the Reserve's public outreach officer, Winter would be your best source. You can contact the district office in Knoxville for more details. She does not work in this office, so she isn't here for your questions."

Everyone was using their official voices today. The last time Macy had heard Brett speaking like that, he'd been lecturing his daughter about protecting her brother instead of running con games on him. Riley Hendrix had the sort of gumption Macy admired. Today with that stern tone, if Brett had rolled up to her campsite, she'd have said "yes, sir" and "no, sir" until he left, and then wondered later what had come over her. Authority came with the badge, but the voice helped.

"Where *is* the head ranger?" Bailey asked.

"He was called to the district office early this morning. I don't know when he will return, but—" Brett looked over his shoulder at Macy "—Ms. Gentry will take down your information so that Ranger Kingfisher can get back to each of you in due course."

Macy waved a pen and pad, as if she was desperate to be writing down names and numbers.

No one was satisfied with that answer.

Brett listened to the jumble of shouted questions for another minute before interjecting. "I have nothing further to add. You can stay here if you like, but we ask that you move to one side. The visitor center and offices are open for business." Instead of hanging around to watch them move, Brett turned and ushered Macy inside.

Their steps rang through the empty lobby as they walked back to her desk. Gleaming hardwood floors and the vaulted cathedral ceiling meant every step echoed.

Macy did her best not to flop into her chair, aware that she had an audience. She perched carefully and crammed a hundred questions into one raised eyebrow.

Brett made a solid wall between her and the reporters, his shoulders blocking the view. "They're still there, aren't they? That's scarier than dealing with an angry bear or finding a lost hiker." His stance was solid, unshakable, but his face showed his concern.

"Between you and me, what's really going on?" Macy asked.

"When we talked, Ash didn't know much, but the chief ranger demanded he report to the district office first thing. Everything else that I know, I've heard on the radio."

Brett tugged off his hat and tossed it on her desk before ruffling his hand through sweaty hair. The pressure had gotten to him. The first week of December was not a sweaty time in Sweetwater, not unless a man was wilting under stress.

Flirting with the panic button reminded Macy she had come dangerously close to cracking herself. Now she was ready to push Brett for answers. Macy crossed her arms over her chest, certain he'd pick up on her body language. "We've got plenty of time. Tell me everything."

Brett sighed. "The new lodge the Callaways are pushing to build? The one the chief ranger's been working on for more than a year with the Reserve planning office and Callaway Construction? Yeah, well…" Brett rolled his shoulders. "The environmental impact report on building the lodge up at The Aerie is about to hit the news cycle. Some anonymous tipster got a copy to the governor, and now he's making waves. He'll use whatever he can to knock Whit Callaway down in the polls before the election, even if we all know Richard Duncan is only interested in conservation as a sound bite."

The Aerie was the highest point in the park and provided habitat for several native Tennessee species. The Callaways had built a reputation as benevolent protectors of Tennessee's history, leaning heavily on the acres of land Whit Callaway's great-great-great grandfather had set aside for conservation. A report that outlined how their new moneymaking project would destroy a large piece of that would not be something they'd want falling into the hands of a political enemy.

And yet, it had, but how?

"That lodge is to be built on Callaway land, even if the land's been held in reserve for public use for five Callaway generations. What can the governor say or do about that?" Brett glanced over his shoulder. "It always comes back to money, doesn't it? Right now, the lodge is on hold until the Callaways decide what to do in the face of the results of the suddenly very publicized environmental impact study. If they move forward as is, the reputation they pride themselves on as generous protectors of Tennessee takes a hit. That's pretty much Whit Callaway's entire platform. 'Good for Tennessee.' If they stop the project completely, their future bank account will be impacted because that lodge will make money."

Nature reserve areas had been carved out of the extensive Callaway lands and were self-sustaining at this point, thanks to programs, grants and daily operations, but the Callaways directed the work at each reserve through the board of directors. The Smoky Valley Nature Reserve was the Callaway family's gift to the people of Tennessee, but they still held all the strings. The planned luxury lodge was a huge undertaking and would change the face of the Reserve near Otter Lake in any number of ways.

Where the rest of the Reserve's activities supported the Reserve itself, the lodge profits would be going to the Callaways. No one could mistake how important the lodge was to the family.

"Why all this interest in Ash? I mean, the project stalls, I guess, but he's got no connection to Callaway Construction or the governor."

"Ash has been the most vocal opponent of the building plans and their impact on the animals and their ecosystems. Even I could see how the public could think he's responsible for the report being leaked. He planned to present the findings at the next Reserve board meeting, but instead, it's out there in the world, blindsiding the Callaways."

Macy tipped her head back. "And neither Whit Callaway will be happy about that." Since they ran the board and the board made all the hiring and firing decisions in the Reserve, the situation could get tense quickly.

"It's so obviously a sabotage, making sure the biggest critic of the Callaways has a copy of the report that might point to greed, or at least a love of profit over preservation. I wouldn't be surprised if Ash had considered doing it," Brett said.

When she started to ask if he thought Ash was that devious, Brett answered, "I don't think he did. Not his way, even if he loves this place. Actually, all it would have taken to convince Ash *not* to do it is to imagine this news frenzy."

"Story's got a bit of a soap opera atmosphere. Wealthy family. Political rivals. Scandal." Macy frowned. No wonder reporters were making the trip to Sweetwater. Was this going to cause trouble for longer than a day?

Brett rubbed his forehead. "Not to mention the society wedding Winter and the Callaways have been planning. Marrying Winter, who's admired by everyone who knows her, was bound to be a big boost to Whit's credibility as a worthy candidate. If Winter goes through with it, there'll still be a rain cloud over her day now."

Macy hadn't even considered that. "Oh, boy."

Brett's rough laugh echoed loudly. "Yeah. That pretty much covers it. No matter what it does to Whit Callaway's election chances, this is going to leave a bruise. And if the Callaways decide to go there, Ash's job could be in danger. They have a lot of power with the board of directors."

"I wish I could talk to Ash," Macy said, "to be sure he knows we don't believe it's true."

"This morning when he called me and told me to get here ASAP so you'd have support, you were the most important thing on his mind. He'll be okay. We'll all work this out." Brett turned to check on the people out front. "He and I must have crossed paths on the road. I was in Knoxville with Leanne. She's thinking about going back to school and Christina insisted she didn't need to go alone for her meeting with the admissions people." He shook his head. "Yes, I took my ex-wife to meet with a college admissions counselor because my girlfriend insisted. Weirdest family in the world."

Macy patted his shoulder and smiled. "Probably not the entire world, but you, your adorable kids, your ex and your new love, who might as well be her sister… Well, weirdest in East Tennessee, at least, possibly the whole state. Hold your head up, kid." Teasing him was normal. After the crazy morning they'd had, it was nice to have some normal again.

Brett studied the floor and then he nodded. "I'll accept that, as long as we're solidly in the running for happiest, too."

Pleased to have something to think about other than the missing Ash and the potential fallout to the story, Macy tapped his cheek affectionately. "That lipstick on your handsome jaw should get you a big head start in that competition."

"You don't expect me to fall for that, do you?" Brett raised an eyebrow.

Macy didn't answer, only widened her grin. He didn't want to believe her, but he had his doubts.

"It's a good color for you, but it's better on Christina." She narrowed her eyes. "I'd wager a month's pay that's why you were late. You had to make a quick stop down at the campground for a good-morning kiss?"

Brett rubbed his jaw to eliminate the evidence. "Maybe." If this had been any other day, she would have hooted with excitement and given him so much grief over the blush staining his cheeks that Brett would have quit the ranger station like his hair was on fire.

As it was, she couldn't contain a wicked laugh. "That woman's got you good. I love it."

He rolled his shoulders. "I love it, too."

"Good thing. When the pictures come out in the newspaper tomorrow, everyone's gonna know you've been claimed." Macy's grin matched his until she noticed the way the reporters were watching their show through the large windows.

Anxious for the protection and control of her usual spot, Macy retreated to her chair. "You staying in the office today?"

Brett motioned over his shoulder. "As long as they're here, I'm here. I've called in an extra officer for campground patrols. There are no tours on the schedule today, so all the guides have the day off. Ash insisted you aren't to be left alone until this is settled."

"I can handle it." Macy straightened her shoulders. "I was thrown off when everything started, mainly because I had no idea what was happening. Now, though, I've got this. You don't have to babysit me."

"I've got my orders, Macy." Brett picked up his hat and stared out at the parking lot. "Ash wants me here, so here I'll stay. The two of us are more than equal to a few pushy reporters and Sweetwater's finest troublemakers."

Of course they were.

"Business goes on, even when scandal hits." She tapped the reports she'd intended to power through before the phone started ringing. "I've got plenty to do. The open house is less than two weeks away, and this place is not close to ready. When we show off the new education panels that Ash has been working so hard on, I want this whole building to shine. I want the parking lot to be filled to overflowing with our neighbors from Sweetwater. With no Ash bothering me to find things in clear sight on his desk, I should make record time." Except she and Ash were a team. Working without him wasn't easy.

"He'll get here as soon as he can. You know he loves this place." Brett pointed at the small office he used whenever he was in the ranger station. "I'll catch up on some paperwork. You call me if things escalate or you need help."

Macy saluted, but paused before digging into her most urgent task.

It had taken a long time to find the place that fit her like a perfectly tailored dress. In the end, she'd had to make it for herself, but she had it now. As work spaces went, hers ruled. Cramped offices formed a ring on three sides of the airy lobby which was filled with educational panels about the flora and fauna of the Smoky Valley Nature Reserve. Ruthlessly straightened and organized maps and pamphlets lined the wall across from her desk. Everything was in reach, which made it simple to keep the place running smoothly.

The boxes stacked in the corner had been annoying her for a week. Ever since she'd met a large snake in the small outbuilding used for storage, Macy refused to enter it. Ash had moved these boxes in for her recently because it was time to put out the holiday decorations.

After Ash's reports were done, she'd get on that. It would distract her from the strange tension in the air.

Ash Kingfisher was as much a part of the fabric of the ranger station as the chair she sat in, the view out the windows and the easy peace she felt when she walked into the lobby. Without him grumbling away at his desk, everything was slightly askew. His absence left a hole.

Her only option? "Get to work, Macy Elizabeth Gentry. There's no time for moodiness." She could hear the words in her grandmother's no-nonsense voice, so she straightened in her chair, set about clearing her missed calls and then compiling the visitor stats for Ash's review.

When he came back into the office, he was going to be impressed with what she'd pulled off. She would raise some stink over being initially left out of the loop, and then things would return to normal.

# CHAPTER TWO

ASH KINGFISHER HATED missing days at the ranger station. The amount of paperwork that shuffled across his desk was enough to drown any strong bureaucrat.

It wasn't what Ash had planned for or wanted. Ever since his first encounter with a ranger on the trail up to The Aerie with his grandfather, he'd dreamed of becoming a law enforcement ranger; getting paid to spend days out on the Reserve, the uniform, even the hat, all of it had seemed his perfect job. But he'd landed behind a desk when a mistake had robbed him of the full use of his leg. Was he good at his job? Yes. That didn't mean he loved the sound of pen scratching across paper as he signed an unending stack of reports.

After three days out of the office? He'd need a life preserver, an unlimited coffee supply and all the organizational ability of the best right hand ever, one Macy Gentry. Most days, she was all the help he needed to make it through.

Today, even *her* skills might not be enough.

This forced vacation reminded him that he missed seeing her every day. Macy was the bright ray of light that cut through his shadow. No matter what happened today, it would be better than the rest of the week because they'd be together.

His visit to see the chief ranger in Knoxville had been predictable. Frank talk, so many questions about who might have released the report if it hadn't been him, a tense phone conversation with Whit Callaway, Senior, followed by the chief ranger's orders to stay out of sight for a full week, answer zero phone calls and knocks on his door, and let Brett and Macy handle the Reserve's business. He hated it.

A full week? Seventy-eight hours was all Ash could manage. He needed his desk, his view of the forests and the comfortable sounds of Macy running the world outside his door. The park guides needed a new schedule. Brett was handling all the incident reports that landed on his desk, doing Ash's job. And Macy was forced to juggle all the tiny crises that hit every day in a busy place like Otter Lake.

Ash closed his eyes and tried to breathe in the peace of the Buckeye Cove along Wattie Run, one of the smaller creeks that flowed into Otter Lake. At this time of year, few animals were stirring in the cold hours before dawn, but the heart of the land was still beating. He tried to concentrate on his own heartbeat. If he was successful, it would drown out the chaos that had taken over his brain ever since he'd gotten an angry phone call from his boss Monday morning.

When the faintest pink of sunrise over the mountains stained his eyelids, he gave up. It wasn't that he was a big believer in meditation, but when times got hard, he knew he had to go to the water.

Very little of his father's Cherokee heritage had trickled down and stuck with him, but this was unshakable. His sister could tell stories and share their history easily because she'd soaked it in. For him, he had to be outdoors to truly feel alive. Today, the sound, the smell, the quiet of his spot beside the running water were necessary.

He needed to absorb enough silence and calm to make it through what would be a hard day.

Winter was his least favorite season, but attendance numbers dropped in the Reserve and there was more time in the day to get outside. To get away from the ringing phone and back to what made him love his job. The land he worked hard to protect. His father's favorite fishing hole. The place his grandmother's youngest brother had told him about the legend of Rabbit tricking Possum, leaving him with a tail without a single hair. The background of the old faded wedding photo his mother loved to show him. She'd been the original hippie, even if she'd come to Sweetwater and Otter Lake on a spring break trip from her Ivy League school forty years ago, about a decade too late to claim the name.

Donna Warren and Martin Kingfisher had met on a hike; as soon as she'd graduated, Donna had left New England behind to find her real home in Tennessee.

She and his father had married with a small group of friends who'd made the climb up to the overlook of Yanu Falls. From his spot, he could hear the falls rustling in the summertime. Right now, the water was more of a slide along a frozen surface down into the lake.

But that was okay. It was only for a season. In the spring, everything would change again.

He'd held on to that promise, that things would change again, for a long time.

Unfortunately, sometimes when the promise came true, things only got worse.

"Dark. Real dark, Kingfisher." Ash forced himself to stand, the ache in his leg worse than when he'd started out that morning. Sitting on cold rock could do that to a man. Eventually, he'd either have to give up his favorite hike, or he'd have to admit old age and bad decisions had caught up with him and find a place with a bench. "So it's going to be like that, is it? Nothing but rain clouds and thunder."

The hoot of an owl stopped him in his tracks. "Oh, fine. That's not creepy timing." If his grandmother had been near, she'd insist the owl was a messenger. Somehow, every omen had to do with death the way his enisi told it. "Could be good news, Ash. And messages are just messages, anyway."

Frustrated with himself, Ash limped back to the Reserve SUV sitting alone in the tiny parking lot. The push to get the Reserve's attendance numbers up hadn't taken off, and this latest catastrophe was going to be a distraction. To address either problem, he had to be hands-on.

As Ash slid into the driver's seat, he gripped the steering wheel. While his leg painfully adjusted to the change in circumstances and the heater warmed everything, Ash muttered, "Three good things."

That was Macy's influence. It wasn't that she was so bright and optimistic herself. She had no time for foolishness. Self-pity? Yeah, that would be enemy number one to his capable office manager.

He liked it like that, too. Without her...

He didn't want to imagine how dark life might get without her.

In the bad days right after the accident, where a friend's decision to climb the wrong spot in the park had gotten them both injured, Ash had struggled against that darkness. The threat of never being able to do what he loved, serving at Otter Lake as a ranger, had been real. Then he'd been moved to his spot in the new visitor center. Eventually, the Administrative Services director had sent young Macy Gentry to manage it and turn his world upside down, mainly by forcing light into dim corners.

They'd made each other miserable before they'd learned to work together.

*Come up with three good things.* That's what she muttered to herself every time someone snapped at her over the phone, or a vendor gave her the runaround, or when he made her mad enough to spit. Sometimes she said them out loud. Sunshine. A steady paycheck. Work that matters. She'd said it; Ash had felt it and he was grateful for the reminder.

Ash backed out of the parking spot. "Number one, your commute is perfect."

Driving in the park was something he enjoyed. Even in the winter, the old growth trees meant lots of shade and sun and the animals of the park were hardy. A little cold only slowed them down. As he turned into the parking lot of the ranger station, Ash hit the brakes hard at the sight of a shadow on the path leading up to the visitor center's overlook. Was it a black bear? The mild temps meant the bear might still be out foraging, but he faded into the trees before Ash could get his binoculars out.

*Black bears mean good luck.* His father had told him that the first time they'd run into one on a hike up Yanu. Ash had never found anyone else who said so, but his father either believed or wanted him to, so Ash went with it. Good luck. He needed it.

And Macy's car was already parked outside. "That's got to be three."

She was usually the first in; he was the last out, only because he insisted she go home ahead of him. He and his rangers and support staff served the visitors to Otter Lake and Smoky Valley Nature Reserve. They were responsible for safety and law enforcement in the park, all education and conservation efforts, and welcoming visitors. If school groups needed guides or researchers needed support or hikers got lost or campers got rowdy or bills needed to be paid, it all ended up on his desk.

Macy made sure all of that fell into an orderly formation. Spending all day with her annoyed was going to test his patience.

Following orders outlined by his boss, the chief ranger, was always important, but it was especially a priority now that he owed his career to Leland Hall. Climbing without the proper safety equipment as a Reserve law enforcement ranger had been dumb beyond belief. Being fired would have made perfect sense. Instead, Leland Hall had recommended him for the new head ranger position. Ash's hardline position on safety procedures was now well known to everyone who worked for him. No one would make the same mistakes he had, not while he was watching over the rangers at Otter Lake. He'd been lucky Chief Ranger Hall had believed in his ability to do more. His boss's questioning about the leaked environmental impact report had been a hard blow. Being ordered away from his post was worse.

"Doesn't matter. Only way out is through." Ash heard his grim tone. He knew that people were saying he'd leaked the report. That he was being disloyal to his sister, to the town and what the lodge might mean for the local economy. "Never met bad news he didn't like." He'd gotten a reputation as Mr. Doom because he was forced to point out problems with the lodge project.

But he did all that upfront, no sneaking around.

The mayor and town council of Sweetwater and other places that depended on the Reserve for tourism wanted the lodge. They could see money coming in, and the guy who'd insisted it was a bad deal for the Reserve itself was never going to be popular.

It made sense that folks suspected he'd stirred up the governor's office.

Ash only wished he'd thought of it. Construction was scheduled to begin in less than a month. All this media frenzy stirred up by the governor might mean nothing, but if it delayed the lodge until he could come up with a permanent solution, it would all be worth the trouble. The architect's plans were going to be confirmed at the next board meeting. His plan had been to present the report he'd commissioned on the impact of building at The Aerie at the same time.

Someone had beaten him to the punch, though.

And while he'd been trying to sleep last night, it had hit him that his sister would be tangled up in the same mess for however long it lasted. What if her job was in danger because of her connection to him? Worse. What if Whit Callaway was stupid enough to blow up their engagement over this lodge report?

After the chief ranger had suggested getting solid support for his position against building at The Aerie, he'd commissioned the report, but he'd talked to Winter about the findings. Showing it to her had changed her middle-of-the-road attitude to firm opposition to construction of the lodge. It could have worked for the board of directors as well.

Would she and Callaway be able to weather this trouble and the suspicion that Ash was sabotaging Whit's political career?

He loved his little sister. This better not hurt her.

The fact that he hadn't heard from her since the news broke made it impossible to pretend he might ever fall asleep again, leaving him plenty of time to make an early morning visit to Buckeye Cove.

"Silver linings to the storm clouds." Ash chose a spot

in the empty parking lot of the ranger station and slowly slid out of the SUV. The lack of a crowd out front was a relief. Leland had been right; with no Ash on hand, the reporters had moved on to other angles for their stories.

What would happen when word got around that he was back at his desk?

Maybe he should have taken the whole week as the chief ranger had ordered.

"I'm here now. Might as well clear my desk." If the reporters or angry Sweetwater citizens started gathering, he could disappear.

Ash grabbed the hat he only wore on official visits and when he was forced to. Safety procedures were life. Uniforms inspired respect and gave his staff a professional image. But the hat? Carrying the thing was good enough, even if it was time for a haircut.

Letting his own standards slip would never do, no matter how off track his whole week had been.

As soon as he stepped inside the open space of the lobby, some of his anxiety melted. He could smell coffee. Macy was nearby. Every inch of the visitor center was in order. His office manager had been busy. Natural greenery framed the line of windows, while a giant wreath with white lights had been hung on the wall behind her desk. The holidays at the ranger station were usually low-key, but this year, Macy had badgered him into hosting an open house. They had new displays. Attendance numbers needed a boost. Everything she'd said made sense.

But now he was the center of a controversy. The last thing he wanted was to issue an invitation for people to stop and stare. Should he reconsider the open house?

Worse, would it turn into a picket line instead of a party?

The new winter educational displays were impressive.

Losing the head education ranger was a blow he'd have to focus on soon. The other park rangers responsible for teaching programs and guiding visitors had picked up the extra work, but someone needed to direct their activities, someone who could expand the Reserve's reach.

He'd move finding that person to the top of the list.

Right after he soothed Macy, figured out how to clear the suspicion that he'd torpedoed the lodge project and found out whether his sister was brokenhearted or not, he'd finish applying for approval to hire a new education director.

Why was he so tired all of a sudden?

"Well, now, I wondered when I might see you again," Macy drawled as she strolled over to block the pathway to his office. That was how she got him to stop: a full-blown barrier. If they were boxers in a ring, she'd be squared up and ready to fight.

Getting over that hurdle was job number one.

He should have spent more time figuring out what to say.

"Yeah, haven't seen you in some time." Ash ran a hand down his nape and fought back a wince as her eyebrows shot up. Not the way to go.

"You think you can make jokes, Ash Kingfisher?" Macy wildly shook her head. "That's just another sign the world is off-kilter. Out. Of. Control. You don't make jokes. You grunt. Sometimes you complain. Other times, you do thoughtful things that keep me from seriously considering doctoring your coffee in a bad way. But now, details. I want them."

"Fine. Leland called me to Knoxville, where he and the Callaways questioned me about the environmental impact study I commissioned on the building plans at

The Aerie. As I hope you've guessed, I had no information to give them. This isn't me, but convincing anyone in Knoxville of that is going to take some effort. Leland told me to lay low all week, avoid the press and the staff of the Reserve, but I couldn't." The urge to tell her he'd missed her smile even more than he'd missed his desk or Otter Lake was strong, but he fought it back. To her, he was just the boss and not…anything else.

He dodged her to head straight for the coffeemaker, grateful his bum leg made it possible. His mug was sitting in front. Like she'd expected him. He filled the fish-shaped mug and covered the Don't Bait Me on the side with both hands as he took the first sip. When he opened his eyes, Macy was propping one shoulder against the door frame, doing her best impression of a patient woman. Not a hair was out of place, but the temperature in the air suggested he was pressing his luck. "The fact that I requested the study, Winter's engaged to a Callaway, the construction company is owned by a Callaway, the Reserve is involved… I'm right in the center of all the speculation and it makes sense to anyone who doesn't know me." He took another long drink of the coffee, acknowledged his burned taste buds and enjoyed the slow roll of caffeine into his system. "Was it terrible here?"

Macy tilted her head to the side. "Nothing I couldn't handle. Would have been nice if I'd had a warning."

That wasn't what Brett told him when he'd called for status reports.

"Yeah, me, too." Their eyes met. She understood him. Neither of them had been prepared.

He should have called her, but that had seemed impossible. With Brett, he could demand facts and make yes-and-no decisions accordingly.

For Macy, he'd want to charge in to the rescue.

Macy took his mug and topped it off. "Let this one cool down first."

This was the reason things weren't quite as simple with Macy. In a hundred different ways, they were more than coworkers. She looked out for him.

He would do the same for her, but he never tried to give his feelings for Macy a name. That could be scary.

"You know I was sure you could handle whatever came up here, right?" Ash didn't meet her stare because he was leaving his comfort zone quickly. Feelings and saying them out loud? Not his MO.

"I did need help." Macy retreated to the doorway. "On the first day. Since then, the calls have died down a bit. A few picketers showed up yesterday, but this cold weather is probably slowing them down. If word gets out that you're back, that will change. What do you want me to say?"

*Lie for me. Tell them I'm not here.*

She would do it, too, because Macy supported the Otter Lake Ranger Station fully.

But asking her to do that would do little to restore his own balance, so Ash didn't.

Macy's exaggerated eye roll would have been insubordination on any other day with any other employee. Today, it made him laugh. "So much respect."

Macy marched over to his desk and thumped her hand on a towering stack of white paper. "Here's my respect. Perfect paperwork every time. Stacked in order of priority. Just like every time." She made the signing motion. "Waiting on you to finish."

She left off the *every time*, but it was present in the room.

"Where are the newspapers?" Ash had never expected to become so set in his ways, but the idea of diving straight into spreadsheets without first meandering his way through the day's headlines further upset his queasy stomach. He sipped his coffee, hoping it would drown the acid of worry.

"On my desk." She planted her feet firmly. "You don't want to see them. Neither does Brett, but I have plans to make sure he gets a good look at a certain photo, lipstick smear in full color, in the *Sweetwater Sentinel*." The gleam in her eyes suggested they might all have a real laugh about something. The warning about the rest of the papers? Not good.

"You better show them to me." He stared hard at the red light on his phone. "I might have messages waiting about them."

Macy nodded once and then marched away. Normally, the noises she made as she moved in the lobby were soothing background sounds. Today each step clicked like hands on a clock.

Or a ticking time bomb.

Instead of plopping the newspapers down and then sailing away, like she would usually do, Macy eased them down and lingered. There was no other word for her watchful waiting.

"Don't hover." Ash sipped his coffee and then carefully stared at her until she held up both hands in surrender.

"I'll be outside if you need me." Macy paused in the doorway, her long blond ponytail swinging to punctuate her irritation. "You never did tell me what you want me to do with callers who ask for you. I'll tell them you aren't here. Give you some time to catch up." Satisfied with her own answer, she turned to go.

"Put them through to me. I'll handle it, Macy." Ash waited for her to meet his stare and nod. He still didn't fully trust her to do as he'd asked, mainly because she was almost always certain she had a better answer, but he'd done the right thing.

It was also the hard thing, but that seemed to be the case more and more.

On top of the stack of newspapers was a shot of Ranger Brett Hendrix standing out in front of the visitor center. He seemed to have full control of the situation. Macy had his back, her pen ready. The two of them were a credit to the Reserve.

Ash slipped on a pair of reading glasses he kept in his desk to study the fine print.

"Lots of questions. No answers. So, basically the same as every other news outlet." Satisfied he'd gotten the main idea, he moved to turn to the next page and caught a red smear on Brett's cheek. Lipstick. On his face. In a photo on the front page.

No wonder Macy was delighted. She'd be back in soon to reclaim her prize.

Brett Hendrix was the kind of employee every boss would be lucky to find. He was dedicated to his job. Smart. Followed procedure without complaint and served with the highest standards.

After a rocky period where family stress caused some distraction for him, he'd settled into the job and performed at the highest level. The guy made no mistakes.

This photo would drive him nuts.

Ash smiled as he set the newspaper down on top of the documents Macy was antsy to have reviewed and signed. When she asked, he'd tell her that the news was causing the delay. Picturing her death glare made him smile again.

Things could not be that bad. Life at the Otter Lake Ranger Station was close to all right that morning.

Then he opened the next paper, saw the governor's angry face, and his own official photograph from the website for the Reserve. It wasn't a mug shot, but it could almost pass as one. What made no sense was why it was there. Ash quickly scanned the content of the article around his photo. The only reference to him was completely true. He was the ranger in charge of the Otter Lake area. So what?

The project had enjoyed almost zero support on the ground here at the Reserve. Even without data and traffic projections, the effect on the habitat of The Aerie from construction alone had raised so many alarms. His objections were on record in the form of easily requested memos and reports, but it was almost like someone was setting him up to take the blame for this covert maneuver. He'd stated his objections publicly. How dumb would he have to be not to understand everyone would focus on him if he'd actually decided to leak the report? Even Ash could understand why he'd be the primary suspect.

If he never objected, everyone would assume he was the anonymous source who'd leaked the report to the governor. He checked for the journalist's name on the story and turned to the computer to find a phone number.

Then he flipped to the next paper. Nothing. The story didn't make the cut. "Finally. Some luck."

When he reviewed his search results for the reporter's contact info, Ash clicked the website link for the article and another photo of himself loaded. This time he was leaving the district office. "And I look like fifty miles of bad road."

His uniform was wrinkled. His hat was missing. And his hair clearly exceeded the Reserve's standards. Besides that, it might as well have been combed with a weed whacker.

Ash closed his eyes, but he could still see his own mess. "Why hasn't the chief ranger called to rain his displeasure down? He told me to lay low and I did, but I'm still all over the front page and looking as if I slept in my uniform." Silence from Knoxville's district office was not a good sign.

"He called. I took a message." Macy slowly reached over to pick up the Sweetwater paper. "You okay, boss?"

"I can tell things are serious when you call me 'boss.' Do I look that fragile?" Ash asked as he scrubbed his hand through his hair. From most of his staff, "boss" was an endearment. She meant it that way, too, but he preferred his name on her lips.

He didn't really want anything putting more space between them, but the reminder of who they were, boss and important right hand, might be a gift.

When he realized he was still wearing the reading glasses, he yanked them off and tossed them in a desk drawer. He couldn't do anything about the gray hair spreading at his temple.

"That's what happened to your hair before they took the picture." Macy leaned closer, the scent of magnolia and soap an easy reminder of better times. "And you don't have to hide the glasses. They make you look... distinguished."

"Another word for old. *Distinguished*." Almost a decade older than Macy. The word twisted on his tongue. "Fits me today. These last few days have aged me at least ten years."

"Anything I can do?" Macy asked brightly. He liked her energy, but today, she was too young, too healthy and strong. Compared to her, he felt brittle. Too little sleep. Too much time cooped up inside his small cabin with his own thoughts. A combination that was bad for him.

Ash braced his elbows on the desk and considered asking her advice on what to do to clear his name. Unless he convinced the Callaways and the chief ranger he'd had nothing to do with leaking that report, his job might be gone. His plan had made sense: get numbers, the data to show the impact of the construction and operation of the new lodge in black and white. Take the emotion out of the equation, all his family's history. That had been his only goal. The Callaways had set aside this land and hired him to do the job of preserving. Ash had only been doing what he'd been asked to do, to request the study on the environmental impact.

But unless someone else came forward, who would believe his claims of innocence?

Macy might be able to figure out how to spin this story, so everything turned out the way it was supposed to. She did that daily with small problems. Could she help with this one?

"Don't know what I'd do without you manning your post, Macy." He'd meant it as nothing but a compliment. The way her face fell made him think he'd missed the mark, but she immediately straightened her shoulders and nodded. "I'll be just outside if you need me."

She disappeared a second before he blurted out something he would regret. What could he say?

*I missed you.*

A few other things came to mind, but that was what he wanted to say. Instead, he buried his head in the reports on his desk.

Visitation numbers were down.

Spending was flat.

Revenue coming in from the education programs and even what had been reported from the campground and marina…all lower than normal, even for December.

Dutifully, he scribbled his name, but it was difficult to continue. After hours of spreadsheets and incident reports filed by the law enforcement rangers over the weekend and So. Many. Emails. Ash leaned back in his chair and stared up at the water spot on the ceiling.

Primer and paint would fix that.

Did they have the budget? He covered his eyes, so weary.

"I'm off to grab some lunch. Want me to lock the front door?" Macy stood in the doorway, half in, half out. Her hesitation was unusual.

"We're open regular hours today. I'll cover the phones and the front." And count the minutes until she got back.

"Should I send Brett for backup?" Macy asked.

Ash waved her off. "You've been stuck here all week. Get out. The paperwork fairy will leave you a gift on your desk."

Instead of laughing or glaring or lecturing or any other Macy thing, she just…left. Silently.

At this point, he had a few choices to make.

He should call his sister. Winter was pretty close to the center of this mess as well and she had as much, if not more, to lose.

Would her engagement survive the storm? Would she blame Ash if Whit Callaway called off the wedding? This lodge was the Callaway family's current cause, an expansion on the Reserve after five generations of conservation.

It would make them a lot of money.

Politicians always required a lot of money.

Another suspect might be all he needed to settle the Callaway family down. All he had to do was think.

The water spot resembled a standard poodle. Further study turned up no other ideas for the report's leaker.

"Well, there's me." Frustrated that he was the only logical suspect, Ash folded the newspapers and tossed them into the trash can. He heard an imaginary Macy bark "Recycle!" in his ear so he pulled them out and dropped them on top of the leaning pile behind his chair. "Since I know I didn't leak this report, there has to be someone else."

Fatigued, yet ready for a project he could complete quickly, Ash picked up his glasses and settled in to read Macy's outline of events for the coming open house. Not because he was concerned she'd forgotten anything, but just because it was nice to live in her organized world. "I should have asked for pie."

# CHAPTER THREE

GETTING OUT OF the visitor center had seemed like a good idea until Macy had to decide where to go. Most days, she spent her lunch hour at her desk. The only difference between a lunch hour and a regular hour was the addition of a turkey sandwich and the fruit of the day.

After three days cooped up and Ash's return—which should have made everything right, but instead filled the air with a new kind of tension—Macy had to do something different. The urge to change things up was getting stronger, but she wasn't sure where to start. Escape, temporary though it was, was a first step.

"A beautiful day for eating at the campground diner. No phones. No worrying over Ash." For December, it *was* beautiful weather. Sunny. Warm enough to forget that Christmas was lurking somewhere in the near distance.

Although spending the holiday alone meant it was pretty much like any other day.

Except there was no work. No ranger station.

No distraction.

No Ash.

"But it gives you plenty of time to catch up on all your projects, Macy Elizabeth. Free time is a luxury you better appreciate." Even her grandmother would have taken off Christmas Day. All the chores could wait. Since she was the last of her particular branch of Gentrys and holidays could be lonely, Macy had already decided she'd spend the holiday hiking Yanu Falls. Getting outside of her apartment would be required.

Her inability to name any projects she was dying to finish was something she needed to think about. She'd moved to Sweetwater when Administrative Services had offered her a permanent position running the visitor information desk at the Otter Lake Ranger Station. During her first year with the Smoky Valley Nature Reserve, she'd bounced around locations, doing a wide variety of temporary assignments. The job she had now, managing the visitor center and administration support, fit her best. Even the months she'd spent in the district office in Knoxville had been less satisfying, although some people would think the ranger station was a step down.

The minute she'd signed a lease on a one-bedroom apartment in town, Macy knew she'd found her home.

Friends were easy enough to claim in the small town. Odella at the coffee shop remembered how she ordered her coffee. She and Astrid, the town's librarian, had spent many a Friday night at The Branch bemoaning the town's lack of night life.

And then there was Ash, the man who…

Approved her timesheets.

Looked like he wanted to pat her on the head now and then.

Needed her.

*Enough wasting time, Macy.*

That familiar voice in her head belonged to her no-nonsense grandmother. Gran had been easy enough for Macy to love, but the whole town of Myrtle Bend, Georgia, and the three cousins Macy claimed there had always trembled when she drove down Main Street.

Gran had been fierce. Tough. Some days, Macy had to remind herself that fierce made people uncomfortable.

As long as she'd remembered that, that it was easier to get along than follow in Gran's tradition, making Sweetwater home had been easy enough.

Still, she'd be fighting that bossy voice in her head until she died.

"Lunch is an hour, Macy. Quit wasting precious seconds," she muttered to herself, a bad habit she wasn't even trying to break.

After days alone at work and at home, Macy was ready to make conversation. The campground diner would have food *and* people, so it was an easy choice.

As Macy pulled into the deserted parking lot, she worried the diner was somehow closed for business that day. Then she realized if anyone should know the schedule for the Otter Lake Campground convenience store-slash-marina-slash-diner, it would be her. She could recite the hours with a second's notice, both winter and summer.

Normally, at least one or two cars would be parked in front of the glass doors, even in winter.

"Business must be slower than usual." Macy slid out of the car and marched inside. "I should do this more often." For some reason, she'd always imagined a wild lunch rush, filled with loud conversations and not enough time.

When Christina Braswell turned to greet her, Macy was relieved. They didn't know each other well, but Christina was a familiar face, and they had a built-in topic of easy conversation: Christina's boyfriend, Ranger Brett Hendrix. "I didn't expect to see you here," Macy said.

"Yeah, I usually handle the breakfast shift, but Luisa asked me to stay later this week because she's on vacation. If she'd known how few people would be through here, she might have shut the place down." Christina held her arms wide. "Pick a spot. Any spot. I suggest the large booth by the window. I can stretch out my legs."

Did that mean she was joining Macy? Macy had only planned to order something to go. Ash was no good with the phones and if a reporter came in...

*Do something different, Macy. He's a grown man, not a child.* Ash Kingfisher would not appreciate her rushing back because she was afraid he couldn't handle being left alone.

"Come on. This once, have a lunch here. At a table. With refilled drinks and everything." Christina folded her hands beneath her chin. "Please. It's so slow. I'm begging."

Macy laughed. "Okay. I'll take the best seat in the house and your finest club sandwich, all the fries you have and a big glass of tea. Might as well do this right." Even out-of-towner Macy had been warned about wild Christina Braswell. Apparently, the people of Sweetwater had long memories, because all the stories she'd heard featured a teenage girl out of control. Granted, Macy's grandmother would have rained down fire if she'd ever been caught stealing. People changed. Macy had seen nothing but positive things from Christina, and the way she clapped her hands in delight when Macy slid into the booth was just charming.

Brett Hendrix was one of the best guys she knew. All signs pointed to people being dead wrong about Christina.

*Never let people tell you what you can see with your own eyes, Macy.* Her grandmother's impatience for all types of foolishness meant she never fell for stupid gossip.

"Friendly company." Christina pointed at her. "I knew I liked you. Monroe, put the cookie dough away. We've got a lunch to make." She turned around to slip an order through the window to the kitchen and then banged around making Macy's drink.

"The kid's been testing cookie recipes for your open house. He mans the grill well enough, but he was born to bake."

"I only asked for drinks. Tea and hot chocolate." When she'd finagled a yes out of Ash for the open house and managed to get the chief ranger's approval, Macy hadn't wanted to push the cost or overdo on the details.

"You *ordered* drinks as I recall," Christina answered. "If we were busy, Luisa would have never offered to do cookies, too, but we aren't and Monroe makes a mean chocolate chip."

Christina set a glass on the table as Macy's phone lit up with a text. It said, Pecan pie. Please.

She shook her head. The man could issue an order using a meager two words in a text. That *please* had been a tacked-on afterthought.

It was a sign of growth.

Macy sighed. "And make sure I leave here with at least one slice of pecan pie." It was a good thing she knew her boss so well. Ash was having a hard day. Things were weird at work and between them, but he could still count on her. Pie always helped.

He depended on her to understand that. "No problem. Brett never delivers bad news without a slice of pie in hand. Plenty of news lately, and it does seem kinda bad." Christina hurried behind the counter to box up the pie. She brought a white to-go bag and two beautiful sandwiches to Macy. "I guess I was waiting to have lunch today for a good reason."

When they'd doctored the fries with ketchup and had

both taken satisfying bites, they turned to stare out over the calm water of Otter Lake.

"It's nice to be slow sometimes. I like a chance to enjoy this view." Christina sipped her water and stretched slowly. "I like sitting down even more."

"I could not do what you do." Macy shook her head. Life at the ranger station was about silence and peace, broken only by the occasional visitor and the chance to tell them all about the reserve she loved. Sometimes school groups came in and the racket nearly blew the ceiling off, but there was something about the enthusiasm of kids that made it bearable. Loud, pushy adults set Macy's teeth on edge. "Your job is hard. Remembering who ordered what. Juggling plates and chairs and all the coming and going. Being nice to people for all that *time*."

"I am a wonder, it's true." Christina grinned. As she chewed, she said, "Pretty sure I used to be the world's worst waitress, though."

"What changed?" Macy asked before she took another bite. Seriously. Why didn't she do this more? It was a sandwich, nothing special, but it tasted better than any meal she'd had in… She couldn't even remember. Had to be the atmosphere.

"Well…" Christina wiped her mouth. "Couple things changed. I needed to keep the job." She held up a finger. "Very important discovery. Then, I realized how little it takes to make people happy. Remembering an order or calling someone by name or relaying a tidbit of a story. That's it. They're convinced I'm awesome, even if I forget they asked for mayo on the side."

Macy nodded. "Doesn't hurt that a handsome man comes through at least once a day to kiss you, either." She grinned. "Right?"

"It has certainly added to my current job satisfaction. Life is weird." Christina sighed before attacking her lunch again.

Macy laughed, having thought the same thing for most of the morning. She and Christina ate in silence. Every now and then, a slow ripple in the water sent a bright flash across the table in reflection. "This is nice. I'd be satisfied here, too."

"Your view at the station's pretty good. Green trees. Enough handsome ranger action to keep the blood perking. We're lucky to be surrounded by beauty." Christina balled her napkin up and stretched back with a sigh as she extended her legs. "Brett says some of the chaos has died down."

"Yeah, Ash is back to work. I wonder if the calm will hold when word gets out." Macy shrugged. "I'll keep an eye out if those reporters come back around."

Christina fiddled with her straw wrapper. "The way gossip spreads around here, there may be a news caravan already headed your way. It's all the locals will talk about lately. Especially whether Ash Kingfisher is responsible for delaying the lodge project that everyone's hoping will bring more people and therefore more dollars to the area. The crowds through here have disappeared. Only the diehards like Woody, Janet and Regina have been coming in for breakfast. Tourists?" She shrugged. "Not enough to speak of right now. According to Woody, there's a lot of pot stirring in town, calling for locals to boycott the whole Reserve, including the campground, until Ash admits he's behind this leaked report. The Callaways will replace him, get the lodge back on schedule, and in will pour the jobs. Brett says when the number of visitors drop and the revenues drop, the district office will want to know why. If all of Sweetwater is pointing at Ash, it could mean trouble." She glanced around the restaurant. "See how all the talk in town is working out here?"

Macy leaned against the booth and considered what Christina was saying and what she meant. "I'm not surprised. People holding protest signs is something I've never seen in Sweetwater before, but they showed up earlier this week out at the ranger station. They don't know him like I do."

Macy returned to studying the golden ripples of Otter Lake. The only thing she was certain of was that Ash Kingfisher had nothing to do with the current drama.

Was she wrong?

"The whole town depends on the tourists the Reserve brings in. The lodge will bring in even more. It makes sense that people are concerned. The mission matters less than the money," Christina said softly. "They want somebody to be at fault, so they can get rid of 'em and convince themselves everything's perfect in their small town. I've seen it before." In the sunlight, Christina was pretty, gorgeous even, but her serious eyes worried Macy. Even with Brett's support for Ash, it seemed Christina had her doubts.

"He didn't do it. Ash has been vocal about his objections to this lodge all along, mainly because of the habitat it will destroy. To build up on The Aerie? It makes no sense. New road. A bridge over the valley, plus the clearing in one of the oldest areas of the Reserve. He was doing his job to object. Anyone who thinks he'd play politics to get what he wanted is wrong." Macy leaned forward. "Is that what you're thinking?" Storming out was a possibility, but Macy's excellent lunch was slowing her down.

Christina snorted. "Me? No way. Brett would say the same in front of a firing squad. He trusts Ash and I trust him. The rest of Sweetwater, though? Man, you would not believe the things I've heard from the morning crowd. Gossip starts out simple enough, but it doesn't take long to get ugly. Believe me, I've studied it for a long time. Got the first complaint about me for the month for setting someone straight about Ash."

"It's a good thing Ash doesn't care about ridiculous gossip like that." Macy dug around in her purse for cash. She needed to get back to work.

"Sure." Christina rolled her eyes. "Brett would be having a crisis if anyone said the same of him, but Ash... Well, he's kind of a mystery, anyway. Doubt he's even heard it, lucky guy."

Macy paused. "What does that mean?"

Christina wrinkled her nose. "Hermit. That was the word I heard someone use. Do those even exist anymore? Must be nice to not have to care about what people say because you don't have to *hear* it, you know?"

Annoyed at first, Macy forced herself to settle and take in the scenery.

"So...what? That convinces people he's guilty? They don't know him." If they did, they'd brush the story off like tabloid trash.

"Listen, girl, if there's anyone in this town who'll step up beside you to protest the way people jump to judgy conclusions, it's me." Christina pointed at her face. "Doesn't change the fact that they can't be talked out of what they think. They have to *see* it." She leaned forward. "They need to see *him* more. I told Brett that, but he laughed like he does when his son tells knock-knock jokes. That's what's changing people's minds about me and about his wild, bad ex-wife, Leanne. They see us working hard, raising good kids. It's hard to believe a story when the evidence right in front of your face tells you something different."

"How? How would we even show Sweetwater a different side of Ash?" Macy crossed her arms over her chest. "He works hard at the Reserve. Long hours."

"Right. And that's all. The last big splash Ash made was when he fell climbing the cliff below Yanu Falls." She shivered. "Why would anyone want to climb up it? When we were in high school, I went out there with Travis Riggs after the Reserve had closed for the night, and he told a ghost story I've never forgotten. How many other girls did that move work on?" Christina shook her head. "Not important. It's too bad Sam Blackburn took that job in Colorado. That guy could say Ash was better than Tennessee whiskey and people would believe the golden boy. Without him, that leaves… Brett. You, I guess." She wrinkled her nose. It wasn't an impressive number of people.

"Doesn't matter. He will never go for… What would you even call that? A publicity makeover? He's innocent. This will all work out. It has to." Ash hated the unnecessary mess and noise of most people.

Unless it had to do with introducing them to the natural wonders of the Smoky Valley Nature Reserve.

"I hope you're right and it happens fast. This place needs Sweetwater showing up here and ordering the usual. Brett respects Ash more than anyone else he knows. He doesn't want to lose the best boss he's ever had."

Macy straightened in her seat. "You think Ash could lose his job, too?" No way. There was no way the Reserve would let silly things like unsubstantiated rumors lead to firing a man who served like Ash did. "Surely this will blow over. The news is dying down already."

Brett had mentioned the possibility that Ash's job could be in danger, but it made no sense to Macy. If the Callaways never came to their senses, surely the law would. Ash had done nothing wrong.

"No idea. To be clear, I do not understand how politics and power work because they've never been a part of my circle, but I know what I hear. It's like they're trying to make him the face of this." Christina frowned. "It seems to me that might be a bad sign."

"Yeah." And if Ash left the Otter Lake Ranger Station, what would happen to the spot she'd made for herself? Technically, she was part of an administrative pool that served all of the Smoky Valley Nature Reserve's different areas. Ash wasn't her boss per se, but he was the person in charge of the ranger station. Until he wasn't.

They could leave her there and a new ranger would take over or they could reassign her.

But it wasn't about the paycheck.

What would she do without Ash?

They had worked together for years. In the early days, she'd annoyed more rangers than she liked by insisting she knew better. With Ash, they could butt heads but never go too far. She'd learned to trust the guy implicitly.

That put him at the top of a short list. Macy didn't need much to get by, just a good job and a safe place to sleep at night.

And Ash.

Christina tapped the bag. "Pie's on me." She bent forward. "I believe you, hon, you do know Ash Kingfisher as well as anyone. Because you work for him." Christina raised an eyebrow.

Macy frowned as she deciphered what the last bit meant. "Yes. I work for him."

Christina made the "go on" motion with both hands. "Okay. I wondered if there was something else." She wagged her eyebrows. "Guy his age and general handsomeness... Seems like he'd have a special woman in his life. Does he?" The way she drew out the words made Macy think of a curious cat, one tail flip the only sign it was intent on prey.

"Huh?"

"You two... Just coworkers?" Christina tipped her head to the side. "Because whoever he dates could have some serious ability to revamp his image. If that's you, drag him out of his cave. Go to dinner. Have breakfast here. Easy. People see him around, they start to think they know him. If it's not you, we could find him one." She scooped up the empty dishes from their table. "Know anybody important? Maybe a woman who could help him if this is political?" Then she straightened. "Janet Abernathy."

Since Janet Abernathy had to be in her midsixties, Macy said, "Don't you think she's too—" she dropped her voice "—old for Ash?"

Christina paused and then hooted with laughter. "I meant she might have some suggestions." Then she frowned. "Ash has gotta be...fifty? It still might work."

Macy closed her eyes and counted to ten. "There's no chance Ash is fifty. Winter is barely thirty." She didn't know how old Ash was, hadn't ever considered it.

"You're right." Christina nodded. "I have not heard a single tidbit of gossip about Winter's engagement. I wonder how that's going." Christina was deep in thought as she took the dishes into the kitchen.

Macy turned back to the water and considered Christina's suggestions. Revamp his image, convince him to date a woman who liked to go out a lot. Wouldn't it be easier to find the person who'd passed the report to the governor? They could prove Ash was innocent, the Callaways would acknowledge his loyalty and whatever happened with the lodge…happened.

Macy could see both sides of the argument: protecting the animals and habitat on the Reserve versus the economic advantage of a nice new lodge. As long as she could keep things the same at the station, she was prepared to be practical about it all.

Easier than finding the perfect woman for Ash Kingfisher, certainly.

Just the thought of some mysterious woman out there, waiting to fall in love with Ash, irritated her.

"Thanks for the advice, Christina," Macy said as she slid out of the booth. Standing next to tall beautiful Christina Braswell made Macy feel a tiny bit frumpy in her uniform, but it was required.

"About staying for lunch? No problem. You chose literally the best thing on the menu." Christina rang up her ticket and then took the cash Macy slid across to her.

"I meant about giving Sweetwater someone else to talk about." Macy shrugged. "And possibly a light PR makeover. Forget the girlfriend."

"Because you've already got that covered?" Christina asked slyly.

"No. Besides, that's up to Ash."

"You'll meddle but only so far." Christina pursed her lips. "I get that. I respect that."

"It's helping a friend… A good boss. It's in my best interest to keep him in place." Macy waved as she headed for the door. Really. That was all this was. It made perfect, logical sense that no girlfriend would be required and that she could help Ash navigate Sweetwater herself.

"Got any ideas who might be responsible for sending the report?" Christina called out, but Macy stepped outside and pretended not to hear her.

She didn't, but it seemed to her that the only other person central to the mess was Winter Kingfisher. She'd grown up at the Reserve, like Ash. That had to mean a strong connection to the land, one that might make it necessary to put a stop to the project.

Anonymity would be a plus for Winter if she wanted to stop the building and marry her fiancé. What if she loved both, the Callaway heir running for governor and the Reserve?

How would she even go about investigating this theory? Winter was in Knoxville. Ash would turn to fire if she suggested Winter had played a part.

Macy could count on one hand the number of conversations she'd had with Ash's younger, ambitious sister. Making this happen could take some planning.

When Christina stepped out behind her, Macy scrambled for a way to end further suggestion of a romance between her and Ash, but the waitress held out the white bag she'd packed. "Pie. Don't forget it. Ash might grumble."

Macy dipped her chin to acknowledge her thanks and then marched around to the driver's side of her car. Christina's grin was big as she rested against the diner.

Ash would grumble, anyway, but the pie would be a bright spot in a long day. He'd asked for it. She was only doing a favor.

And the next big, big favor she was going to do for Ash he'd never expect. She was going to find another suspect, someone to lend some support to his denial of guilt.

That person couldn't be Winter Kingfisher, not even

for Ash's protection. Ash was proud of his sister. Even if Winter was responsible for the leak, Ash was the kind of hero to take the fall to save her engagement.

That didn't change the fact that Macy was certain the next step was to talk to Ash's sister.

## CHAPTER FOUR

JUMPING EVERY TIME the phone rang had gotten old early on. Doing it for two days straight was enough to make Ash irritable as a wounded bear. The number of phone calls he'd returned had to be reaching world records. Halfway through the afternoon on Thursday, he wished he'd started counting the number of times he'd said some version of "I don't know the answer to your question" and "Direct all requests for information about Smoky Valley Nature Reserve business to the district office in Knoxville" and "I have no further comments." Over and over, on a loop.

The question he hated the most was "Who else had access to the report and good reason to slip it to Whit Callaway's opponent?"

The answer to the first part of the question was short: the team that had prepared the report, his sister and Macy. That was it.

Ash studied the list of names on the report. A couple of hours of research on the scientists and engineers involved had turned up no obvious red flags. Before he'd commissioned this team to prepare the environmental impact study, he'd done his research, determined to hire only the best experts on the Great Smoky Mountains.

Short of making public accusations with no evidence to back it up, he was out of ideas.

That, along with hiding behind his desk for too long, made him short-tempered.

Since Macy was one of the few people left who'd have his back in a gunfight, he hated that he was snapping at her.

Fridays were normally nice, the coming weekend lifting everyone's spirits. Guides had been in and out, preparing for the busiest days of the week, Friday and Saturday. None had stopped by to say hello. The cloud above his head had dampened the ranger station's mood. Even the mailman, a guy who normally sang a Friday song of his own composing, had come and gone with a subdued "Have a nice weekend." Macy's reply had been too quiet for him to hear at his desk.

It was time for a break from his office. He stood, straightened his shoulders, prepared to pretend he wasn't nervous about his reception and headed out to Macy's desk.

"Did you come by to tell me that my plans for the open house are terrible and you're not sure how I ever got this job in the first place?" Macy asked sweetly. "Because that's definitely where this day is headed."

"I've been short-tempered. I'm sorry." He didn't apologize often enough for it to be easy. In fact, the words burned all the way down his throat. Her reaction told him his pain was obvious.

"Well, now," Macy drawled, amusement making her lips twitch, "I can tell it's genuine because you seem horrified that this apology is happening." She crossed her arms over her chest. "I've been trying to be patient."

Ash pinched the brim of his hat. "You don't do patient."

"I do not. What I do instead is make sure everything is moving along. I've confirmed refreshments and that the press release for the open house went out. I've made invitations for the shops on Main Street to display. I've already contacted them by phone, so this is just a reminder. Maybe they'll talk up the open house to all their shoppers this week. I will deliver them ASAP. I have talked with Brett about security and Hank about the tours running that evening." Macy pursed her lips. "I did all that while you snarled at every question. This place looks great. These displays you researched and put together about the animals in the park and how they weather the cold temperatures are good. Interesting. Informative. You've worked hard to prepare a program to draw visitors in. I want to show off the displays. For you. You do so much here. Let's blow the horn about it. Stop acting like a frazzled toddler, okay? Or else. And I mean that with respect and as a genuine threat." She'd relaxed in her chair, although her eyes still glinted like she was ready to murder him with a million tiny papercuts, but she reached across the desk to squeeze his hand. Before she could pull away, he wrapped his fingers around hers.

And everything settled.

For him, this public attention was too much, too strange, and it rattled him. Macy calmed all that. The connection between them was strong. Too strong for a little thing like his ruined reputation, and snapping at her, to break it. She released his hand, and he was surprised at how much he hated the feeling of her hand slipping away.

"I appreciate it." Ash forced himself to move away from her desk. His boots on the ground. That was the only way to know, day to day, what was happening in the Reserve. Visitation and incident reports, revenues, those told only part of the story. Driving through the trailhead lots, talking with visitors, making sure he remembered all the people behind the statistics mattered. Those people, this place, made him love his job.

And he needed to get out of the office. It seemed his staff was also avoiding him. Only Brett had stuck his head in so far all day long. Were they convinced he'd anonymously sabotaged the lodge, too?

Here, he could avoid…whatever. He wasn't sure what the consequences within the ranks would be of the firestorm that had yet to fade.

"Are you headed out to patrol?" Macy asked. "Patrol" was her word for his "making the rounds." He was a law enforcement ranger, but most of what he did was management instead of enforcement.

They both knew he had to spend time on the trails of the Reserve to make it through some days. She'd been telling him he needed to do that at least once an hour all morning.

Being a part of the Reserve's team was important to him. His first job at the Reserve had been summer help at the marina, and he'd loved it, but being able to combine the service of a policeman with the mission of the park had been his calling. When attendance was up, having another park ranger SUV on the roads and uniforms actually in the campground and on the trails, with the signature hat and holstered weapon, kept troublemakers on their best behavior.

Today, this "patrol" was just for him.

"The fire chief wants me to check out the photography backdrop you commandeered for the open house. I'm not sure why we couldn't stand next to a…tree or something to have our pictures taken with the kids, but I'll bow to your creative planning. I also don't know why I have to do it when it's your…" Her cleared throat interrupted the flow which was a good thing. She'd raised one eyebrow. "Then, I'll head into Knoxville to the district office. We've got to get a full-time park guide on staff to handle the volunteers and part-time guides, and Chief McKesson's had a personnel request in for weeks. We both need the chief ranger's approval to move forward."

Macy nodded, but the fear that he could remember in her eyes during their early days flitted across his memory. She'd always been able to eventually control it. After all this time, Ash had decided that Macy Gentry only feared one thing: failure. He'd seen less of that fear lately; he wanted to keep it that way.

"I bet the phones at the district office have been busy. Surely that's the holdup. I'm guessing the chief ranger doesn't like the lodge's construction delay. He'll be hustling to get everything back on track. I can't believe anybody in Knoxville would blame you for all this." Macy propped her hands on her hips. "It beats all I ever saw."

Her loyalty was a nice boost. "All you ever saw, huh? You must be from around here." He liked to tease her about how she spoke. Most days, Macy was completely professional, letting little of her firecracker personality slip through to anyone but him. Being that person to Macy was nice.

"My grandmother used to say that. She had this little run-down farmhouse with enough land to kill us both as we tried to keep up the garden." Macy slumped back against her chair. "I'll never forget the torment of picking green beans in the hot sun. Can't even eat those suckers from a can now."

Ash leaned an elbow on the high ledge of her desk. They didn't do a lot of personal talk, so this glimpse was rare and sweeter for it. The lilt of her voice changed when she talked about home. Listening to her talk was easy.

"Why don't I know where you grew up?" Ash asked,

surprised there was something he needed to know about Macy. They'd talked about all the favorites: music, movies, books, candy bars, ice creams and assorted baked goods.

But he didn't know where her family was.

Where a person came from could tell a lot about them.

"Myrtle Bend, Georgia. About thirty miles from nowhere and as fancy as you'd imagine. At least the indoor plumbing came along before I did." Macy wrinkled her nose. "I don't like to talk about my family or lack of one too much. That's probably why."

Ash had a hard time picturing such a place. He'd grown up on a very nice street in the middle of Sweetwater, the kind of place people imagine when they daydream about the good old days.

"Do you ever go home?" Ash asked.

He'd helped her move. She made him coffee every morning just because. Once he'd asked his mother to make chicken noodle soup for her, even though Macy refused to take a sick day.

He knew Macy. So well.

But they'd never talked about her history. Why was that?

"No home to go back to. Home is my apartment in Sweetwater." Macy cleared her throat. "Grandma died when I was nineteen, so…" She shrugged a shoulder. "I was the only one left. Had college and bills and I couldn't keep up the place, too." She tipped her head down. "She wouldn't have wanted me to give up school just to keep a small farmhouse. I'm pretty sure." The way she bit her lip suggested she wasn't as certain as she wanted to be.

Uneasy because the emotions were changing so quickly on her face that he was afraid she was about to be overwhelmed, Ash said, "Surely she'd want you to be happy."

Macy frowned. "Actually, happiness wasn't high on her list of priorities. Busyness. Usefulness. Those things ruled, and she had zero tolerance for anything that interfered."

Ash considered that. It was so far outside of his own experience, he had a hard time imagining it. When he was growing up, his mother had taken him out of school so that he could experience perfect weather or she'd kept him up too late watching shooting stars to make his first period and she'd refused to let him take a required shop class because the main project was a gun rack.

For Donna Kingfisher, life was about loving each day. Work was a part of that, but not the biggest part. She'd been a successful lawyer, but she'd retired at sixty, determined not to miss out on all the things she'd been putting off. His father had put on a suit and tie and been an accountant at the electric company for forty years.

But there was no doubt in Ash's mind that his father had enjoyed his job and loved his life, too. Macy's grandmother would have been appalled at how much time his family had spent sitting beside a campfire and staring up at the sky.

This conversation also explained a lot about Macy. He wanted to introduce her to his mother, to ask his mother to take Macy under her wing. She deserved some of Donna Kingfisher's wacky fun, moments that were about nothing more than enjoying life fully.

How lucky he'd been to have that.

Macy deserved some of that good luck.

"Nobody works harder than you do. She'd be proud of you." Ash had never seen anyone else as efficient at organization as Macy. She didn't sit if she could straighten. If something was broken, she kept fiddling until it started again. And she couldn't understand why everyone didn't treat their jobs exactly the same way.

"I hope so." Macy laughed. "Even if she was still here, I'd have to guess that she was happy."

Uneasy with the emotion but determined to put some of the shine back in her eyes, Ash said, "If it helps, I think you're amazing. At all this." He gestured around awkwardly. "And I want you to be happy. You deserve it."

Her mouth dropped open before she shut it with a click. Ash ran a hand through the hair at his neck, while pink spotted her cheeks and his ears. He was terrible at speaking to women.

"What happened to your parents?" Ash asked, desperate to change the subject to anything else.

"They were long gone by the time I hit elementary school. Thus, Grandma and the garden of doom." Macy tried to make it a joke, but none of the smile on her lips made it into her eyes. "She was no fun, but she was there."

He wanted to tell her he was sorry. He wanted to wrap his arms around her and squeeze her close, just to make sure she knew she wasn't really alone. No one should be alone. Macy deserved a rambunctious family that she could lovingly organize.

Macy took pity on him. "Your face, boss. It's so… worried. It's okay. I decided this week that it's been too long since I've been to the top of Yanu. That'll be my Christmas treat. I hike only because I love it. It's taken me a while, but I'm learning to do things for me, just for me. You should try it, only go into town. Have a bite to eat you didn't pour from a can."

How did the conversation switch to his issues? Ash

had to wonder if his own face was showing the whirling emotions that he was losing control of.

That never happened to him.

"Too many people. I'm fine with my own company." He was a law officer, trained to assess situations and take charge if there was any kind of danger.

She deserved the same thing, though, a nice dinner prepared by someone else. He could almost picture it in his mind.

But why was he the man seated across from her? They were wearing street clothes, no uniforms in sight, and she was smiling. What a great night that could be.

Staring at her soft eyes, the brave smile she wore, he was losing the threads of the conversation.

"Right. You're now off to go out into the park to speak to *people*. Then other people. More people. So, when will you be back?" Macy asked. "And should I tell reporters where you are or lie like a rug?"

Ash twirled his hat on his hand and considered her options. "Send anyone who calls for me through to my cell. Make sure Winter does that if she calls the office instead for some reason."

The fact that Winter had yet to return his messages? Yeah, that worried him. If he hadn't been catching small glimpses of her on the news that was still trickling through regularly, he'd have been mounting a search. If he didn't catch up with her over the weekend, he still might.

"If I'm out of cell range, take a message." Ash sighed. The park had plenty of dead spots. "Unless it's an emergency. Send them through to the radio if you judge it to be an emergency."

"So, business as usual, then." Macy nodded. "You can count on me."

Satisfied that they were back to normal, Ash turned on a heel and headed for the door, but instead of marching through it, he paused to look back.

He didn't do that, get sentimental or emotional.

But looking at Macy perched on her throne behind the polished wood desk in the airy lobby where she'd been every day for years made him pause.

"Did you forget something?" Macy asked. She leaned forward in her seat as if she was ready to launch into action to assist him.

"Just…" Ash wanted the right words, but he couldn't figure out what they were. "Thanks for your help, Macy."

Her eyebrows shot up. "Well, now…" She frowned. "It's my job." Her confusion suggested no thanks were needed. She'd do what had to be done. Like always.

That dependability made her invaluable.

"And you do it well." Ash waved his hat and stepped out onto the sidewalk, determined to shake off the worry that had settled over him.

Walking down off the curb next to his SUV sent a sharp twinge through the twisted muscles of his leg. Ash stopped with one hand on the car and waited to make sure the leg would hold.

The feeling of someone watching him made him check over his shoulder again. Macy was hovering.

She did that sometimes, waited and watched for him to ask for help.

If she hadn't stepped up to the door, he might have waited until his leg cooperated. As it was, he couldn't stand there like a statue any longer.

"Not when your pride is at stake," Ash muttered to himself through gritted teeth as he limped over to open the door and slid inside. Macy saw him at his most irritable daily. Why did it matter if she watched him limp away?

It just did.

He managed to get the leg inside and himself buckled in without too much trouble, so he raised a hand at Macy. She was no longer in the doorway.

Because he'd snapped at her often enough not to fuss over him like a nurse and an invalid.

So she did her best to be sneaky about it.

"Probably why we get along as well as we do." Ash closed his eyes for a minute, wished again he'd been smarter when he was younger instead of foolhardy and too cocky to back down. Soon, he started the SUV. There was no sense in beating himself up for old mistakes. "Plenty of current mistakes to regret, idiot."

On his way down the mountain, toward the station where the fire trucks and equipment were stored, Ash scanned the forest and studied the parking areas for the campsites. "Still empty." The winter season was a slow time in the Reserve, but not often this slow. The open house could be a big boost in attendance if Macy had her way and she usually did. Having the chief ranger see their efforts as a move in the right direction was key to getting his approval to add staff.

Asking him to approve anything right now would be dicey. The Callaways were angry. They'd stir up the board of directors. Any request Ash made could be shut down.

"Burying your head in the sand won't change a thing, Kingfisher." He'd delivered bad news before. Today, he'd return to the district office in Knoxville and hope to get back to business as usual. They'd already questioned him about the environmental impact report and any connection he had to the governor. He had nothing else to say about that.

If the chief ranger couldn't resume daily operations

at the Reserve, Ash needed to know whether his job was in jeopardy.

Ash parked in front of the firehouse garage where the guys on duty were gathered. In addition to using his Reserve SUV, Macy's grand plan for the ranger station's first ever open house included the fire truck with light bar flashing. Kids loved machines. He was sure she was right about them being big draws. She'd asked the firefighters to put together a fun photo booth, someplace kids could pose with either a park ranger or a firefighter and have their pictures taken. Parents would love it. Kids? Ash had no idea what kids loved.

Ash had pictured a simple piece of large plywood with holes cut out for folks to put their faces. Maybe a cartoonlike cutout of a park ranger and a bear with a picnic basket or Santa with an otter elf. Goofy pictures people would laugh over.

Apparently, he was wrong. Three men were scrambling to attach some kind of plastic sheeting over a metal rigging while the fire crew chief, Phil McKesson, judged their efforts.

Ash paused next to him silently. Neither man spoke as they watched the guys decorate the sheeting with artificial trees and eventually Ash got the idea. "Is that Yanu Falls?" Something about the shape of the miniature mountain and how the trees were grouped to suggest a trail along the cliff's face made it easy to imagine the waterfall that cascaded into Otter Lake on warmer days.

"Yep." The chief pointed at a large round indention in the fake rocks lining the bed. "That's the lake. Gonna fill it with water." The chief shook his head like he couldn't believe he was saying the words out loud.

"Running water? Like, it will come down the side and then pool and…" Ash rubbed his forehead as he tried to imagine how that would work. The water had to go somewhere, didn't it?

"Cho says it recirculates." The chief spoke slowly as if it had taken him a while to get a handle on the word. "Runs down into the pool before it's pulled back up to the top. Haven't seen it in action yet."

Ash propped his hands on his hips as he watched the guy he recognized as the new mechanic pointing to places that needed to be covered or rearranged.

"New mechanic builds models, landscapes with water features and such. Even restores muscle cars for fun. Cooks a mean tiramisu." McKesson cleared his throat. "So when the guys were half a second from throwing in the towel on this project, even though Blackburn is going to be in town to see it all and they'd like to impress the hotshot, Cho stands up and says, 'I have an idea.'"

Sam Blackburn had been a member of the wildland firefighting team before he'd moved to Colorado to join a hot shot crew, the daredevils who fought the biggest blazes. Ash hadn't been surprised when the kid applied for the position or got it, because he was that good at his job. He had been surprised at how much he'd missed Blackburn badgering him to get out of his cabin now and then.

Blackburn had been the guy the firefighters trotted out for all photo ops and community service. Women and children loved him.

Ash wondered how easy it would be for a new guy to be accepted into the tight group of wildland firefighters who worked to protect the Reserve and restore the native habitat. Apparently, not too difficult. Every guy working listened intently to what Ronald James Cho said and then asked for approval before moving to the next step.

"He any good against fire?" Ash asked. If the kid had

skill and this kind of leadership ability, they might be looking at a good candidate for training.

"Cautious. Solid." Chief glanced over at Ash. "Nothing like Blackburn's flair, but if you need a guy you can depend on to follow protocol and execute a plan, Cho's got it." He shrugged. "Big city roots, though. Comes from New Orleans by way of the national park system. Not sure Sweetwater will make the cut for long."

"What brought him here?" Ash asked. Competition for all park service, national, state and even small places like the Smoky Valley Nature Reserve, was tough. Cho would have had to fight for his spot.

McKesson raised an eyebrow.

He hadn't asked. Of course. It didn't matter.

"Chief, we're about to flip the switch. Want to do the honors?" Cho yelled from his spot atop mini Yanu Falls.

"Head ranger, would you be interested in turning on the waterfall?" the chief asked before bowing deeply. Everyone smirked, but the way they watched convinced Ash they were proud of the work they'd done.

"Glad to." Ash walked over to take the box that Cho handed him.

"Press the button when I say." Cho didn't wait for Ash to agree but bent to study the apparatus. "Steady. Good." Cho nodded. "Okay, hit it."

Ash pressed the black button and, at first, nothing happened. Cho cursed under his breath and then muttered, "Water hose. I need the water hose."

The scramble on the ground was quick but Cho carefully arranged the hose and said, "Turn on the water. Slowly."

A trickle of water poured from the hose down the smooth sheeting of the mountain before pooling in the fake rocks below. Cho motioned to turn off the hose and then stared hard at the top of the waterfall.

Half a second later, Ash could hear the tiniest gurgle and water poured up over the top of the mountain to roll back down into the pool.

"Lights!" Cho eased his way carefully off the mountain to join Ash and the chief on the ground. White twinkle lights under the sheeting gave the water a glisten that would make it truly pretty after sunset.

Ash held out his hand. "You did it. That's an amazing design there."

Cho clamped his hand hard and gave it a shake. "Thanks, Ranger. I like to tinker."

"And you're good at it. I hear this was all your idea." Ash watched red cover Cho's cheeks.

"Yeah, he's as good at big ideas as Blackburn ever was, boss." Rodriguez tossed his arm around Cho's shoulders. "My girl is going to lose her cool when she sees this. She loves otters."

Ash turned to the chief. "Otters? How are you managing that?"

"Costumes." Cho cleared his throat. "Two or three people in costumes. Gotta have people to take the photos, manage the line, hand out candy." He ran a hand over his close-cropped hair. The sign of nerves was unexpected. The kid obviously had skill. He motioned at stacks of plywood leaning against the building. "We're going to put up a temporary wall. Those will include facts about the Reserve's restoration work with otter populations. Waiting on the public outreach office to give us those figures. Education. That's part of the goal with the open house." Cho glanced around. "Right?"

The men who'd been carrying out his orders all nodded seriously.

"And are you guys part of the photo op?" Ash asked as he offered Cho the magic box that controlled the water flow. "Kids love firefighters."

"Some of us will be there, decked out, to show off the engines and whatnot. We can take shots if needed." McKesson propped his hands on his hips. "Gonna have some law enforcement rangers on hand, too. Photo op with a park ranger ought to be somebody in charge, right?" He bent his head closer. "Think you could ask Chief Ranger Hall to drop in? We don't want another time like the Fourth of July parade where Whit Callaway snagged the spotlight."

That little bit of grandstanding had stuck in Ash's craw, too. The Reserve belonged to the Callaways, but most of the time, they used it as a talking point about their gracious generosity.

Which was nice and all, but when they made sure to get every single attaboy they thought they deserved, his team had a reason to grumble. They'd worked hard on the parade float; all Whit Callaway had done was step in at the last minute to hog the glory.

"Let's avoid a Callaway takeover. Any ranger on hand should be representative of the park. I'll talk to the chief." Ash studied the smooth flow of the water until he realized everyone else was watching him. "What?"

"Head ranger would be a good representative for the Smoky Valley Nature Reserve, too." McKesson watched him closely.

Ash would rather eat kale than have his picture taken all day long, and he hated kale.

"Not for me, not this year." Not ever. "You want celebrity, someone people will look forward to seeing. Considering my press right now, I'd only bring the party down. I can ask the chief ranger his feelings. Might get us some extra points. Or Macy will do it. Officer Hendrix. I will order them to, if necessary."

The disappointment on the faces of the fire crew was another blow to Ash's confidence. If he kept this up, every ally he had would be ready to dump him.

"It's next weekend, right?" Dumb. He knew exactly when it was. Macy wouldn't let him forget. "Well, let's think on it. This idea, though? It's great." Ash clapped his hand on Cho's shoulder. "Impressive work, everyone. I'm proud to have you representing us."

The response was subdued as Ash retreated to his SUV.

"Nothing to feel guilty about. I'm saving them the grief of having Sweetwater's least popular citizen ruin their hard work." Ash realized he was muttering to himself half a second before he hit the highway out of town. "Get a grip, Kingfisher."

Ash made the short trip to Knoxville without remembering much of it. The district office for the three private, Callaway-owned reserves in east Tennessee was in a squat brick building with only one claim to fame: the beautiful view of the Tennessee River. The river was still that afternoon, the calm surface reflecting the Henley Street Bridge. Ash slowly limped forward, but stopped to take a few minutes to catch his breath at the overlook.

"No good comes from procrastination." His father had said that to him in a variety of tones for separate occasions, so Ash had learned the phrase by heart. Today, he wanted to put meeting with his boss off for a week. Maybe two. But the Reserve needed a new educational director.

"Afternoon, Ranger," Kayla, the smart redhead who manned the district's front desk, said with a bright smile.

Ash dipped his chin. All his conversation skills had been spent for the day.

"I'll let the chief ranger know you're here." She tapped the small earpiece that was nearly covered by crazy curls and said, "Ash Kingfisher to see you, sir."

*Sir.* Ash didn't shake his head. He didn't blink in confusion, although he had to fight that urge nearly every time he stopped in. It wasn't that Chief Ranger Hall didn't deserve respect. He did.

But requiring titles like that would never be Ash's way.

Loyalty should be earned and come from a team for its leader naturally.

Still, he'd do well to remember that Hall did require it, no matter how the meeting turned out.

"He's ready for you." Kayla nodded toward the open door. "Can I get you something to drink?"

Reminded of how well Macy ran the ranger station without turning it into…this, Ash held up a hand.

"Sir. Thank you for making time to see me this afternoon." Ash reached up to take off his hat and realized he'd left it on the front seat of the SUV. Off to a great start.

"Not quite regulation uniform, Kingfisher." Hall pointed at the seat across from his desk. "Or haircut. Thought you would have taken care of that by now. Splashed across enough news sources that surely you've noticed."

Ash refused to wince. He deserved the criticism and needed to make visiting his barber in Sweetwater a priority.

"It's on the top of my list to correct." Ash perched on the edge of the seat, realized what he was doing, and forced himself to relax as if he had no cares in the world.

No matter how this went, he was going to hold on to his pride.

"Good." Hall tapped the stack of papers in front of him. "Numbers are low for November."

Ash nodded. "Right. That's why I'm here. You should have received my request to fill the open spot for an educational director. We need someone with a strong education background and an interest in the flora and fauna of the Great Smoky Mountains. In addition to programs for school-age children, I'd like to explore activities geared toward seniors and hobbyists like birders who would be drawn to the park at times like this." Ash had rehearsed his opening statement on the drive into Knoxville. It was impossible to read how well his boss was receiving it, so he continued, "I have rangers on staff who can lead hikes and point out the animals and plants, but in the winter, that's more challenging. We could clear the room at the back of the lobby and set up tables for hands-on workshops. An experienced guide would develop and lead those." Ash ran his hands down his uniform pants to dry them and smooth away the wrinkle he could see from the odd angle he kept his left leg at while he drove.

Hall turned to glance at his computer screen. "Your budget is tight, but there's some room. I expect you know that." He clasped his hands over his stomach as he swung back around. "Go for it. Can't think of any other reason why the numbers would be suffering. Can you?" He studied Ash's face carefully and it was clear this was the tricky part of the conversation.

"Well, I have heard that the people in Sweetwater are…" Ash studied the crisp, clean white of this office's ceiling. His had water stains that they'd delayed repairing because paint was a low priority. "They're concerned about the news stories."

The chief ranger tipped his head to the side, but he had no other reaction. He was at ease with the tension in the room. Wouldn't a nervous man blink or twitch or do something else? Ash was on the verge of all three.

Hall leaned forward to rest his elbows on the desk. "You know how I feel about the lodge, Ash. If we want to continue the business of preservation, pleasing the Callaways matters. As I explained a few days ago, I'm not sure I can continue to support an employee who doesn't understand the importance of that."

"And, as I explained, I didn't put a bug in the governor's ear. I'm not sure I can continue to support a boss who believes I could or doubts my commitment to the job." Ash straightened in his seat. "Sir."

Hall's eyes narrowed as he studied Ash's face. He wasn't convinced. "I'm not sure how this is going to shake out. The governor's not happy with the Callaways because the kid running for election has been critical of his record. We work with state departments for support and grants. And the Callaways…" He sighed long and loud before placing both hands on his desk. "As I said, this could go one of two ways. The governor keeps hitting Whit Callaway hard in his reputation and the lodge stalls. You know how well that would go over with the Callaway family and the people of Sweetwater. I've had three calls from the mayor this week." Hall met Ash's stare. "Or the Callaways push ahead with the lodge, please the voters in Sweetwater and ignore the smudge on their Tennessee heritage reputation."

"I'm prepared to serve at the Otter Lake Ranger Station either way." Ash heard how loudly he'd said it and forced himself to clear his throat and take a breath. "Sir."

"That's the question, isn't it?" Hall said with a shrug. "Is there any possible outcome where the Callaways let this go without firing the man responsible for disturb-ing the hornets' nest?" Hall met his eyes steadily. "Why would you do this, Ash? Everyone wins if the project goes forward."

"Sure, winners. Except for the copses of old-growth hardwoods that will be torn down and the animals who rely on that habitat." Ash squeezed his eyes shut. "I can't imagine how this idiotic project made it off the ground in the first place. Building at The Aerie would require struc-tural supports and clearances that would devastate hun-dreds of acres. Every report I wrote was against it. Every ecologist and not-for-profit we work with was against it. The first time I raised my objections, you told me to do the environmental impact study. At your suggestion, I hired the team. To suggest this is all on me is…not right." Unfair. That's what he'd wanted to say.

"Progress versus protection. That's where we are. That's been clear to us in Knoxville ever since the Cal-laways announced their plans. To keep the rest of the Re-serve, the lodge goes in." Hall shrugged. "It's a battle, but the thing about those battles is, when you know you're beat, you gotta stand back up, pick up your weapon and hold the fallback position, Ash."

That was as clear an explanation of what was happen-ing at the Reserve as Ash could expect.

The Callaways were ready to profit off the land they'd protected for five generations and everyone from the state of Tennessee to Ash Kingfisher better fall in line.

"I did that, Leland." Ash shook his head. "I stated my objections plainly. With honor. But I love that place, even with a lodge perched on top. Someone else slipped this report to the governor. My intention was always to pres-ent it to the Callaways, as you and I discussed. Then I would do the job I was ordered to do. That's it. This was never supposed to be a bone that two politicians would fight over. Someone turned my concern for the Reserve into a political bargaining tool. Find him."

A smart man would try groveling, keep his head down and do whatever it took to keep his job.

When he had a minute, he'd try to remember if anyone other than his mother had ever called him smart.

The Callaways were one of the richest families in East Tennessee thanks to a long line of successful business ventures spanning generations building on that wealth. The Callaway name was on college buildings, hospital wings and enough politicians' election funds that only one reason would have kept their donations out of the current governor's coffers: his days were numbered because a Callaway was about to take his office. The governor had every incentive to fight them hard and dirty.

"If you think you can find him, I suggest you get to it." Hall tapped one finger slowly on his desk. "A man who loves his job on the Smoky Valley Nature Reserve will get behind the people who make it possible."

"Or find a new job," Ash said, ready to have it all out on the table.

Leland tipped his chin up. "We've worked together for a long time. I'll do my best for you, Ash, but if you think there's something else out there you *can* do, maybe polish up your résumé."

Before he could make his escape, Leland added, "Might do some more whispering in ears. Them Callaways, they're big on loyalty. If they come for you, not sure they'll stop with you."

Ash frowned. He hadn't considered who might also be collateral damage. He had to get back to Sweetwater and make some decisions.

"Hey, Ash, keep me in the loop." His boss propped his hands on his hips. "On the new programs."

Their eyes met for a second before Ash nodded. Determined not to limp on the walk out to the SUV, Ash concentrated on every step. As soon as he was behind the wheel, he checked the time.

If he pushed the edge of the speed limit, he could make it back to Sweetwater and the ranger station before Macy left for the day. Hall had been right about one thing. He'd fallen back; now, it was time to battle from the new position he found himself in.

Macy Gentry was the first person he thought of when he realized he was going to need some help.

# CHAPTER FIVE

UNDER NORMAL CIRCUMSTANCES, being by herself in the lobby of the ranger station gave Macy time to tackle the projects that took too much concentration under the normal flow of visitors and phone calls and all of Ash's requests.

But on that Friday afternoon, Macy stared out the window. Leaves were falling, and the cold gave every color of the landscape a sharp contrast. "That sky is the perfect shade of blue."

As soon as she heard herself, Macy pictured her grandmother's disapproving head shake. "Wasting valuable time, Macy Elizabeth Gentry. I'm ashamed of you."

Normally that was enough to set Macy in motion.

Today, she'd spent a lot of time staring out at the view she loved while she tried to come up with a plan to save Ash Kingfisher's job. Finding the person responsible for sending the governor the environmental impact study was a long shot. Convincing Sweetwater to support Ash in any battle over his job... That might also be a long shot. She'd created the perfect setup here at the ranger station; losing it wasn't an option.

Neither was leaving Ash in charge of his own fate. Was he smart enough to plot and plan? Yes, but he lacked the killer instinct. If anyone could offer an alternative to Ash as the person behind the news story, it was his sister, Winter.

Three different times that afternoon, Macy had picked up the phone to call Winter.

She'd only muscled up the gumption to press the numbers in once, only to find out that the public information officer had already left for the afternoon.

Now Macy was back to wasting time by admiring the view while she worried about losing the perfect employment arrangement: lots of independence, respect and a boss who could deal with her bossiness.

Macy took a deep breath. "Visitor reports are done. All the park materials are restocked. Open house is a go, except for putting up the invitations around town." She'd already made plans to do that on Saturday. If she managed to sneak in some shopping as well, the ghost of her grandmother could be ignored. There wasn't a minute to waste. Really, all she'd done was ask for some ideas and a bit of effort from the different areas of the park, and people had stepped up. Why hadn't they been doing this all along? If she had her way, this first open house would be so successful that Ash wouldn't be able to argue when she offered to organize another one in the spring.

If they were both still here in the spring.

"Find something to do, Macy," she muttered as she straightened the pens in the Reserve mug on her desk and then stared at the dark doorway to Ash's office. More than once, the idea of snooping had floated through her brain. She was pretty sure he hadn't been the guy who'd contacted the governor, but... Well, if she glanced through his paperwork, maybe another suspect would come to mind.

Her grandmother's ghost didn't need words to stop that plan in its tracks. Picturing her disapproving frown was easy enough.

The sound of tires on dry leaves helped Macy to focus

on the parking lot again. The sedan parked in Ash's spot was an unusual sight. Most of the rangers and senior staff drove white SUVs emblazoned with the Reserve's logo, a mountain range composed of a bear, an otter and a fish outline. This gray car had the same logo but was much smaller.

When Winter Kingfisher slid out of the vehicle, her dark suit a contrast to the Reserve's uniform, Macy straightened.

Winter Kingfisher, head of the public outreach team, dressed like a corporate queen in a slim skirt with matching black jacket and heels that Macy admired but could never pull off. Winter's concessions to the uniform were a brass pin with the logo in miniature and a legal-sized leather portfolio with the Reserve's motto in silver: Tennessee's Treasures Today and Tomorrow.

The Reserve's mission was to preserve the habitats unique to eastern Tennessee and the Great Smoky Mountains and to make sure visitors enjoyed the natural beauty of the land. The people in Winter's office worked as a public relations team to get the Reserve's news covered by the press and address any bad stories as well as they could. Winter's role was essential because fund-raising kept all three ranger stations operational. Because she loved Otter Lake as much as Ash did, Winter was good at her job.

The few times she'd come into the ranger station, Macy had been able to pinpoint the exact second she herself had faded into the background. It was unusual for her, but if Ash's focus made Macy feel strong, Winter's gaze made her a bit anxious.

The stress around Ash's sister's eyes, revealed when she removed her unnecessary sunglasses, suggested that her job, although it might often require extra hours and even crisis management, had taken a turn for the worse.

And Macy was only going to have more bad news. She hadn't heard from Ash since he'd left for Knoxville.

As Winter stepped inside the lobby, she seemed to be assessing whether there were any potential problems looming. That was her job: finding solutions to thorny problems. It seemed second nature, like maybe Winter didn't realize she was doing it. She surveyed the space carefully, critically before turning to Macy.

"No cameras. No reporters. Just me. If you're looking for Ash, he went to Knoxville to talk to the chief ranger."

Winter paused as if considering Macy's words. "I tried calling his cell. Maybe he was in a dead spot."

"Or had the ringer turned off for his meeting. He forgets to turn it back on sometimes." Macy wanted to keep the conversation rolling, mainly for her own nerves, but could only clear her throat. "Texts are his preference." Macy shrugged. "But not when he's driving." Her voice trailed off and the awkwardness almost choked her.

Winter placed her portfolio down and tugged on the sleeves of her suit.

"I could patch you through to his radio if it's an emergency. As you know, it's the Reserve's policy to prohibit abuse of that capability because distracted driving is dangerous to the ranger and other drivers. However, in an urgent case, I can certainly do that. All you have to do is say the word and I'll be happy to—"

"Macy. Stop." Winter held up one hand. "There's no emergency. Ash has been calling me ever since the story hit. Everyone in the world except the one person I need to talk to has been calling me since this story hit." Winter closed her eyes. "Never my fiancé, though, which has to mean something, right?"

Macy knew her surprise was written on her face. She had no advice to offer, though.

Winter tilted her head to the side. "Cat got your tongue?"

Macy tried to laugh, but it was a strangled jumble instead.

"I'll go sit at his desk for a minute, if that's okay. I'm not quite ready to hit the road. I've been called to an emergency dinner at my parents' house and that is going to require more intestinal fortitude than I have at this moment. I'm running on empty." Winter seemed to be studying Macy's expression, while Macy wished she could find the right words to make the conversation easier. "Guts. I'm going to need more guts for that. That's what I'm saying."

Macy nodded. "I got that."

"Do I make you nervous or something?" Winter asked as she dragged over one of the polished rocking chairs that normally sat in front of the observation window. So, she wasn't going to disappear into Ash's office. Fine. "Also, did you know there's a bear back there?"

Macy darted around the desk to the window. Careful study turned up no bear, but that didn't mean Winter was wrong. "He's gone."

"So disappointed. He a friend?" Winter sighed as she kicked off her heels. "Let me know if a visitor pulls up. Can't be seen like this by the public." She stretched her legs out. "The bear? A friend?"

Macy wandered slowly back to Winter. She'd never seen Ash's sister so...comfortable. Casual. On the verge of relaxed instead of sharp and powerful.

"When I first started working here, Ash told me bears were good luck." Macy sniffed. "After the week we've had, everyone would like to see their luck turn, you know? Plus, who doesn't love bears?"

Winter stretched in her seat. "Fish. All animals smaller than bears. People who meet bears. Lots not to love about bears, but I get it. We don't see them often enough to ever get over the thrill of it, do we?" Winter rolled her head against the back of the chair. "Word to the wise, though. Don't trust everything Ash tells you. In college, I did my best to study every Cherokee tale and as much indigenous folklore as I could. Thought I might be a teacher or a writer or…something. Bears are sacred, symbols of strength and courage. Meeting a mama with her cubs would not be lucky." She wrinkled her nose. "Also, I was bamboozled enough by Ash as a kid to learn to verify everything he tells me. I ended up owing him money and doing his chores entirely too many times to forget he can be convincing when he wants to be."

"I have a hard time picturing Ash as a… What? A practical joker?" Macy had spent too much time with him. How had she missed something like that?

She wanted to see that side. How amazing would it be to know Ash in a way most people didn't?

Winter leaned forward. "Okay, I'll agree I haven't seen much of that Ash lately, either. It's like the accident robbed him of any ability to enjoy life. Work. That's all he does. In high school, he was class president. Not that that's a great indication of a fun-loving guy, but he got out there, you know? People knew him. Now, he's so… focused on the job. He was always serious, but there were some things he loved. I don't know what those are now." She pressed two fingers over the frown line between her eyebrows. "Except here, in the Reserve. When we stand next to Yanu, I see him, all of him. And I think that's where the bear good luck charm story came from. Our grandfather probably told us that so we'd stop shaking in terror every time he took us up to the falls." Her face was somber as she added, "It's too bad Ash got over that fear. Maybe he wouldn't have tried to climb up the face to the overlook without the proper safety equipment."

Macy gasped. She'd never heard the full story. "Ash did that?" It didn't fit the man she knew. He followed protocols to the letter, and required that of everyone who worked with him.

"He used to run with a different crowd. A little wild. For Ash, these mountains are about connection and… history. For me, too. But other people are about challenge and risk and…" Winter closed her eyes briefly. "It's easy to do dumb things for the people you want to impress." She clasped her hands over her waist. "Know anything about that?"

Stuck trying to mash the two different pictures of Ash together, Macy lost the thread of the conversation. Winter was watching her closely. "Ever changed the way you act for someone else? I mean, outside of the crush you had on the most popular boy in high school." She rolled her eyes and muttered, "Or the college of business, if you're me."

Macy puzzled over Winter's question. "What do you mean?"

Winter's huff of breath was loud in the quiet lobby growing dim. Soon it would be completely dark outside. In the winter, shadows stretched slowly all afternoon, but as soon as the sun sank behind the tall ridge of mountains, the valley went black.

Macy hoped Ash was close to home. Still, driving the mountain roads in the dark would be no challenge for him. He knew them.

She preferred he not have to do it more than necessary.

"I guess I don't know what I'm asking. People pretend

to be something they're not sometimes. I'm guessing you don't. Neither does Ash now." Winter shrugged. "Maybe you were never as silly as me, falling for someone so different from you that you can never shake the worry that it's a terrible idea. You could say you've found the man who loves you as you are and I could hate you for that unless you mean Ash. In that case, I would swallow my bile over true love and celebrate my brother's good luck. Because he needs something or someone other than all this mess." Winter's head thumped against the rocker. "I've lost all ability to follow a train of thought."

"Your brother and I are not a couple, true love or not." Macy wanted to drop the subject. Any relationship with Ash would be a mess of…tangled strings. The fact that other people saw potential in it was silly.

She and Ash butted heads over everything. Love wouldn't change that.

Would it?

Macy clasped a hand over her suddenly topsy-turvy stomach.

"What is it with speculation on my relationship with my boss?" Ignoring Winter's suddenly alert expression, Macy stomped behind her desk and plopped down in her chair.

"Someone else is asking?" Winter dragged the rocker next to Macy and leaned forward, her eyes sparkling anew.

"No one that matters." She waited for that to sink in. "I don't appreciate all this mess he's in, mainly because I know it makes him unhappy. How do I know? I bear the brunt of his surly attitude. He's worried for the Reserve and for you." Determined not to back down on Ash's behalf, she muttered, "Which you would know about if you'd answered any of his phone calls."

Winter shot her an irritated frown. "I've had a few things going on."

"So has Ash." Macy tipped her chin up at Winter's annoyed glare. She would fight for him because he wouldn't. Not against his sister.

But Winter had been in the eye of the storm, too. Macy wasn't sorry she'd said what she had, but it was impossible to ignore how defeated Winter looked. "Do you want to talk about it?" Macy asked.

Macy didn't smack her forehead, but she thought about it. There was no reason Winter Kingfisher, important public outreach officer for the Reserve, fiancée to one of the heirs of the richest families in Tennessee, would want to spend time discussing her feelings with Macy.

But it was clear Winter needed someone.

Winter lifted her bare feet from the cold tiles and tucked them under her. Macy winced and tried to calculate whether frostbite was even possible indoors.

"All week I've answered calls from news outlets and tabloids alike, politicians demanding answers and a few testing to see what I might know about the environmental impact report and who released it to the governor." She turned. "But no call from Whit. My best friend. The man I might marry."

This was the issue. Macy had a feeling Winter could juggle all those questions and still have time to cook a four-course dinner. She'd be good at everything she tried.

More than anything, Macy wanted to come up with something encouraging to say.

But there was no way to spin a man leaving her alone in the middle of a mess. Challenger for the office of governor and beloved heir to one of the most powerful families in the state or not, Whit Callaway should have been by her side, making problems go away.

If he loved Winter.

Macy frowned as she shifted in her seat. She wasn't sure she believed that kind of love existed, the kind that weathered storms and came out stronger. Did Whit blame Winter's brother for damaging his campaign? Logically, it made sense.

If he loved Winter, couldn't they work through that?

Somewhere inside, Macy wanted to believe that there was a kind of love that would look at that mess as a mere temporary inconvenience, not a final end.

"No matter how I look at this, I can't see how my brother and my fiancé ever come to terms." Winter shrugged, standing and walking over to the windows. "And where does that leave me? I've either got to tear everything to the ground or I've got to…stand back while people make Ash a scapegoat and then destroy this place."

Macy sighed. "You really aren't good at keeping secrets, are you?"

Winter laughed. "If you only knew how many I've skated around for the past few days, you'd see that I'm better at it than you think."

She'd wanted to investigate Winter as a possible option for the guilty party. Now she was almost certain Winter would have been the last person to hide behind the scenes. She was bold, not sneaky.

Macy was relieved to cross Winter off her list of suspects.

Winter covered her face with both hands. "I'm not certain why I'm unloading on you."

After a lifetime of similar conversations, the ones where the grocery store checkout lady told her about her terrible hysterectomy over the coupon exchange and her hairdresser asked for advice on investments, Macy didn't even pause to wonder anymore.

"The thing about bears being good luck…" Macy stood, wanting to be brave enough to force Winter away from the chilly windows. Coffee would help. Coffee always helped. "I didn't hear many of those pieces of… whatever you call them…while I was growing up."

"Lies?" Winter asked. "Legends. Folklore. Or superstitions, if we're being academic."

"Whatever. My grandmother, who was the most practical woman you'd have ever met, would have told me meeting a bear was what I deserved for slacking instead of doing my chores." Macy nodded at Winter's shock. "Yes, imagine that lecture for ten years and then someone mentions something to believe in, like bears are good luck, something that may or may not be true, but that it doesn't hurt to have some hope in. All I'm saying is, seeing that bear might not change my luck, but believing that it could will."

Winter considered that, and Macy was pretty sure what she'd said made zero sense even though it was an attempt at capturing what was in her heart. These Kingfishers were hard to read and even harder to convince. Winter, with all her degrees and experience with important people, had probably seen and heard it all.

"I'm saying…" What? Why had she started this? "You saw the bear. You can either believe it means nothing or hope for better luck. What does it hurt to believe something good is about to happen?" Macy blinked for a minute after she finished speaking. Where had all that come from? And did she actually believe it? She crossed over to stand next to Winter, shivering at the cold penetrating the glass.

When she realized she did believe every word, it was

impossible to ignore how her time in Sweetwater had changed her. "Hokey nonsense, my grandmother would say." She watched Winter's reflection. "But that's better than despair any day, I'd say."

Winter's slow smile was enough to make Macy's mood lighten. "I'm happy you're here, Macy. I needed to hear that. I don't know what to do with it, but I believe we're here together for this conversation. And when you and Ash fall in love, because that's what I'm going to pin all my hopes on for the future, I can't wait to tell the world you're an optimist at heart."

Macy shook her head. Somehow the conversation had taken a turn that she hadn't expected.

So, she decided to take the wheel. "Love? No way, but I was going to do my best to get close to you so that I could investigate whether you were responsible for this mess with the lodge. But that doesn't seem to be the way to go anymore." Macy rubbed her forehead.

"You're not great with secrets, either." Winter crossed her arms over her chest. "Good to know. No one would believe you were lying to cover for Ash if it comes to that." She paced in a small circle. "I've been thinking all week on how to move this attention away from Ash, but he's right in the middle of the story. Pointing the finger at someone else only works if there's proof. He's my brother, so of course I'd defend him. I can't let the Callaways fire him. I can't. He loves this place. Otter Lake needs Ash."

"If he's fired..." Macy stared hard out the window, desperate for a bear distraction.

The faint trail of lights signaling someone turning into the parking lot was a relief.

"Someone's on their way in." Macy checked the large clock over her desk. "Even though the ranger station is officially closed." This time of year, park gates were locked at eight, but the visitor center closed promptly at five, no matter the season. "Grab your shoes and head for the coffeemaker. We'll give Ash another call as soon as I lock the doors."

Winter bent to pick up her shoes without any argument, but before Macy could get the door locked, Ash's SUV swung into the parking spot in front. He killed the lights and limped slowly in, and no matter how many times it happened, Macy got the same feeling of relief.

Rain or shine, light or dark, good day or bad, when Ash was near, she relaxed.

Then she realized she was about to have a front row seat to a family drama and wondered if she could get her purse out of the drawer of her desk and slink past him before the tension choked her.

Growing up as she had, with her grandmother who had no patience for drama of any sort, the prospect of diving headfirst into this gave her a nervous knot in her stomach.

"You lost your phone and had to get a new number at exactly the same time you tripped on your heels, hit your head and got amnesia, so you didn't remember that you had an older brother who would worry after a few days of you dodging his calls." Ash narrowed his eyes at Winter. "That's it, right? You would never believe what other people are saying over what I've told you myself."

Macy knew her eyes were round, but she was certain her mouth was clamped shut. They didn't hesitate but launched right into battle.

"*Or* I've been doing nothing but talking on the phone, one obnoxious call right after the next, and so I needed time to call you back." Winter dropped her shoes with a loud clatter before she marched up to Ash. "Or I needed you in person, not over the phone." She wrapped her arms around her brother's neck and pressed her forehead to his shoulder. "Be quiet and hold me now."

Watching Ash hug his sister tightly was shocking. Winter no longer seemed capable of striding right over the competition. She'd needed her brother. Envy brought a sting to Macy's eyes.

Being so alone wasn't too difficult most of the time.

Standing on the outside of this, though... Macy pinched the end of her nose, desperate to chase the tears away. Then Ash tilted his head up and their eyes met. He was asking for her help. Without words, Macy understood that he needed her.

"Let me lock the door. Then I'll make coffee before I leave." Macy took her key ring out and pressed her hand to Ash's shoulder as she reached around him to lock the door. "It won't take a minute."

Before she could ease away from them, Ash bent his head closer to hers. "I know it's Friday and you might have plans, but I'd appreciate it if you'd stick around." He glanced down at his sister who was studying them both suspiciously. "Both of you."

"What about dinner at Mom and Dad's? It's a command performance, some kind of emergency meeting," Winter said as she stepped back, her arms wrapped tightly around herself.

Had she realized she wasn't as tough as she'd imagined?

"I called it." Ash glanced at the window. Was he seeking the solace from the view? "If I'm going to fight, I need my allies. Dinner seemed the easiest way to get everyone there."

"So, we're your team." Winter motioned to Macy. "The two of us."

"Yes, the people I trust most." Ash gripped both of

their shoulders and it was hard for Macy to shake the feeling that something was shifting between her and Ash Kingfisher.

Not that it mattered. He needed her. Whatever it was, she was in.

# CHAPTER SIX

MACY WASN'T QUITE convinced how great an idea it was
to be strapped in beside her boss for the drive to his parents' house for Friday night dinner and strategy session,
Winter Kingfisher's taillights leading the way into Sweetwater, but it was better than what she'd had planned for
the evening, so it was easy enough to go along.

Except for the crushing silence.

Ash had yet to say a word.

The tension between them was new. They were outside of the office, on their own, in the close confines of
the dark SUV.

Something about it made Macy think of a first date. In
her mind, she could picture Ash showing up at her door.
Instead of the Reserve uniform, he was wearing a jacket.

Macy had to blink at how easy that was to imagine,
Ash wearing date clothes. She saw him every day, but
that would be a new side of him.

A date with Ash would be a mix of old-fashioned good
manners, conversation like pulling teeth and so much
time to enjoy his handsome face.

No wonder this felt like a date. She was already there.

If one of them didn't speak soon, Macy was certain
she'd just forget how from all the stress of scrambling
through her brain to find something to say.

Ash cleared his throat and Macy froze. He'd get the
ball rolling.

When he merely shifted in his seat, Macy huffed out a breath. "Could this get any more awkward?"

Ash's rough laugh made it easier to relax. "You should have ridden with Winter. I bet she has plenty to say. Questions, anyway."

"I didn't have to ride with either of you, but you insisted." And she was still irritated about it.

Ash held up a hand. "I don't like the idea of you driving after dark."

Since the comment echoed her own thoughts about him a short while ago, Macy took a deep breath and tried to understand. "Except my car is still at the ranger station. You'll drive me back to it and I'll... What? Sleep in the station until the sun comes up?" Macy crossed her arms over her chest, still irritated but curious to see how this played out.

If she'd been able to see his face, Macy was certain she'd see the expression he always wore when he was corralling his patience to answer calmly. Even in the dark, she could almost hear his thinking.

"I'll follow you back home to make sure you're safe."

Macy pursed her lips as she considered pointing out the poor logic behind his plan. He could have done that with this trip. Instead, he was going to make two trips, one with her and one following her. Did he not see that?

"I wanted to talk to you. Just you," Ash said quietly. "This was the best way to have some time, just the two of us."

The heated wave started somewhere in her midsection and landed in her cheeks. Pleased that he thought of her as...

Unsure how to fill in the blank, Macy bit back a smile and tried to wait patiently for him to continue.

But silence filled the space again. Macy wasn't sure how long she could give him to get on with the show.

Finally, exasperated, she asked, "Well, then please talk already."

If she'd been thankful for the dark before, now she wanted bright sunlight. Most of what Ash said had to be deciphered through the emotions that showed on his face. By the light of the dashboard, Macy thought the muscle in his jaw was twitching. Twitching, that couldn't be good.

"Leland won't be the guy taking photos with kids at our open house, that's for sure." Ash's voice was tight. Macy wasn't sure she'd ever heard that before. His answer also had nothing to do with what she'd asked. Did it? "I have the okay to hire a new educational director. I never got a chance to get the okay to find the fire chief an administrator, but I'm going to do that, too. What can the guy do if he doesn't agree? Fire me?"

Was that squeak the leather of the steering wheel creaking? Macy pinched pleats in her pants as she decoded his answer. "That's what you were hoping for. Both things are good news, right?"

Ash's grunt was not an answer. He usually did that when he didn't want to reply.

"I'm guessing you approved what McKesson and the firefighters have put together for the photo booth at the open house. I knew it would be good." When Ash didn't say anything, Macy added, "No, don't tell me about it. I want to be surprised." Rolling her eyes helped nothing but it made her marginally happier. Macy wasn't concerned at all about whatever the fire house came up with, but she wanted to keep the conversation going. Anything would be better than letting the question she most wanted to ask escape.

*So, what do you think about all this relationship spec-*

*ulation? You and me? The two of us?* She'd try a care-free laugh which would strangle her and he'd have to perform CPR.

It would be one way of breaking the ice.

"They suggested the chief ranger take center stage, but I made that decision for him. Never asked. We only talked about the education program." Ash's voice was rough when he added, "And the lodge project some more."

"How did that go?" Macy asked as she leaned closer. This was the source of the whole change of atmosphere between them. She was certain of it.

"Let's talk about the chief ranger with Winter. I need everyone on board, but we're going to have to...possibly..."

Macy inched closer to him, one arm on the console between them, ready for whatever he was struggling with.

"Either way this turns out, I'm probably going to lose my job." Ash glanced at her before returning his eyes to the twisting road ahead of them. "Since that's the case, I've got nothing to lose. I might as well try to save The Aerie. Stopping the Callaways from building there is the only thing that would make all this worthwhile."

Caught off guard at how certain Ash seemed that he was on the way out, Macy had to catch her breath. All week, she'd tried to convince herself that this was going to blow over.

Ash had just calmly stated that nothing was going to return to normal. Ever.

"I want to talk to Winter about it first," Ash said, "but Hall still believes I've stirred up the bad press. He won't be able to save me, anyway, not if the Callaways want me out."

Macy licked her lips, desperate to find some positive encouragement that might convince Ash there was another choice. "What if we could find the person who *did* talk to the governor? The Callaways would be forced to leave you alone if you were cleared of suspicion." But how?

"For a time, maybe." Ash was so quiet in the close quarters of the front seat. "I don't think they'll forget this. Publicly challenging the Callaways is going to mean damage to careers. Mine. Winter's." He cleared his throat. "That's why I need Winter in this discussion."

Macy cleared her throat. "She's pretty amazing. Scary, but amazing."

The Kingfishers were both impressive. No matter what happened around him, Ash was the same. Steady. Solid. She respected that.

"Do you have a plan?" Macy asked. Day to day, she was the plotter; he was more about direction.

"Nope," Ash said with a sigh, "but I've gathered the greatest minds I know. You, Winter, my parents. We'll come up with one and then…we'll see."

"It figures that the first time you acknowledge my superior planning skills could be what leads to my swan song, Ash Kingfisher," Macy said, determined to set them both on the right foot and reassure herself that she did have something to contribute, "but you've come to the right place. I managed to get elected homecoming queen of my high school by polling groups and negotiating concessions from the administration. If I can unite Myrtle Bend High School in the pursuit of a second soda machine and chocolate chip cookies in the cafeteria— things that cost a pretty penny, I tell you—in order to subvert a popularity contest, I can manage bad press, greedy politicians and a bad-tempered boss."

When he didn't laugh, Macy wondered if she'd gone

too far in the pursuit of tough-minded talk like her grandmother would have used on Macy.

Then Ash offered her his right hand.

Half a second after she slipped her left hand in and gave it a squeeze, Macy realized he'd meant it as a handshake and she'd turned it into something else, something more.

First, she froze; then she tried to yank her hand back, but Ash tightened his grip and then rested his arm on the console between them, their fingers tangled together in a connection that shifted her whole world sideways.

"Homecoming queen? I never would have guessed. You're so…" Ash trailed off but there was no way Macy was going to let him leave that sentence unfinished. "Practical."

Macy stared hard at their hands for a second, the green light from the dashboard doing very little to clarify what it was about. "What if I told you that both my grandmother and the meanest girl in Myrtle Bend High School told me I couldn't do it?" She memorized how her fingers were linked with his, determined to analyze it. Later. When she was alone again. This connection was rare. Special. "That's all it takes, one person to say I can't."

His soft exhalation was some version of a laugh. Macy squeezed his hand. They could be the only two people in the world.

How sweet would that be, the two of them to… Do what exactly? Everyone else seemed to think they had couple potential. Ash was holding her hand. Did he think so, too?

"Macy," Ash said as he turned his head, "stop thinking so hard. This is enough for right now." His fingers tightened on hers and it was impossible to imagine pulling away from him at that point. "For ten minutes, hold my hand and be with me."

Getting her tongue to make conversation was nearly as difficult, so she shifted in her seat and did her best to remember how the butterflies in her stomach had transformed into something else, something more like the connection she'd always wanted and never found. Ash was one of the few people she trusted and even fewer that she depended on.

If their relationship changed, what would happen to that? What she loved was the safety she'd found in Ash's friendship.

When his fingers shifted and the warmth spread, Macy realized it didn't matter. Nothing mattered. The future would be what it would be. Her grandmother had told her that a thousand times whenever she'd fretted over this thing or that. The future would take care of itself, and no matter what happened, worrying over it wouldn't change a thing.

Besides all that, Ash Kingfisher was the kind of man that a woman took risks for. She'd never have to worry about him changing his mind or losing his way. Ash was kind, strong; a smart woman wouldn't toss away a chance for a relationship with him. The future would be whatever it would be.

"Tell me about your parents." Macy heard the roughness in her voice and knew she had to get herself back under control. Ash needed that control. "If I'd known I was meeting them, I might have…" What? Dressed differently? Like a woman Ash would date? How did she dress, that saint Macy hadn't even been able to imagine?

"I can't explain my parents." Ash squeezed her hand. "They'll love you. They love everyone. I've been thinking about introducing you to my mother all day long, just to watch your reaction. I doubt you've ever met anyone like her, but she's going to love you. That I'm sure of. You can't prepare in advance. Just be with me right now. I know that doesn't work for you because you organize your shoes by mileage or whatever, but I like this." He squeezed her hand.

Macy absorbed the shock that he'd considered introducing her to his parents as a good thing, something to look forward to. It was sweet, a compliment like she'd never received before, and the little girl who'd been abandoned by her own parents had spent some time imagining what it might be like to find a new, loving family.

Ash and his sister were tight.

At the first sign of trouble, Ash called on his family for help. And he wanted to bring her into that circle.

Macy struggled to regulate her racing heart.

*Say something funny. Don't make this bigger than it is.*

"I only organize shoes by color. Now, my sock drawer is arranged by age and I rotate them exactly through the laundry to make sure they all wear evenly. Anything else is ludicrous." Macy sighed. "I'm nervous. I don't like change, Ash. That's what makes me, *me*."

"No, what makes you, *you* is so much more than that. I need you to be planning, but right now, I need this." He shifted their hands. "Except…" He started untangling their fingers, but Macy refused to let go. "I realize how that sounds. I'm sorry. You're an employee of the Reserve. I would never want to make you uncomfortable by making advances that you could feel you have no power to reject or to make you fear for your job. You don't have to help me. You don't have to hold my hand." He blew out a frustrated breath. "I'm so focused on what I need. I'm sorry, Macy. Let me call Winter and tell her I'll be late. I'll take you back to your car. You deserve time to think about this, whether you want to get any more involved. We're alike in that way. I should know better. What is wrong with me?"

Macy knew her mouth was hanging open. When he applied the brakes to slow the SUV down and put on his turn signal, she snapped out of it. "Ash, do not stop or turn around. I want to go to dinner. I want to meet your mother. I want to be included. You know I can't stand to be left out of things." She giggled. For the first time in a week, it was impossible to contain the laughter and it felt good. "That's the longest string of words I've ever heard you put together. All of it nonsense, but it was truly amazing to see that you can speak in paragraphs. I mean, long sentences are rare enough but that was a full paragraph."

When he didn't answer, Macy squeezed his fingers. Holding Ash Kingfisher's hand in the dark night could become a habit if she let it.

"Are you sure you don't want me to take you back to your car?" Ash asked quietly. "There's a good spot to pull off coming up."

Thankful for the darkness now, Macy said, "Of course not." She stared straight ahead. "You don't scare me, Ash Kingfisher, not that you'd ever try. We both know I could find another job. If there was something—" she motioned between them because she couldn't put it into words "—between us, I'd only be worried about what happened if it didn't work, not that you coerced me into anything. You're awesome, Ash. I am, too. Maybe…" She drew the word out as she tried to decide how brave she was. "I don't know how to fill that in. I want to work at the ranger station. If something between us makes that too weird…" Macy shrugged. *I want to hold your hand, too.*

After a long beat, Ash grunted. "Maybe we leave the question hanging for now." It was hard to read how he felt about his suggestion, but he didn't sound content. That was nice. She wasn't content with it, either.

"Otter Lake is my home, too. And I need it. Let's settle this lodge question first. Then we can talk about what happens next. For now, I need the ranger station." *And you.* The words were right there, trembling to escape but she bit them back. "I can't imagine the place without you, so I'll do whatever you need. You might not know it, but that's the kind of friend I can be."

Macy let go of his hand to tangle her fingers together in her lap and ignored the fact that it was a lot less satisfying than Ash's warmth.

"Friends." Ash was silent long enough that she was almost sure that it was his last word on the subject. "That's what we are."

Macy couldn't tell if he meant it as a question or something else.

"Friends," she said, "who snap at each other over empty coffeepots and late reports. I mean, those exist, right?" Ash had been the fourth ranger she'd worked for and the only one that stuck. Not that he needed to know that. If he understood how rare it was for her to get along with a boss, he might be harder to handle. Right now, he thought he needed her and she wanted to keep it that way.

The lights of Sweetwater were at first a faint glow, but Macy was glad to see the town in the distance. As soon as she knew Ash's plan, she could figure out how to improve it, ensure its success.

Then life would go back to being comfortable, with nothing out of the ordinary.

No one asking her whether she and Ash were dating.

Winter would return to a mysterious godlike creature on stilettos instead of a woman on the verge of a nervous breakdown, thanks to work and a man who might be a ruthless politician but was certainly a bad fiancé.

And there would be no more holding Ash's hand.

It would be up to her to ask the questions and to reach across the space between them.

Could she do that?

The click of the turn signal drew Macy's attention back to the road in front of her. She wasn't certain what she'd expected of Ash Kingfisher's mother and father, but this fairy-tale older suburban street filled with holiday inflatables and a million lights in all the colors wasn't it.

"Whoa," Macy whispered, already in love with the Kingfishers because they lived on the prettiest street in the world.

"Yeah, the neighbors take their decorating seriously." Ash parked behind Winter in a long, narrow driveway. It was lit on both sides by lampposts wrapped in twinkling white lights. "And my father can't stand to lose a competition. Any competition." Ash wrapped his hand over her arm to stop her from throwing open the door. "If he sees me let you open your own door, we'll waste the first fifteen minutes of the meal on a lecture about the proper way to treat a lady." As he opened the door, the interior light showed his completely serious expression. "Just let me open your door."

Macy squirmed in the seat, uncomfortable with the experience. It made no sense. It was the kind of gesture a man might make to a woman he was dating. Maybe. Did any men do that anymore? Before she could decide, Ash had her door open. Macy wasn't sure what kind of expression was on her face, but it was enough to provoke a genuine laugh.

"Sometimes, you have to go along to get along, Macy." Ash closed the door and met Winter on the driveway.

"I'll follow your lead, big brother," Winter said and motioned him forward. She fell into step behind Macy, but it was easy to hear her say, "Meeting the parents. That's a big step, Macy."

Amazed to hear such a bratty, little-sister tone from cool Winter, Macy turned her head to glare over her shoulder. She didn't want to be teased about this—the one thing she'd discovered she wanted and couldn't have. Macy missed Ash's sudden stop. They made a three-person pileup, Macy grunting as she smooshed her face against Ash's back and again when Winter did the same to her, just as Ash's father opened the door. He was as tall as Ash, but salt-and-pepper hair was cut into a neat style. He wore a plaid button-down, making Macy wonder how Ash dressed in his off-hours. He'd helped her move once. After work. So he'd still been wearing his uniform.

"Well, now…" Ash's father frowned down at them. "I don't recall ordering any stooges. Donna, did you order holiday stooges?" Then his wide grin lit his whole face and he yanked Ash into his arms. "Never mind. A good stooge is something a man never turns down."

Macy was rubbing her chin, when Ash's father wrapped his arms tightly around her. "We've not been introduced. Martin Kingfisher. Father of these two, proudest father you ever met. And you are Macy Gentry, the woman who runs the Otter Lake Ranger Station."

He squeezed hard and Macy grinned at Ash over his father's shoulder. If she was right, there were red spots on his cheeks. "Mr. Kingfisher, I must say it is a pleasure to meet you. I might drop by every day for a hug like that." Macy returned his second squeeze and then stepped away. What was it about the Kingfisher men? Ash was maybe the one person she trusted absolutely. An introduction and a hug, and already Macy was certain whatever happened, life would be better for having been in Martin Kingfisher's company.

That was an amazing thing to find.

After Martin set his daughter down, three complete twirls with her giggling like she was six years old completed, he clapped his hands. "Hugs are free, Macy. So is advice. Anything else will cost you."

Before she could ask what else was available, Ash's mother stuck her head through the narrow doorway over the small saloon-like swinging doors. "Martin. You'll scare her to death with talk like that, although if you can get her to clear out a few of these baskets, I will not complain." She shoved a ragged blond braid over her shoulder and wiped her hands on a pink calico apron. "Don't scare off Ash's friend. Dinner's ready." Then she disappeared.

"Scared? Of what?" Macy mouthed as she exchanged a glance with Ash and he shrugged his shoulders. Whatever should have scared her went right over her head and Ash had no explanation to help her out. Instead, he had the face of a sixteen-year-old suffering his parents at a school open house. Macy loved it. Of all the things she'd seen and done in her life, stepping foot in the Kingfisher home for the first time was one she'd remember forever. Ash was hard to know; meeting his parents blew wide-open a window into his personality and who he was.

"What? I'm not scaring her. I only meant chores. Tax advice, charging for stuff like that. I make these amazing woven baskets, Macy." Martin Kingfisher leaned forward to murmur, "And I'll give you the friends-and-family price. You see anything you like, anything at all, make me an offer, 'mkay?" Then he whacked his hand in the center of her back, hard enough to jostle her into Ash's side, and shoved through the swinging doors.

What was the deal with the baskets? Macy replayed

the conversation in her head, but she was more confused than when this had started. Plus, she had a headache. Macy rubbed her forehead and turned back to Ash for direction.

But she couldn't form a question that made sense, either.

Ash grinned. He steadied her with one arm around her shoulders. "I couldn't have prepared you for this, could I?"

Grateful for the solid warmth against her side, Macy shook her head. "I don't see how. If you'd tried, I wouldn't have believed you."

Winter bumped her shoulder from the other side. "Just think, all this could be yours." Then she sashayed through the saloon door. Curious about Ash's reaction, Macy shot him a glance. Whatever he was thinking, Ash had no way of untangling it all.

"They're smart. They love me and Winter. They can help. No way would I bring you here otherwise."

Macy laughed. "I believe you, one hundred percent."

"Me, monosyllables and grunts, from this…" Ash trailed off and shook his head. "Yeah. It makes no sense." He took a deep breath. "You haven't met my mother yet, either. It's only getting weirder, Macy. Are you sure you want to do this?"

"Just try to stop me, Ash Kingfisher. This is more entertainment than I've had in years." And it was. Macy refused to let herself dwell on what it might be like to have a family like Ash's: close, supportive, fun and funny.

She wouldn't miss her chance to experience it firsthand.

Watching solid, tight-lipped Ash Kingfisher squirm through every minute was going to be a definite bonus.

## CHAPTER SEVEN

STANDING IN THE entryway of his parents' house, Ash realized the thing about Macy Gentry that made it impossible not to consider her the most beautiful woman he'd ever known: she met every challenge with a sparkle in her eye. On most days, he was the challenge she was trying to corral into submission, and it was nice to be locked into the give-and-take that made their relationship work.

Tonight, the pure energy that blazed from her pretty blue eyes was mesmerizing. Before he could stop her, she'd put both hands on the out-of-date saloon doors his mother loved and pushed right into the warm, cluttered kitchen. If she was nervous, it didn't show.

Considering what he might have said to make it easier to understand his mother preoccupied him for only a second. It was a futile brainteaser. He'd grown up in this house and he'd never come up with the solution.

Determined to follow her and run interference if necessary, Ash halted abruptly when Winter stepped in front of the doors to stop him. Only her head and shoulders appeared over the tiny doors; her wicked grin was enough to send a chill down his spine.

He might be four years older than Winter, but she'd always been the cleverest of the two of them.

"Macy tells me there's absolutely nothing between the two of you," Winter slowly drawled. Her eyebrow raised.

She spoke volumes with the eyebrows. She went for expressive; he was stuck on stonewall.

"Macy tells you the truth." Not that he was happy about it. Still, she'd surprised him when she'd taken his hand, and something had clicked in his head. For too long, something had been missing, teasing around the edges of his brain, as if he could catch it if he turned quickly enough. In that second when she'd put her hand in his, a new vision had come into focus.

Then she'd made it clear how unprepared either one of them were for the world to tilt toward something more than coworkers by thinking so loudly he couldn't ignore it.

Winter's grin made it easier to be content with a delay. His sister had no trouble believing they could be more. When he had a minute, he could return to the question with Macy.

"Tonight, she called us friends, so I guess that's better than employee and boss. Which we are. In your official capacity, I think you should warn me away from her."

"But…" Winter dipped her head down, clearly waiting for the real scoop.

"But." Ash shook his head. That was it. For the first time in a long time, someone tempted him to take chances, assume the risk in order to gain the reward, but he realized only a fool would push the issue when she'd marked her line clearly in the sand. She loved her job. She wouldn't risk it. "Nothing else. Friends."

"Classic blunder, brother." Winter whistled. "The worst decision she could make would be to turn my big brother down. I thought she was smarter than that."

"One of the two smartest women I know. Timing. That's what we're looking at here. First thing's first—dinner with Mom and Dad, manage to save your career while we torpedo mine spectacularly. Dating after that. Maybe." Pinning his hopes on "after this Reserve problem was resolved" was dangerous. Ash crossed his arms over his chest. "Macy's half a second from sprinting from that kitchen because Mom is washing her chi or some such and you're standing here, annoying me. Do you want that on your conscience?"

Winter sniffed. "If she's terrorized by some innocent chi talk, she's not the woman I thought she was." She huffed out a breath. "You're half in love with her already, aren't you? You wouldn't gamble on the embarrassment of the parental units otherwise." Winter patted his shoulder. "It's your luck that you'd find the female counterpart to your workaholism and obliviousness to what has been right in front of you. Still, I agree with you about timing." She wagged her finger at him. "First, we'll tackle this little problem at the Reserve and save both our jobs. You can't stop true love, just delay it awhile." Her sympathetic expression melted into laughter as she backed away and Ash slowly followed.

Instead of Macy being confounded by his parents, which he expected, Macy, his mother and his father were doing a cramped version of some Motown dance moves between the refrigerator and the oven while they set the table. "Turn the music down. The cops are here," his mother cried over Stevie Wonder's "Signed, Sealed, Delivered, I'm Yours." Then she dropped the bread basket on the table, scooted around the table, twirled Winter over to her father and wrapped her arms tightly around his neck. "My son. I've missed you."

Ash dipped his head to rest his chin on her shoulder and closed his eyes. It didn't matter if it had been five hours or five days since he'd seen his mother, her greeting never changed. He never knew what color her hair would be because she liked to play with dyes and lengths and wigs and a million other things that were part of her personal style, but she always smelled of the lavender soap she made herself from the gardens she tended.

And she always hugged him like she'd never let him go.

"Mom. The food is burning." Ash squeezed her tightly and glanced up to see his father doing his level best to dance with both Winter and Macy. Since he switched to a two-step when the song shuffled to Patty Loveless singing "I'm That Kind of Girl," it had turned into a free-for-all. "And we have company."

Macy's grin was impossible to miss. When she and Winter spun away from his father to do their own two-step, she was pure sparkle. A little bit of music and his parents' fun-loving party shuffle had wiped out some of her intimidation. Winter promptly stepped on both of Macy's feet, and they both giggled.

"Macy? She's not company," his mother squawked. "You talk about her enough that I'm certain she's already family."

Ash cleared his throat as he watched Macy's jaw drop. Winter's wicked laughter was enough to bring the heat of embarrassment back up to his cheeks. At some point, he'd have to get a handle on the blushing. If Sam Blackburn or Brett Hendrix were here, they'd be hooting louder than Winter. Both men had done enough talking about the women in their lives to Ash that they'd relish having the tables turned.

Ash resolved then and there to solve his own relationship questions.

"Now, I know we have serious business to discuss, so I made a proper dinner. Spaghetti. You can never go wrong with pasta, am I right, Macy?" His mother pointed at the seat directly across from Ash's usual spot and said, "Have a seat. I'll pour you some rosehip tea."

Macy blinked slowly and then hurried to take the seat she'd been assigned.

He should have warned her.

But what would he have said, really? While he was considering telling his mother Macy needed a glass of water or coffee or something a little less healthy and a little more common than rosehip tea, his father sat down next to Macy.

"Macy, you like that basket?" his father asked as he leaned over to talk quietly and pointed at a shelf over the door. Ash had a feeling the low-key sales pitch was for his benefit. No doubt his father expected him to put a stop to the hard sell that was coming, but Ash was too worn-out to come up with a defense. Instead, he picked up his glass of "healthy" tea and forced himself to sip.

When Macy did the same and followed with a quick version of the "blech, what is that" lick of her lips, Ash struggled to hold the laughter in.

And it felt so good, he was afraid it was going to escape.

Watching Winter roll her eyes while Macy played along with his father was enough to make a man think life would go on.

"Mr. Kingfisher, that is a very nice basket. Did you make it? What did you use?" Macy asked politely and then took the basket he offered her to trace the lines of color worked into the side. "I love the colors. I see… mountains." It *was* nice work. His father had too much time on his hands, thanks to retirement, and turned it into a passion for weaving. Unfortunately, he was also a businessman at heart and was always looking for some cash flow. Martin Kingfisher had never met a sales opportunity he hadn't seized.

"I did. Handmade. In the tradition handed down from my mother to me. I even made some of the dyes, but I'm still learning." He tapped Macy's hand. "You know, the Cherokee woven basket spans generations, the tradition passed mostly through the female line. My mother had no daughters, so I was her unwilling student. As a kid, I didn't think much of it. Now it keeps me busy and I enjoy it. That's good work." *Take it from me*, his expression said.

His mother huffed out a deep breath. "It is very good work, Martin. In the classes you're teaching, the neighbors you show them to, everyone tells you that, so you don't have to force visitors to our table to stroke your ego. You aren't selling Macy one, either. I'm *giving* her at least three before she goes, so stop pushing." She bugged her eyes out at her husband. He stuck his tongue out and winked at Macy.

"Donna's my biggest fan," Martin said.

"I really am," she said with a nod. "And the one who keeps him in line and loves him more than anything. That's called a 'wife,' am I right?" She looked around the table. "Call me Donna, Macy." Then his mother dished a serving onto Macy's plate. Macy would never eat that much pasta in a week of meals and her face said so, but she wasn't going to argue.

"Well," his father said as he leaned back in his chair, "she has family who'd like a nice gift. It is Christmastime, you know. I'm only trying to help, and you're always telling me to try to *sell* them."

"No family, and all my closest friends are right here." Macy wrinkled her nose at Ash, ignoring the look his parents exchanged at her words. "But you can bet I'll take my basket and show it off to anyone I can think of. I could start a collection." She picked up her fork and pretended to be absorbed in her spaghetti.

Ash could see on each parent's face the regret and embarrassment at pushing Macy to admit she was on her own.

"Why don't you tell us what happened with the chief ranger today, Ash?" Winter said from her seat to his right.

Grateful to have the conversation turn, Ash cleared his throat.

"I went to talk to him about hiring a new education director, someone to bring more schools or civic groups in during the slow season and to work with the park guides." Ash took another sip of the terrible tea. "But I had to... I should back up. I wanted to stop the project, but I'm not the one who got this mess started. Leland Hall told me to research, find the best firm and commission an environmental impact study that could be presented to the Callaways. I followed orders. No one at the Reserve was enthusiastic about the lodge, but we needed something to hold and say, 'This is the problem.' I did that, but what benefit would I gain by telling in advance and putting all this heat on myself and jeopardizing my job, not to mention hurting Winter? You'd have had to threaten to do me in before I would have even considered doing something like that." He glanced over at his sister. The district office was generally in favor of the lodge project, but Winter wanted to protect the Reserve, even if the addition meant new growth opportunities. They'd discussed their concerns over the habitat destruction more than once. "I don't know if I would have released the report early if it had occurred to me, but I hope not. I know it's causing trouble with the Callaways, and it's not just your wedding in jeopardy."

"But the tip-off to the governor was anonymous," his father murmured. "Why all the focus on you?" He rested his chin on his hand as he watched Winter. "And, my girl, what does your fiancé say about all this?"

Winter sighed. "I don't know the answer to that one. We talked the morning the story hit, but as soon as he mentioned Ash…" She cleared her throat. "I told him clearly what I thought about any attempts to make Ash the face of this story and he didn't appreciate it. Now he's not returning my calls, probably because he's waiting on his father to decide what happens next. But all of Whit's campaign plans revolve around heritage, history and family values. As soon as Richard Duncan had the means to punch holes in that, he took it. Making my brother the face of it? That's good television, strong ratings, easy for voters to remember. And my brother as the leading opponent? It's too juicy." She shook her head. "A lodge that destroys the land it's built on is going to run against the Callaway reputation for protecting Tennessee's past and pride. Founding fathers of the state capital, benefactors of so many organizations and the reserves… It won't do for them to be seen chasing the almighty dollar like this."

"Even if Ash did do that—" his mother snapped before raising one hand. "Now, I don't want to say 'I told you so,' but the minute you introduced me to Whit, I had the skeeves." She tapped the table. "Skeeves don't lie."

Macy's slow blinks indicated she had no idea what the skeeves were. That's because it was something his mother had latched onto when Ash was in the third grade.

"Skeeves. Like getting the shivers, but about someone you think is a criminal and you don't have the proof," Ash translated. Macy listened carefully and then answered with a firm nod.

"Like the bully who chased Ash from the bus stop for

three weeks until he told me about it. Too young to have a criminal record but I could see it looming in his future if we didn't change his path, you know?" His mother waited for Ash to agree. "And what did I do?"

Ash didn't want to say it.

His mother raised her eyebrows.

She'd wait until dinner got cold.

"She cleared the skeeves." Ash bit his lip as he watched Macy's slow blinks turn to fast ones. First, she'd been confused; now she was trying not to smirk.

"Burn a few of the right herbs, make a case to the universe, and the skeeves can be turned away." His mother jumped up. "I've seen it happen. That bully? He's a pediatrician now in Nashville. Nice family pictures on Facebook. I've got enough sage to work something out." Before Ash could stop her, his mother had stepped out of the room into her patio greenhouse.

Ash slumped back against his chair. He should have had this conversation with Winter and Macy at the ranger station. Anytime his parents were involved, the whole plan went through some detours.

His father sighed. "While I believe the skeeves are a real thing—" he put both hands over his heart and waited until the three of them had nodded their understanding "—I also know that sometimes you have to call the principal, go to a meeting your wife knows nothing about with the parents of the little runt trying to be a big man at the bus stop, and handle things a different way, like with a full week of chores wherein you have multiple conversations about all the wrong paths a person can take and how hard work is the only key to success. Sage is good. Refusing to back down is sometimes the only real option, though."

Ash took a bite of his pasta as he absorbed the fact that the antiskeeve ceremony had had some help.

"Here's what we're going to do." His father tapped the table. "Whatever you want, Ash." Then he leaned back and shrugged. "Your job. Your future. Your decision."

Ash turned to Winter. She wrinkled her nose. "He's absolutely right. In this, we do what you want. If you decide to keep your head down and let this play out, I'll handle calls and we'll both keep our jobs until the end. But if you decide to fight, then we'll just see who wins. Maybe we'll both be looking for new jobs. If we have to move back home, I'm calling dibs on the biggest spare bedroom."

Ash braced his hand on her chair. "The job isn't the only thing in the balance."

Winter took a bite, chewed it slowly and washed it down with some of his mother's brew while she stared down at her twinkling engagement ring. "That'll be *my* decision. Whit and I need to talk. Then I'll figure out what to do from there. The one thing has no impact on the other."

"But it does," Macy said softly. "How can it not?" Macy, ever practical and thinking of others. He was glad she'd spoken up when she did.

Winter closed her eyes for a minute. "Some relationships can survive big tests." No one at the table could be convinced that her engagement was one of them. His sister's face displayed her own doubts plainly.

His mother came back in with a wad of greenery in her hand. "I'm short a full bouquet of what I need to burn, but this should send things back a bit, give us all some breathing room." She dropped the bundle on the floor and took her seat. "We'll light that after dessert. I have apple pie. I tried a new recipe." She settled and then took Winter's hand. "Ash is going to do the right thing. Before, he was going to do what it took to keep his job. Now we're going to stop that lodge from being built. We love Otter Lake. I stood at the top of those falls and married the only man in this world who could ever make me happy. Someday, I hope each of you will do the same. Or, I don't know, at least kiss the people you want to marry or something." She waved her hand. "Winter, skeevy Whit is not that man and I'll stake my reputation as a healer on it." She studied her daughter's face. "This situation has come about to make your decision easier and clearer."

Anxious to take as much pressure off Winter as he could, Ash said, "Winter's right. She's got to have more information before she makes any decision."

His mother obviously wanted to argue further, but his father headed her off. "What's our first step?"

Ash propped his elbows on the table and waited for his mother to squawk about his manners. When she didn't, he decided they all had a lot on their minds. "That's why Macy and Winter are here. Strategy."

"Good. Something to do." Winter cracked her knuckles. "First thing, you start talking to every reporter you can get a hold of. You tell the truth. You had no contact with Richard Duncan, the chief ranger suggested the study be done as a way to support your views in front of the Reserve's board of directors. And of course you're glad there's more conversation about the lodge because of the harm it could do to the Reserve."

Ash waited for someone else to say something. "And I start looking for another job ASAP, then."

"Nope. We start truth telling ASAP. You gain nothing and risk everything, an everyman standing up to the wealthy family that pulls the strings. Your only hope is to take this to the full board. Callaways are in charge there, but they don't have a majority. If we can get Caleb Callaway to show up for a vote, you might even have an ally. The problem is going to be when they decide to play dirty. How can we fight that with only Ash's honor and integrity?"

"No good comes from ignoring the truth." Ash watched his father nod as Ash repeated the words he'd heard so many times.

Then he realized his father had done some ignoring of his own, mainly when it came to fighting the skeeves honestly, but now was not the time to launch into that point.

"I have a suggestion," Macy said. When everyone turned to her, she cleared her throat. "First thing Monday, let's fire the first shot. Can you get a press conference together, Winter? You could say it's regarding the winter open house next weekend, but everyone will be ready to dig into Ash's involvement." Macy held up a second finger. "We'll go from defense to offense. Instead of hiding away, Ash will hit them with the truth, say he had nothing to do with getting the governor involved, but he can quote statistics about the environmental impact of building at The Aerie. We'll hand out copies. We'll challenge the governor's record directly, question what he's done to protect the state's lands himself. We can call on the Callaways to reconsider the project while reinforcing our gratitude that the Reserve exists, thanks to the family." She tipped her head to the side. "Before any of that happens, Ash will get a haircut. There's no sense in tweaking the chief ranger's nose by cheating on the regulations, you know?"

Before he could object to the valid comment, Winter nodded. "It's bold. The Callaways prefer agreement to even supportive opposition." She chewed spaghetti as she considered the plan. "I'll set it up. We pick up the chips, wherever they fall, and make a plan for phase two. That will be when the Callaways go low. I'm not sure what that means, but I have a feeling it will happen. And yes, Mom, that totally gives me the skeeves, the fact that I can predict that the family I'm about to marry into will do whatever it takes to win and I have no idea how to stop it. They need to blame someone, even if they can't find the deserving target. That's why the media is coming after Ash. Whit was the first to throw his name out there as the person who'd betrayed their trust."

Ash squeezed his sister's shoulder. That had to hurt. Add the fact that they'd argued and hadn't spoken since, and the wedding was clearly in danger.

"Still, I love Whit. We've been best friends and partners in his political career for a decade. He wanted to get married as soon as we graduated. If we'd done that, just… Things might be different. If he's still that guy, the one who attended so many political rallies with me and got excited over the same causes I did, I need to make my decision with that guy, not the one you think you know. Just be patient, please. I'll figure this out." She blinked as she waited for her mother to speak. When their mom made a tight line of her lips and mimed throwing away the key, Winter softened. "I'll drag him up to Yanu if that makes you happy. There, I'll either kiss him or shove him over. Poetic justice." Winter grinned.

"My girl. You are my girl, through and through. Couldn't be prouder." Their mother lunged across the table to hug Winter's neck, rattling silverware and glasses. Ash and his father exchanged a look, one they'd shared more than once. In their small family, it was most often Winter and his mother that butted heads, because his sister couldn't be any more practical if she tried and his mother had her own set of rules. When they were aligned, though, the female Kingfishers were fierce. The one time Ash had wanted to dump a girl in high school, Winter had disapproved of him doing it over the phone. She'd told his mother, and they'd tormented him until he'd made an in-person explanation of why he and Charity Scarborough should not go to the prom together. The fact that she'd already started dating someone else, the biggest jerk on the football team, had not swayed the female Kingfishers in the least.

Throughout his life, he'd understood that most families were probably different from his, more predictable.

As he watched Macy try to pretend that she was absolutely comfortable with all the family-ness flying around the table, Ash knew he had a lot to be grateful for. He could have decided to be an unemployed beet farmer, and his mother would have applauded. His father would have given him advice and worked circles around him until he was building a steady income from his combination beet-and-organic-juices roadside stand. That was who they were. Winter had pieces of each of them; he had other pieces. Together they were unstoppable.

If he lost his spot at the Reserve, it would take some time to figure out what he'd do next. There wasn't much call for a park ranger with a limp, not when the competition for both state and national park service jobs was so intense. Law enforcement would be a long shot and the fact that he could be in harm's way daily would give his mother a strong case of the skeeves, stronger than all the sage in the world could battle.

But at least he knew his safety net—his family—would catch him and it would hold until he could stand on his own.

Macy was alone in the world. Her safety net was... What? Did she have one?

"How long will it take for you to have everything ready to distribute, Macy?" Winter asked as she picked up the notebook she never traveled without. "We want to give the reporters enough time to make it to the ranger station, but without giving anyone at headquarters enough notice to make it to the ranger station before the press conference."

Macy pursed her lips. "I've filed everything to do with the lodge project, so it'll be easy to prepare. By ten, I'll have coffee hot and waiting. Do we need snacks?"

Everyone turned to face him.

"No." He was reminded of Leland's expression during his last visit to the district office. "No coffee. No snacks. This is official business. Very serious."

Macy wasn't an event planner. She was the administrative powerhouse that kept everything on schedule.

"And I don't want Macy anywhere near it. You're going to take the day off. I'll go in and make the copies tomorrow." Ash nodded at her shock. "Myself. I will make the copies myself. You are going to be sick and you are going to stay home. Yes, this will ruin your chances of winning the nonexistent award for perfect attendance, but you will be far away from the ranger station on that day."

The blaze in her eyes suggested she had a few choice words to give him, but she glanced from his mother to his father and said, "Did you mention dessert, Donna? Ash and I can figure out the details later. I'm glad we have the makings of a plan."

His mother blinked slowly, but whatever she read on Macy's face was enough to convince her to go along.

Was it some indefinable signal only women understood? Ash had a feeling that Macy was biding her time and that his mother understood that and bowed to her ability to wound an idiotic man with words alone. When his father gave him a sorrowful head shake, his hunch was confirmed.

Not that his impending scolding mattered. Macy needed protection. She had no one who would catch her if things fell apart.

So he would make sure that didn't happen, keep her away from the ranger station when it all went down.

Figuring out how to convince her he was right would require some brainpower and he should let his mother burn all the sage she had.

He was definitely coming down with a case of the skeeves.

# CHAPTER EIGHT

MACY HAD BEEN staring out the passenger-side window with her nose tilted toward "extremely annoyed" for so long that she had a crick in her neck and a throbbing pain at her temple.

And Ash still hadn't said a single word since they'd left his parents' lovely little house.

"Bet my parents weren't what you expected," Ash spoke, leaving Macy with a difficult decision. It wasn't an apology. He hardly ever made them without her explaining in depth why he needed to, so unless she unbent, she was going to permanently freeze in this condition.

"Most of my friends in high school loved hanging out at our place." Ash cleared his throat. Was he going to share something with her? Macy leaned back against the seat, grateful when the belt stopped digging into the side of her neck. "Of course, I had to fight some of those same guys in elementary school for supposedly *joking* about my being Cherokee."

Macy glanced at him and noticed he was watching her.

"I don't get it. Why would they do that?" Macy turned her attention back to the road. She'd ask questions; Ash would keep talking. That didn't mean she forgave him.

"Kids are dumb. So many families around here have some Cherokee ancestors and there are plenty like me and Winter who still have the name to prove it." He shook his head. "When you consider my mother's awful baking, they should have been teasing me about her gross muffins and cupcakes. Elementary coincided with my mother's refined sugar-free phase. Those were some rough years."

Reluctantly, Macy laughed. "I can imagine. Particularly since you never met a piece of pie you don't love."

"My dad fixed that. Very sweetly, he talked her around and I'll never forget the first Christmas where she served pecan pie again. It's one of my favorites. Can't remember what Santa brought, just the first bite of syrupy goodness."

"I bet that was amazing. I'm always so surprised when I hear someone mention Santa like there was a time when they believed the myth."

The silence between them was nice since the anger was gone. He'd been able to do that almost from the first time they'd tangled. Ever since, he could always slowly turn her away from annoyance and irritation to amusement.

"You never did? Grandma didn't believe in giving you Santa, either?" Ash asked.

Macy's snort was louder than she meant it to be, so she quickly said, "Not only didn't believe, but she didn't cotton to allowing other parents to fool their kids into thinking it, either. I'll never forget the first meeting at the principal's office I attended. It was a Thursday, just before the holiday break started." Her grandmother had worn her apron into town that day. On the Wednesday afternoon before that, Gran had informed both teachers monitoring the pickup line and a dozen parents waiting for their kids that lying to children should be a criminal act and that encouraging them to believe in something so senseless as an elf who delivered free gifts for acceptable behavior was bad parenting. Macy had been six. Luckily, she'd also been the only child within hearing distance. If she'd had to remember the faces of kids who'd had their illusions shattered, along with the expressions of the stunned adults, she'd hate it. As it was, she could laugh.

"Macy Gentry got called to the principal's office?" Ash's teasing voice was rare enough that it was especially nice to listen to it when it happened.

"My *grandmother* got called to the principal's office. I was just waiting for her to arrive." Macy laughed because it was funny now that she didn't have to live the embarrassment anymore. The town of Myrtle Bend must have already forgotten she existed and she'd keep it that way. "Turns out, school authorities frown on parents lecturing each other in the pickup line. My grandmother didn't believe biting her tongue was ever the right decision." At Ash's whistle, Macy shrugged. "The principal didn't have much to say to her, though. I guess the shock was still there." Macy sighed. "Still, he did explain why it was better for me not to repeat the truth about Santa to other kids, even if I knew it." As if she'd ever ruin someone else's fun like that. Fun was to be cherished, not squashed.

Truth mattered, too.

So did joy and hope and learning those things as a child because holding on to them as an adult would be a battle.

When Ash had nothing to say, she turned to see that he was watching her again. "What? It's a cute story. You gotta admit that, not that that's what I want to talk to you about."

"Cute now, maybe, but sad, too. I can't imagine growing up in a house where you're expected to be an adult from…birth? Were you ever allowed to be a kid, Macy? To daydream about impossible things?"

"Daydream?" If she'd been asked to come up with the last word Ash might use in a conversation, *daydream* might have been on the list. When he said it like that, he made her wonder if he thought there was something wrong with her.

"When I have my own family, I'll run it differently, Ash, but you gotta admit that I turned out to be a perfectly capable, highly functioning human being, so my grandmother didn't mess up too badly." Macy told herself that often enough the words rolled off her tongue. This might be the first time she heard the defensive tone, however. No defense was necessary, was it?

"My parents are still putting up Christmas lights, even though there have been no kids in their house for decades. My father puts a black bear on every other basket he makes and sells them as good luck house-warming presents. Basically, he's trying to start his own myth, one person at a time. It's hard to imagine what it must have been like in your grandmother's house," Ash scoffed. "For that matter, my grandmother, a woman who was always pointing out omens of death, would grab my hand every time she saw a rainbow and drag me off to chase the pot of gold." Ash tipped his head to the side. "Cherokee do not traditionally believe in leprechauns, Macy, but they do believe in fun and whimsy and joy in life. Or, at least the Kingfishers did."

Since she'd spent a day watching the clock count down to the weekend and wondering what she'd do to fill her time until work started on Monday, Macy understood that she was missing something important. Other people worked to live. Her life was about work. Sure, her grandmother had kept her clothed and fed, but what about the rest of life?

"My kids will dream, Ash." Macy cleared her throat.

"What I don't understand is why we're all...'Macy's childhood was terrible.' I want to talk to you about your decision that I'm going to be out sick on Monday. Because I'm not. I don't call in sick. I don't *get* sick." She didn't want to be defensive. She also didn't want to spend time considering what her life might have been like with a family who'd welcomed Santa and chased rainbows and danced as they prepared dinner and welcomed guests to their table.

Ash held out his hand, but changed his mind before she could decide whether or not to take it. She wanted to, but she didn't understand what that might do to their relationship.

"Start. Call in sick on Monday. This one time, it's a good thing." Ash's flat voice was the same one he used when he was done talking about options she presented him with. At this point, he was sticking to his decision. "I know you're afraid of an entire three days without work, but I'd like you to see if you can manage it. Trust me, if you can't, you will hear 'I told you so' when you fail."

Macy crossed her arms over her chest and bit back an angry answer. This wasn't Ash.

His words reminded her of Winter's description of her older brother. He was pushing buttons to get what he wanted: her safety. Macy knew what he was doing. He was pulling the homecoming queen maneuver on her, telling her she couldn't do something in order to make certain she'd do it or die trying.

A twisted bet that she couldn't stay away from the ranger station when he wanted her to was his only shot.

She was going to give Ash what he wanted. She'd prove to them both that there was more to her life than the Otter Lake Ranger Station.

That didn't mean she had to make it easy for him.

"When you call to beg me to come in because you can't find the reading glasses that are on top of your head, rest easy and know that I have an 'I told you so' in my pocket for you, Ash Kingfisher. You're going to miss me, see if you don't." Macy sniffed and turned to look resolutely back out the passenger window. The hardest part of winning an argument with Ash Kingfisher was learning when to rest. She had a solid last word as long as she didn't ruin it with more talking.

"You're absolutely right," Ash muttered. "I am going to miss you. Why aren't you being more grateful for this sacrifice?"

That was nice, but she couldn't forgive him. Not yet. They spent the rest of the trip back to the ranger station in silence. When he put the SUV in Park next to her car, he eased out of the driver's seat pretty quickly.

As she watched him limp around to the passenger side, she bit back the urge to tell him how silly it was to insist on opening her door when it hurt him.

Ash wouldn't relent, not over a little thing like his own pain. And that's where their disagreement over her attendance was coming into things. He thought he was helping her.

"The copier is finicky. Sometimes you have to shut it down, let it rest for a minute and then restart it. If you run out of paper, there's a full box in the closet next to the restrooms. The new ink cartridges are stored on the filing cabinets, remember?" What else would he need to know? Macy could think of a long list of points, but… "Just text me when you run into trouble."

When she paused next to her car, he shut the SUV door quietly. That strange tension was back between them. This might as well have been the end to a first date, filled with the exciting wonder of "will they or won't they have a goodnight kiss?"

"I can handle the printer, Macy." Ash studied her face before turning away. "I just can't let anything bad happen to you."

It was hard to stay mad at the man, not when he said sweet things like that. Macy took a chance because it was dark and they were alone and it was time to take chances. She moved to stand in front of him and wrapped her arms around his neck before resting her head on his chest. "I loved dinner at your house."

She wasn't sure he'd answer. Maybe he was frozen in surprise, but eventually his arms settled tightly around her, squeezing her closer. "You fit. Almost like you're the missing piece, Macy."

Her heart thumped hard against her chest at his soft words. "Next time, will you dance with me?"

Ash's rough laugh shivered across her nerves like a caress, but he leaned down to say, "I don't dance, but for you, I'd give it a shot."

Macy wanted a kiss. She stared up into his face, lit only by moonlight and the security lights around the ranger station parking lot.

"Let's get you on the road. You've got a whole lot of fun to cram into that sick day that's coming up. You need to plan it all out." Ash studied her lips as he spoke, but he stepped back.

It was almost impossible not to sag against her car without his support, but she got the door unlocked and slid inside. He carefully closed it. "I'll follow you down, wait for you to get in your apartment." At her nod, he returned to the SUV.

Macy started the car and made her cautious way back to Sweetwater. When she was inside her apartment and

Ash was gone, she leaned against her front door and closed her eyes.

Her whole world was upside down thanks to Ash Kingfisher. Being apart right now hurt, but she'd give him what he'd asked.

Mainly because she never had taken losing lightly. And the man was prepared to use that against her.

It had been an amazing night.

She wanted more time with this Ash Kingfisher.

# CHAPTER NINE

NERVES HAD BEEN a part of Ash's job, on and off, ever since he accepted the position of head ranger at the Otter Lake Ranger Station. When he was out on the trails, he was in his element. He understood the forests around the lake, the climb up to Yanu and other popular spots, the animals living here and there, and the places in danger from climate change and human interference.

Even talking to groups about what they did on the Reserve to protect it and address the challenges from climate change was easy because he understood the end goal of every project he and his team undertook.

If the fire module identified an area for a prescribed burn, they prepared detailed reports about the necessity and timing that he read until he understood. When they partnered with conservation groups to improve otter habitat or to clear trails that made areas of the Reserve easier to access for visitors, he asked questions and he researched until he was certain his information was solid. Nothing about his job could surprise him because he'd done his best to make sure that no one knew more about the lands inside the boundaries of the Smoky Valley Nature Reserve than he did.

But standing in the lobby of the ranger station while he watched a small group of reporters mill outside had turned his stomach into a battlefield and he wasn't certain he was going to be able to keep all the action there contained.

When vomiting was an attractive option, the world had gotten completely out of hand.

"Is the coffee ready yet?" he mumbled with no real target.

Silence was his only answer at first.

"I hope you weren't expecting me to make it. I can't drink the stuff unless it's a critical situation," Winter said. She was standing in front of a large map of the Reserve next to the observation window. When she traced a trail and tilted her head sideways, Ash wondered if she was plotting her escape route.

"Is that something I should do?" Nicole asked, one hand held up to cover her mouth as if he'd caught her stealing. She hovered, half in, half out of Macy's chair as if she couldn't decide which direction to go. "I'm sorry." Nicole was the only part-time administrative support person in the Reserve system. She filled in as needed, and the only other time she'd been at the ranger station, Macy had been, too. They'd collaborated on a large project to update how the number of visitors to the various areas of the Reserve was tracked.

These statistics were important in evaluating the Reserve's programs and amenities which helped the rangers and the board of directors determine budgets and which areas needed shoring up. Nicole had helped with data entry when they made the changeover from their old paper logs to the new computerized system.

He remembered Macy saying Nicole would be coming to help out and that the project was completed early because of it. Why couldn't he remember Nicole doing the work? How she tiptoed around him and jerked every time he addressed her made him think she'd done her best to avoid him that time.

Did she miss Macy as much as he did?

Ash realized Macy had acted a lot like Nicole when she'd landed with him at the ranger station. That suggested the problem wasn't with Nicole.

"You know, if I hadn't grown up with you, that frown would be giving me fits, too," Winter murmured. "Unless you want to be answering your own phone, take it down a notch."

Ash held up a hand. "No worries. It's no one's job. The first person who wants a cup makes it. That'd be me this morning." After the weird smile he attempted and missed, based on Nicole's wide eyes, Ash stepped inside the small break room, grateful to have something to do with his hands. He'd been at the ranger station most of the day on Sunday. First, he'd had to hunt up Macy's files. One call to her would have cleared up his confusion, but he refused to do that. He was half afraid she wouldn't answer his call, anyway. In typical Macy fashion, she'd filed it in a small pocket of files in the drawer in her desk instead of in the large file room where all the vendor payments and countless pieces of paper went. It was an ongoing project, like all the other files she kept close at hand.

Smart.

Why didn't he know that part of her system?

In his frustration over not being able to pull everything out of the filing cabinets there, Ash had settled in her seat. The view of the beautiful, quiet lobby was satisfying.

Not as nice as it would have been if Macy had been in her usual place, but nice. Then he'd seen the drawer marked Current Projects and shaken his head. It was the largest current project on the Reserve at that point. She needed the file at her fingertips. Duh.

From that point, all he'd had to do was manhandle the copier which obviously knew someone other than Macy was at the helm. He'd lost count of the paper jams he'd cleared and written himself a note to make sure next year's budget could handle a new copier.

If he was still here, they'd replace the possessed copier.

As the coffee percolated, he heard Brett Hendrix come in and greet Winter. He hadn't called Hendrix in; that made him wonder if news had gotten out somehow.

"Hey, boss, Christina called after the second news van passed the campground. You've got a little party building out front. Need me to do…something?" His expression was concerned and alert.

That alertness was the sign of a good law enforcement ranger in Ash's experience. Knowledge was critical, but without the ability to scan the situation and make quick adjustments, many rangers got tangled up in challenging situations. Hendrix was his best ranger on the force. Having him there was reassuring, but it would be bad visually if things turned sideways.

"You can hit the patrol, Hendrix. We're going to have a press conference, try to get out some good information regarding the open house and shut some gossip down." Ash did his best to keep his face expressionless. Hendrix had less experience reading his face than Macy did, but he was sharp.

"Shut down the gossip," Hendrix said slowly, "but not the lodge project itself?" Like Ash and most people who supported the role of the Reserve to protect Tennessee's lands, Hendrix had never wanted the habitat at The Aerie disturbed. Brett wasn't a fan of any change ever. That was part of the reason why he and Hendrix got along so well.

"No way I can shut it down. Only the Callaways can do that. Today, we're going to ask them to reconsider the project in front of those reporters out there. Probably will be the last nail in my coffin with the Callaways, but might as well take my swing for the Reserve." Ash sipped his coffee and turned to watch Nicole who was fidgeting nervously with the phone cord. Hendrix shifted to study the crowd and turned back to Ash, a question on his face. "Best thing for you to do for your career is to stay out of the picture, Hendrix. When I go, I need you here keeping the Reserve safe."

Hendrix ran a hand down his nape, his own dissatisfaction with his choices clear. "I'd rather stand with you. I owe you that much, Ash."

Ash didn't answer because there was no sense in trying to convince Hendrix otherwise. It would be nice to have another friendly face close by.

He was certain removing Macy from this mess was the best thing for her.

That didn't mean he didn't miss her and want her there fiercely.

Because he did. Macy steadied him.

If he said that out loud to anyone, he was sure they'd be stunned. How much steadier could a man get than Ash Kingfisher, the guy who never smiled?

Only he knew the difference in his confidence when she was around.

"It's time, Ash." Winter stuck her head through the doorway. "We can't keep them waiting any longer, not in these temperatures. I know you don't want them inside the ranger station, but we need to get the show on the road. Reporters with frostbite are bound to write unflattering articles." Winter raised her eyebrows. "If I'd known she was your backbone, I'd have insisted Macy be here. You aren't yourself without her. Stop stalling. Time to roll."

She was gone before he could snap at her that it was entirely too late to be telling him such a thing because there was nothing he could do to fix it and why hadn't she taken that side of the argument at their parents' table instead of burying her head when things got so icily polite and it wasn't that Macy was his backbone but that he was more himself when he was in her company.

Ash held off, reminded of their teenage shouting matches.

Neither one of them had been able to let things go.

Annoyed, nervous and afraid of the consequences headed his annoying little sister's way, Ash closed his eyes and took a deep breath. From there it was easy to picture Macy's face. Her security at the Reserve depended on how he handled this. He would take care of it.

"Don't yell at your sister. You asked for *her* help, genius," Ash muttered.

The fact that he also needed Macy in that second to bolster his resolve was something he'd have to think about later. A little calmer, he motioned at Hendrix. "Either hightail it out or stand back, Hendrix."

Hendrix propped his hands on his hips and slowly surveyed the lobby. "I wondered where you'd hog-tied Macy to keep her from coming in to work. This is why she's not here. You're trying to protect her job and mine. I can't believe you managed to talk her out of being here for this. I expect she'd guard your back if nothing else." He narrowed his eyes as he studied Ash. "Macy? I bet she gets even." The pity in his tone was too thick to be genuine.

Hendrix studied him like a man who'd already been down the road Ash was on with a woman; his expression was a mix of regret, delight and concern that Ash did his best to ignore. He had to get out, say his piece and get behind a closed door before the muscles in his leg reminded him that standing was not their favorite pastime.

The clock was running out, and Hendrix would make his own decisions.

"Let's do this." Winter reached over to pick up the stack of copies he'd managed to put together. "Short. Simple. You've objected to the lodge project from the beginning, but you're a man dedicated to performing the requirements of the Smoky Valley Nature Reserve. Those requirements are developed by the board of directors. At the suggestion of the chief ranger, you commissioned the environmental impact study to present to the board in order to support the best decision for the Reserve. Here's a collection of other communications where you've made your feelings clear, but you would never resort to underhanded politics to subvert the will of the board of directors. But you know, use your own words." Winter held up a hand in a "that's all we can do" motion that was a contrast to the tight lines around her mouth.

His sister had her doubts, but she wasn't going to let them win that morning.

When she said it all like that, it seemed so reasonable. Ash turned to study the crowd outside. There were television cameras and people holding microphones and lots of notebooks and pens moving around. Why had he thought this was a good idea again?

"You can do this." Winter bumped his shoulder with hers.

"How do you think this will end up?" Ash asked. Why? The answer didn't matter. She was right; he was stalling.

Winter wrinkled her nose at him. "It's a gamble. That's

the truth. Remember what Enisi would say when she taught us to play bingo at the family reunions?"

"You pays your money, you takes your chances." Ash smiled at his sister as they repeated it. Thinking of his grandmother and her winning bingo dance reminded him of his conversation with Macy. How could grandmothers be so different? He'd imagined they were all special kinds of angels who brought baked goods and special wisdom but mostly the fun that parents didn't. His mother would be that kind of grandmother to his kids, if he ever managed to have any.

"I saw an owl on the way up here," Winter said and tapped her temple as their grandmother had done. "Important message is coming."

Ash frowned. "What does that have to do with anything?"

Winter shrugged. "I don't know. I was trying to distract you from whatever was making you nervous as a cat a minute ago. They're people, Ash, not monsters. If you mess up, apologize and correct yourself."

Ash nodded once and stepped forward but Winter stopped him. "Get. The. Hat. Are you serious right now? You didn't get a haircut which was like one of the most important things you had to do on a short list and you're still going to step outside without the regulation uniform." She glanced over at Hendrix and shook her head. "Can you believe this guy?"

Ash was muttering under his breath, even if he was grateful Winter was there, as he stepped back in his cramped office and slapped his hat on his head. He immediately stood straighter and felt the authority of his position settle around his shoulders. "Which is the point behind the uniform, Kingfisher."

He'd pursued this career for a reason: Smoky Valley

Nature Reserve mattered to him, his family and future generations. He'd grown up here. Ash wouldn't be the man he was without the days exploring the trails and woods and Otter Lake with his father and grandfather. Neither would they. Nothing could change those facts. They were the bedrock that formed the foundation of his choices, and this was no different. He wanted to keep his job, but protecting the Reserve came first.

Resolved to do his part, Ash turned to march through the lobby. Winter and Brett Hendrix fell in behind him, an army of three, and he was almost certain there was no way he could be defeated.

Ash stepped out on the sidewalk in front of the ranger station and immediately squinted against the flash of cameras. At least his uniform was spotless.

"Good morning, everyone. Thank you for coming out to the Reserve on a cold Monday. I won't take much of your time. My name is Ranger Ash Kingfisher. I am the head ranger here at the Reserve. You may know my name and position already and I may have spoken with you on the phone. Or listened to your message and intended to call you back." He paused, hoping for laughs. He did get a tentative smile here and there and had to consider that a win.

"Everything I do here at Otter Lake is done under the leadership of the chief ranger, Leland Hall, and is undertaken as part of the service the Callaways established when they set these lands aside for Tennesseans to enjoy and explore. The Callaway reserves exist to protect land from development, particularly in areas of the state that are growing quickly. Green spaces are becoming a luxury in many spots of the country. Years ago, Montgomery Callaway carved out some pieces that would be protected. We do that here. In addition, we do our best to make improvements, to protect animals that are native to this land and offer opportunities for anyone who would like to see them or the forests that have been here for centuries. We protect the land. We educate the people. We do that at the pleasure of the board of directors. All of the men and women serving there have been chosen by the Callaway family."

Was he doing this right? He was so far from the script Winter had given him, he wasn't sure how to find his way back. She motioned with the stack of papers she held and he nodded. "Winter is distributing copies of the reports I signed, requested or authored myself regarding The Aerie lodge project. From the beginning, I have questioned it because the damage it will cause to one of the oldest areas of this reserve is significant. You will see that I've stated that more than once. At the chief ranger's suggestion, I requested a formal impact study to benefit the board of directors as they voted on an important decision." Ash waited for everyone in the crowd to get the documents and tried to prepare himself for a flurry of questions.

Instead, he watched as the first couple of people, a news crew from Knoxville, turned away. Then he realized what was stealing the focus.

A long, dark sedan had turned into the parking lot.

Winter leaned forward. "I don't know what this is, but it can't be good."

She was right. The element of surprise itself, the one thing they'd been trying to grab for themselves, was being turned against them.

When Winter's fiancé slid out, looking picture perfect in a tailored suit, Winter stiffened. "I didn't call him." She shook her head. "Okay, I called him, left a message like I have daily for a week, but I didn't tell him what we were doing, Ash."

He squeezed her shoulder. "Of course not." The small group of reporters reluctantly made a path for Callaway to step up on the sidewalk next to Winter. He bent to press a kiss to her cheek, and Ash could hear the whir of camera lenses and the scribble of pens on paper.

Callaway offered Ash his hand to shake. Suspiciously, reluctantly, Ash shook and then propped his hands on his hips.

"Well, isn't this a surprise." Whit Callaway clapped his hands together and smiled at the crowd. "I dropped by to say hello to my fiancée because it has been a wild week, hasn't it? And I stumble on this little gathering. I'm guessing y'all are here talking about that exciting lodge project." He shook his head. "I'm not sure how this has turned into such a big deal. The Callaway family remains committed to preserving green spaces. My father said it last week. I'm saying it again. Callaway Construction would employ every safety measure possible in building the new lodge. Richard Duncan has taken a logical, well-planned expansion project and turned it into a means for political gain. It's disappointing to see a friend lose his way like this, but The Aerie lodge will continue to move forward." He placed his hand on his chest and Ash almost believed his "I'll make this all right again" look. Ash studied his sister's face and realized she was not buying it. Winter didn't do wide ranges of emotion, but she had a hard lock on cold anger. He'd memorized that look growing up. Was the engagement over?

His mother would do a dance if it was.

Kingfishers and Callaways did not belong together after all. Skeeves don't lie.

"As will the wedding between the Callaways and the Kingfishers." Callaway wrapped his arm over Winter's shoulders; the reception must have been as chilly as Ash imagined because his arm slowly dropped away. "Two families who care about the history and people of East Tennessee."

"Mister Callaway, Bailey Garcia, channel six out of Knoxville—"

"Of course, Bailey, I recognize you. Remember that time I won you in a charity auction?" Callaway smiled, his grin friendly and charming.

"You paid for a date with me. Dinner, I believe. And it benefitted the children's hospital in Nashville." Bailey Garcia's smile was almost as cold as Winter's, and Ash was starting to understand he wasn't the only guy in the hot seat. "I remember. Could you tell us whether you've seen the information Ranger Kingfisher has distributed?" She motioned with her pen at the stack of paper in her hand and then stepped out of reach when Whit Callaway tried to take it from her. "Because, if I'm understanding Ranger Kingfisher correctly, he is saying plainly that he was against this lodge from the beginning. Is that right, Ranger?"

Ash refused to meet Whit Callaway's stare and nodded.

"I have not, but I'm sure Ash is telling you the truth. The man doesn't lie to curry favor," Whit said slowly.

That should have been a compliment. Whit Callaway meant something else.

"Mr. Callaway, I've been unable to get an official statement from the Reserve's board of directors," Bailey continued. "I am curious about the board's decision to break official bidding protocol for large projects like this, a safeguard against conflicts of interest which might result in fiscal malfeasance. Do you have an official statement on behalf of the board?"

No one in the crowd spoke, but they turned to Whit

Callaway expectantly. Ash watched him wilt as if this was the most shocking question he'd ever heard. Finally, a dent in Whit's armor.

"I can't…" Callaway frowned. "Obviously, I'm not prepared to make a statement on behalf of the whole board. I'll need to review these reports myself…" He grunted as Winter shoved the remaining stack in his stomach. "But I am certain there's been no intentional… m-malfeasance? Is that the word you used? Bailey, that is one of those impressive words, isn't it? Seems like we talked about your education over dinner. Was it Columbia?"

Her stone-faced expression suggested Bailey Garcia was not playing his game. Ever.

Callaway's charming grin was back in place when he turned to Winter. "I wish your brother had talked to you first, Winter. We might have figured this all out before it hit the front page."

Winter didn't smile back, but she accepted the arm he wrapped around her shoulders.

When the reporters turned back to Ash, he shrugged. "As far as the governor's involvement and his new commitment to conserving Tennessee lands, you know what I know. If his concern is real, and not manufactured to gain votes, I invite him to the Otter Lake Ranger Station to find out more about the work being done here. For now, I serve the Smoky Valley Nature Reserve as ever. I'll be in the office to answer questions today. Tomorrow? Not sure. I do hope you'll all come back out to the ranger station this weekend. We'll be having our first annual winter open house, starting around three. Hikes. Fire trucks. Party things. I think there will be s'mores and lots of fun for the kids. Come join us." He held up his hands, but no one moved. Selling the open house hadn't been his strong suit, obviously. Neither was sending people on their way.

Brett Hendrix opened the door to the ranger station. "Mr. Callaway, would you like to come inside to warm up?" He didn't smile, but motioned them all inside. Nothing about Brett's stance suggested there was another option. As soon as Ash, Winter and Callaway stepped onto the hardwoods of the ranger station's lobby, Brett swung in behind him to block the open door. "As before, you kind press folks are welcome to wait out here on the sidewalk. It's a chilly day. Lunch and warm drinks can be found down at the campground diner. We remain open for business until five o'clock, and I ask you not to impede entrance and exits from this doorway."

Then he stepped inside and pulled the door shut.

"Callaway, let's all talk in my office. Away from the cameras." Ash yanked off his hat. "Nicole, if I have any calls, please put them through. We are open for business as usual."

Her jerky nod made him miss Macy all that much more. If Nicole passed out from the tension in the air, he wouldn't blame her but he'd have a hard time finding a replacement.

As soon as he, Winter and Whit Callaway were crammed inside his small, cluttered office, Ash shut the door and motioned at the two mismatched chairs. Winter sat behind his desk and Whit Callaway dropped down in the closest chair. Ash gritted his teeth as he moved to lean against the closed door. His leg, always angered by inaction, twisted under the strain but it would hold with the extra support.

Or else.

"Why are you here?" Winter asked, her cold eyes focused on her fiancé. Since that was the question Ash most dearly wanted answered, he was content to let his sister take the lead. "Who told you what was happening?"

Callaway grimaced. "I would ask first why *you* didn't tell me what was going on? I mean, we're engaged, Winter. I can't believe you're here." He motioned over his shoulder at Ash. "Him? Going off like this, I get. He's got nothing to lose." He wagged his head. "Well, his job. I'm going to make sure of that. No one goes around me, not without feeling the effects."

Winter pointed a finger in Callaway's face. "Leave my brother alone, Whit."

When Callaway swatted her finger out of his face, Ash straightened. "Watch it, Callaway. Right now, I'm still an officer of the law here on the Reserve."

Then Winter swung around to glare at Ash. "And what about you? Encouraging Richard Duncan to come, to dig harder into this story. That wasn't a part of the plan."

"Whit made it clear my job is no longer part of the equation. The Callaways will see to that. Someone needs to make sure the board of directors examines the placement of this lodge thoroughly. If the governor can slow the project down, give us time to talk to the board, then whoever did this, did us all a favor." Ash crossed his arms over his chest. Winter narrowed her eyes but she didn't argue.

Callaway held up both hands. "Listen." He took a deep breath. "In the interest of family loyalty, which is important to the Callaways if not the Kingfishers, I will try to understand what's happening here." He scrubbed his hands over his face. "If you'd just come to me, this could have been resolved easily, Ash. The lodge goes in, we all profit. It's Callaway land, has been since before the state was a state, and a Callaway company, and a new

Callaway project. She's going to be a Callaway." Whit pointed at Winter. "Or she was. We're in this together."

Winter crossed both arms over her chest. Ash wished he could tell what his sister thought about that, but she'd assumed the Kingfisher deadpan glare. His mother was the undisputed champion of the expression, but Winter was improving daily.

Callaway slumped in his chair. "You were perfect for me. We were perfect *together*. So polished. Your pedigree wasn't all that lofty, but you have a good story, Winter. And I'm from one of the first families of Tennessee."

Winter shook her head. "Why didn't I see this coming?"

"Don't make this into some kind of scheme on my part. We fit together from the minute you sat across from me in that accounting class. The fact that you were worse at it than me was confirmation you were the woman I was looking for. We fit then. We always have." Whit gripped her elbows. "And my parents actually liked you, Winter. Think of how good we looked together. How far we might have made it. The White House. First lady. You could have that. Imagine what you could do from that platform. If we can save this, I want to do it, you and me and the plan we've been working on for years." He tapped his chest. "My father will have it, one way or another, a Callaway in the White House."

"But you got greedy, didn't you?" Winter said slowly. Ash shivered. Her frosty voice was brittle but strong. If he was sitting across from her, he'd be scared. "World domination is nice, but you could do better, was that it? And as long as I don't object to the Callaways destroying a place I love and my brother's career, I'm still welcome to join. How nice."

"We need the money, Winter. We *always* need the

money. Campaigns are expensive and the price keeps rising." Whit scoffed like he couldn't believe how naive Winter was being. "We'd take back some of the money we've put into the Reserve over generations. It's not like we're thieves. We're reclaiming an investment. The land still stands in the Reserve. If anything, we're building a firmer foundation here in Tennessee."

"Yes, a new business would lead to opportunities to boast about new jobs and tourism dollars. Right? Let's follow the logic." Winter turned to Ash. "I really want there to be logic because if this lowlife has broken my trust, hurt the Reserve, ruined the wedding I've wasted six months planning, not to mention the ten years we've been together where I've grinned at some clearly not nice people on behalf of winning their votes, and there's not good logic to this plan, I will lose my cool." Her words were precise and snapped at the end, like an icicle that loses its hold, breaks and falls.

And in the near future, Winter might shatter. Ash limped over to stand next to her, one hand on her shoulder. No matter what happened, he'd back her up.

"I get it," Ash said. If he could let go of yes and no and embrace the maybe, Ash might have been convinced by Hall and Whit Callaway. But sometimes a person cracked open the door to the maybe variety of thinking, and that's when all kinds of bad choices flooded in. "You're only claiming what's yours after all. The land is Callaway land. So is the company working on the expansion you want. We'll lose some animal populations. The bird habitats up there would sustain some damage. One of the most popular climbs in the park would be paved over for a parking lot. But you're only spending money to make money and who does that hurt?" Ash held up both hands as Winter shot up to stand, color in her cheeks. "If you take a minute to look up from your wallet, you'll see, Callaway. Number one—it hurts her. I can't believe you didn't think of that."

Losing his job would hurt; watching his sister's heart break was much worse.

"Why?" Whit asked. "It has almost nothing to do with Winter."

"Until I disagree with you. You'll absolutely cut me loose then. I can have everything I want, and all I have to do is lie for you and say the project's a great idea. But one of us, Ash or me or both of us, will have to change our story, change how we feel. Too late, Whit." Winter narrowed her eyes. "You would have destroyed things we'll never get back, here at the Reserve and between us. Worse, you don't even see it now. I've made a career here, dedicated time to supporting the Reserve because I love it. When I think of all my favorite times, they happened here."

Callaway stood. He was a man clearly at a loss as to how to navigate the situation. "What do you want me to do, Winter?"

"Postpone the project. Get Callaways off the board of the Reserve so a logical decision can be made. Leave my brother out of this." Winter squared up across from her fiancé.

"And you'll come back?" Whit asked. "I don't know if my father will go for any of that, but I'll give it a try if you'll stop here, turn back to me and our plan." He offered her his hand.

Her snort wasn't kind but it was very clear. "No. That was so you could do the right thing, Whit. That's all."

"I want to fix this, Winter," Whit said. "Why don't you?"

Winter squeezed her eyes closed. "Why haven't you

returned my calls? All week I needed to talk to you, wanted to fix this, too, but couldn't get you to answer. I really needed you."

Callaway ran his hand through his hair. "My father thought you needed time to cool off and think. The more we argued, the harder it would be to get over, so I gave you space."

Winter nodded. "Well, more space now would be good. Get out."

He bent his head, his lips a tight, angry line. "You can both expect to hear from the chief ranger today. I'd go ahead and start clearing out your desks. That will save you some time. Since you're about to be all over the newspapers again, you'll want to make a quick getaway."

Ash hadn't thrown a punch in a decade.

Whit Callaway had him testing his fists for muscle memory, but he left the office before Ash could make the final decision on whether punching him was a bad idea or the worst idea ever.

When his sister plopped back down in his desk chair and buried her face in her hands, Ash wished once more for Macy. "I'm sorry. I should have offered to..." He wasn't sure how to complete the sentence.

Her eyes were dry when she craned her neck to glare up at him. "You think I would have told you to... What? Keep quiet so I could have my society wedding?" Her frown left deep lines on her forehead. "I would yell at you right now, but my head is killing me." She dropped her head back down on her arms; Ash squeezed her shoulders and did his best to be patient.

"At least we'll be infamous now. Should make it easier to find new jobs," Ash said drily and smiled as his sister chuckled.

"To think, I could have been first lady. I could have

slept in the Lincoln bedroom or walked barefoot in the Oval Office or…" She sighed. "I can't even think of interesting things to do in the White House."

"Well, not as the president's *wife*." Ash squeezed her shoulders again. "If you were the president, on the other hand, you could…" He tipped his head back to study the water spots on his ceiling. "I don't know, prank call England's prime minister or…" He snapped his fingers. "Change out all the fancy bread bowls for some of Dad's lucky baskets."

"Can you imagine the amount of sage Mom would need to eliminate the skeeves from that place?" Winter laughed as she straightened. "You're right. I'd make a much better president than first lady."

Ash was quiet as he moved back around to sit across from her. "Okay. We found your next job. What should *I* do?" He propped one foot on his desk and straightened his aching leg out beside it.

"What if I'm not joking?" Winter said as she propped her chin on one hand. "Maybe not president but… What if we could give the Callaways a hard time in the next election? It would be sweet."

Ash shrugged. "I'm not sure I was joking, either." Their eyes met across the desk and the sudden stillness was filled with expectation. "You're about to have some time on your hands."

Winter didn't immediately answer. How she traced the lines on his desk calendar made it clear she was weighing the possibilities.

Ash grunted as he leaned forward. "Hey, Winter, what am I going to do?"

She rolled her eyes. "You are going to stay here. Seriously."

Ash raised an eyebrow, ready to hear whatever she had to say.

"Board of directors. I'm not sure why I didn't think of it before. Well, I thought they might be the answer, but couldn't see a way to make it work. The Callaways have some pull, but they aren't the majority. All you have to do is fight for the votes of the board of directors and win." The corners of her mouth turned up. "I have an idea on how to make that happen."

"Couldn't you do the same thing?" Ash asked, confused. "We could both stay here. Nothing changes." He paused. "Except you're single again, I guess."

"Sure, but I don't want to." Winter wrinkled her nose. "There's too much Callaway involvement. I need something new."

Ash sighed long and loud. "Are you going to help me with whatever your plan is or am I going to have to call Mom?"

"Running to Mommy," Winter said, her eyes filled with laughter. Ash wasn't sure he liked where he was, but he was certain that his sister was going to recover and fast. That was something he'd been too afraid to consider. He should have bet on Winter above all else.

"I'm going to transfer Macy out." Ash winced as he moved his leg, but the pain came more from the center of his chest. If she wasn't here, would this be a fight worth winning? "She's got to keep a job. When things settle down, I'll see if I can get her back."

"You better clear that with her first," Winter said drily.

"Then what do I do?" Ash asked.

"All you gotta do is make sure Sweetwater loves you. Well, East Tennessee to be safe. I mean, the people on the board are from other small towns but they're all connected to Sweetwater somehow. You win this place, get it behind you and no one else, I think you stand a chance of keeping your job."

"And remaining in an uneasy standoff with the chief ranger and the Callaways," Ash huffed. That didn't sound like fun.

Winter tapped his hand. "Soon, the Callaways will have a bigger problem. We're both going to be winning hearts and minds, brother. I can challenge Whit, you wait and see. There's still all those reporters investigating. We make you look like a hero instead of a hermit, and this all turns out like it's supposed to—Kingfishers saving the world, one precious piece of it at a time."

Ash gulped. "The world. We're going to save the world. I was just hoping to protect one small part of Tennessee."

Winter's sly smile would have scared him, but he was sure she was on his side. "Sure. We'll do that first, okay? It'll be easy."

She stood, smoothed down her skirt. "I bet the reporters are still waiting on a final quote. I'll handle that, Ash. You stay here." Before he could argue with her, she'd swept out, her head held high. No matter how this turned out, Kingfishers on top or Callaways, she was going to be okay. He believed that.

And he'd roll with the punches.

Before things got too wild, he had to get Macy out of harm's way. He'd never forgive himself if she was hurt in the fallout.

# CHAPTER TEN

"MY FIRST SICK DAY," Macy said as she plopped back against the headboard. "What do I do now?"

Weekends were for errands. Sleeping late. Brunch at Smoky Joe's Café. Good naps. And good books.

Macy had never had any trouble filling the Saturdays and Sundays that interrupted her work at the ranger station, but this unexpected day to do nothing seemed to stretch out before her. Waaay out before her.

"What should I do with this unexpected gift?" She rested her head against the headboard and stared up at the ceiling. "I could paint." But not before clearing it with the landlord. The laundry was done. Why could she name seven different things stacked on her desk that needed her attention, but she couldn't find a single fun thing that excited her? "Knoxville? Shopping? Maybe a movie."

When Macy closed her eyes again, all she could imagine was a sea of aggressive reporters tearing into Ash.

He'd said she couldn't do it. Taking a sick day was not her style.

Letting Ash be right on something like this wasn't her style, either.

He liked to make too many sweeping pronouncements. She had to prove him wrong about this.

"Get dressed. Get out. Do not go anywhere near the Smoky Valley Nature Reserve." Simple. Macy liked lists, so she made a list of the only things she had to do that day.

Since the Reserve wrapped around Sweetwater like a hug, it might be nearly impossible to avoid the park if she stayed in town, but she'd worry about that after she got dressed. As she slapped hangers aside one by one, ignoring jeans and comfy sweaters, inspiration hit. She could avoid the ranger station all day and flout Ash's sick-day strategy. There was still plenty of ground to cover in Sweetwater, and there were plenty of business own-ers to sweet-talk into posting the open house invitation.

As she slipped on her uniform, Macy could feel the smug smile curling her lips. It was going to be a good day.

When she bent to pick up her phone to slide it into her pocket, she had to check for a text message from Ash. There wasn't one. That wasn't surprising, but the defla-tion of her hope was.

"He's busy." Macy chastised herself for her own needi-ness and wandered into the open area that functioned as living room, dining room, kitchen and graveyard for all her failed hobby experiments. "And this place is a wreck." In a quick blitz, Macy separated the library books she'd snatched up on Saturday in an attempt to forestall this "what do I do with myself" morning. When she was done making piles, she had three knotted skeins of yarn, knit-ting needles, crochet hooks, her laptop and a guitar she'd picked up at a garage sale three years ago because she wanted to learn to play.

As it turned out, learning to play guitar by reading about it in a library book was impossible. Or impractical. Or just not advisable. The same was true of knitting and crocheting, and the role-playing game she'd attempted on Sunday afternoon had sucked the life out of her lap-top in no time.

Apparently the quest to become the kingdom's ruling

wizard warrior required more firepower than she had at her disposal.

"No hobbies. No problem. I'll go back to the library. I love that place." Macy walked into her bare kitchen. So bare. Grocery shopping was one exciting adventure she could add to her Monday to-do list. "Oh, boy. The thing I hate the most." Cookbooks. She could check some of those out. Her grandmother hadn't experimented much, but cooking was one of those things that had a useful end. Even Gran had watched chefs whip up miraculous appetizers while she folded laundry.

If Macy could overcome her aversion to the grocery store and the hurdle of preparing every meal for one, cooking could be fun.

"Ash could take all the leftovers. That might work, not that he deserves any sort of treat." But it was easy to imagine Ash seated at her tiny bar while she scrambled eggs and brewed coffee. Breakfast was her go-to meal, no matter the time of day. She would talk; he would listen.

Why did something so simple seem so out of reach?

Especially when she was annoyed with the man.

Macy rubbed her forehead as she stared hard at the few items in the almost empty refrigerator, the worry and disappointment over Ash's lack of communication tangled into a messy knot in her stomach. What time had they settled on for the press conference? Had he managed to find all the reports and sweet-talk the copier into producing enough sets for the reporters who showed up? Of course he had. Or he hadn't. Why hadn't he called her? She could have helped over the phone or gone in to make sure everything went off correctly.

That's what she did for him, ensured a smooth operation.

But he stuck her on the sidelines.

Unless she ignored him and went charging up the mountain to the ranger station. She only wanted to help.

Worn-out and frosty from staring in the refrigerator while she argued with herself, Macy made a decision. "You can't stay here, obviously."

She had to get out of the apartment. Nothing would improve if she stayed here by herself. Since the campground diner was off-limits because it was smack-dab in the center of the Reserve, breakfast would have to come from Smoky Joe's. Macy grabbed her keys, her purse and the stack of copies she'd made of the open house announcement, and hit the door. She was halfway to her car when the first wave of cold air convinced her to run back inside for a jacket.

*Catching a cold when you're out running around instead of staying home like you've been ordered is what you deserve, Macy Elizabeth Gentry.* Why was it that her grandmother's voice was so easy to hear at some points? If she'd looked over her shoulder to see her grandmother standing behind her, Macy would not have shrieked in surprise. What did that mean? "You are becoming your grandmother."

As she slid into her car, Macy closed her eyes. That was one thing she'd have to fight to prevent. Her grandmother had been a good woman. She'd also been humorless and a disappointment as the loving, caring type. Macy would do better on that score.

"Smoky Joe's. Shops on Main Street. The library. Grocery store. Then we'll see." Macy nodded and made the quick trip into town. Parking should be easy on a Monday. Weekends were big business, but during the winter, weekdays were slow even along the tourist strip. Today, instead of wide-open space, both sides of the street were already lined with cars, so Macy made a second loop to find a spot right next to Sweetwater Souvenir. It was still early enough that the shop was closed, but the windows showed some fun, kitschy stuff. The bear wearing a park ranger hat needed to come home with her. He was too cute.

Why hadn't she ever been inside? Today was the day. She'd ask Janet Abernathy to hang up a poster.

"Coffee. Must have coffee." Macy entered Smoky Joe's and immediately sniffed long and loud. The place always smelled like Macy imagined heaven would: warm coffee in the air along with the hint of banana nut bread.

"Well, now, ain't seen you in some time." Odella, the café's owner, was behind the counter, bustling around to clear up nonexistent crumbs while she waited for the next customer. Macy was a bad guesser of people's ages, but if she had to pin a year on Odella, she'd guess one hundred and eleven based on her white hair and the years on her face, but by energy level, she was only eighteen. "What can I get you, Miss Macy?"

Macy smiled. That "Miss Macy" had such a lilting, songlike quality that she smiled every time Odella said it. She might look a lot like Macy's grandmother had, stern and just…old, but the twinkle in her eyes and how she said Macy's name was different.

"Big coffee. Bigger slice of that banana nut bread, please." Macy pulled her credit card out of her wallet and remembered she was there on business. "Can I talk you into displaying one of these announcements about our open house this weekend?" Macy pointed at the Reserve logo on her shirt. "The ranger station is going to have hikes and the fire trucks, a cool photo opportunity, activities for kids." She took out a copy and fluttered it to demonstrate how ready she was to give it away.

Odella didn't immediately answer. "'Spose it could

go on the bulletin board." She motioned at the far wall near the bathroom.

The lukewarm reception concerned Macy, but she hurried to hang the paper before Odella changed her mind.

After she'd paid and Odella handed her a cup and a bag with her bread inside, Macy paused. Should she scurry back to her car?

Odella was watching her intently from behind the counter. Macy glanced around the room, ready to stare down anyone who wanted to make a thing of what was happening at the Reserve with Ash.

Lots of locals very obviously didn't look back at her. Macy didn't know any of them well enough to force the issue, so she slid into the nearest booth and decided to focus on her own breakfast. Specifically, the breakfast she'd treated herself to and hadn't talked herself out of.

At some point, she'd be able to waste money on "frivolous" purchases without a mental image of her grandmother shaking her head in disapproval.

As she took the first bite, Macy sighed happily. If she had been sick, this would have restored her. Then she washed it down with a sip of strong black coffee and knew without a doubt she'd live forever. This was Odella's secret: magic breakfasts that gave her eternal life and endless energy.

"It's good." Odella had followed her, coffee pot in hand, and was leaning against the booth, her arms crossed over her chest. "I know it."

Macy nodded, unwilling to waste mouth time with speaking until every bite was gone. "Yes. This is the key to world peace, Miss Odella. Why are you hiding it here?"

Odella's lips flattened into a smug smile. "Wouldn't want none of that paparazzi following me around. This bread would make me famous and I ain't got time for that." She wagged her finger. "Didn't expect to see you here on a workday."

Macy sipped her coffee. "I'm going to see if I can get some of these flyers handed out. This open house is my idea, so I want lots of people to come by. The whole town, if possible."

Odella pursed her lips. "Not sure that'll happen. Some of them news vans been through town this morning." Odella pointed to the large plate glass window, then propped her hands in the middle of her back. "Easier to see what's going on when the streets are clear, but I ain't complaining about the business. I know for certain my food's better than the campground diner's, but I sure can't compete with the view of Otter Lake." Odella nodded at someone who raised a coffee cup, but she didn't hurry to refill it.

"Is this an unusual crowd for Monday?" Macy fiddled with the edge of her napkin and wondered why the knot was back in her stomach.

"Unusually large and even more unusually quiet," Odella said. When she turned toward the room, more cups went up in the air, but no one said anything.

"The scuttlebutt was bound to either draw the morbidly curious or keep the high-browed away. Hard to call these things. Folks are pretty done with Ash Kingfisher, though. Ain't nobody got the patience to deal with that boy's shady dealings." Odella reached over to grab a folded newspaper from another table. "Them Kingfishers got a lot to answer for, I guess." She waved the folded paper. It was the same copy that showed Brett Hendrix and his lipstick smear.

Seeing it in this moment was less funny than when she'd shown it to Brett at the ranger station. He'd blushed darker than Christina's lipstick. Odella's grim face robbed Macy of all the joy she'd inhaled via warm, sweet bread.

Macy held up one finger as she finished the last of her coffee. It was clear she was about to make a Statement on behalf of "them Kingfishers" and she'd have to stalk out in a huff. However, she didn't want to miss a drop of the goodness in her cup. When it was finally empty, Macy wiped her mouth, calmly folded up all the trash on the table and shoved it inside the empty cup before offering it to Odella. When she slid out of the booth, she was glad she'd worn the official Reserve uniform. It made her braver, as if it were a superhero's cape.

Macy cleared her throat and immediately felt the pressure of the gaze of all the people in the room and the weight of expectation.

"The Kingfishers have done nothing to harm the Smoky Valley Nature Reserve. You will see that tonight when you turn on the news." A split second after she said it, Macy hoped the press conference was scheduled soon. The story of her speech would spread quickly enough that the chief ranger might even get a whiff of it soon. "If you're avoiding the diner or the campgrounds or the lake because of this story, you're endangering the success of the Reserve. Whether the lodge goes in or not, there are still people working in the diner and the marina, at the campgrounds, rangers on staff, shifts of firefighters and search-and-rescue teams, educators and even kids who run the snack shacks around the lake during the summer. Ash Kingfisher is already giving you all of that, and he's doing it in a way that you enjoy while he and his team protect the place you love. When you consider how long he's served Otter Lake, how can you ever believe he has anything but its best interests at heart." She didn't look at anyone directly. She could only handle public speaking if she never really noticed the people in the public. "Since your job or the job of someone you love is directly dependent on the tourists brought in by the Reserve, I'd suggest you do your best to support it and Ash Kingfisher, the ranger in charge of the operation of Otter Lake." She cleared her throat again and wished she'd prepared a script for a situation like this. Instead, she was winging it.

Macy Gentry didn't ever wing it if she could help it.

"Any questions you have should be directed to Ash or Winter. Both are happy to answer. Both are proud to work for the Reserve and to be from Sweetwater." *So you should have their backs instead of waiting anxiously for juicy news to gloat over.*

Macy thought the last part, but she could never say it. The people in Smoky Joe's were neighbors and they loved their town, too. Being committed to the Reserve was something most of them shared, even if they disagreed over what was best.

And they didn't know Ash, not really. Or her, based on the theatrically whispered, "Why should we listen to her?" that floated from somewhere near the front door, according to Odella's narrow-eyed stare.

"My name is Macy Gentry." She shifted her purse over one shoulder. "I've arranged pavilions for your birthday parties and told you the marina's or diner's hours a million times over the phone. I know the ranger station and I know Ash Kingfisher. While he's in charge of the Reserve, you can trust that it is in good hands." *And if he loses his job, you can't.*

Macy dug around in her pocket and slapped down all the cash she had for Odella's tip. "Really good banana nut bread, Odella."

Odella lifted a shoulder to acknowledge her due while

her hand snaked out to grab the tip before sliding it into the pocket of her apron.

Macy knew it was a weak parting line, but she'd already used up every bit of bravery that she had and she wanted out.

"Ain't you gonna invite us all to your party, Miss Macy?" Odella called before Macy made it to the door.

Frozen in her tracks, Macy nodded. "Right. There's some information on the bulletin board, but we've got new exhibits in the visitor center at the ranger station, and we want to celebrate. Come find out what's happening in the park this winter. There'll be firefighters and face painting. Please bring your kids. They're the reason we're all hard at work, making sure Otter Lake is around for their kids, too." Macy backed out the door.

As soon as her heel hit the sidewalk, breathing became easier. She didn't turn to look back in the window of the coffee shop but shifted her purse and marched to her car.

Janet Abernathy was on the sidewalk in front of Sweetwater Souvenir, talking with Leanne Hendrix about the window display when Macy reached into the tote bag of library books. Her first foray into pulling in the local businesses had been rocky, but she'd had a chance to improve her sales pitch.

"Morning, Macy," Janet called and pointed over her shoulder. "Come give us your opinion on the window display. Leanne here's working some magic."

Meeting the former wild girl of Sweetwater at nine o'clock on a Monday came with a few warnings, but Macy was relieved to have some kind of real business to conduct. She hoped all the people in Smoky Joe's had their noses pressed against the windows. Macy pasted on a wide grin. She marched across the sidewalk, her hand held out in the universal sign of "good to see you."

Janet thought nothing of it. Leanne Hendrix stared suspiciously at her hand for a hard second before she shook it.

"Leanne. This window is great." Her handshake was strong, but there was a hesitation that convinced Macy that Leanne was even more uncertain than ever.

"Macy here works out at the ranger station. With Brett." Janet smiled. "But I expect you know that." Unconcerned with the meeting, she returned to admiring her shop window.

"I don't think we've ever met officially, though." Macy straightened.

Leanne blinked slowly before her smile spread. "Sure, I know who you are. And Christina's mentioned you."

"I noticed the window as soon as I parked." Macy pointed at a beautiful painting of sunset over The Aerie, the hardest trail on the Reserve. When a hiker reached the summit, they felt it in every muscle. She needed to get back up there soon, especially if the lodge project got up and running. The place would never be the same. "Is this a local artist?"

Janet Abernathy shot one hand up in the air with a victorious whoop while Leanne turned bright red.

"So local you can't even believe it," Janet said as she danced in place. "Leanne did it. It's. So. Good!" Janet clapped wildly as if she were leading a standing ovation.

Leanne seemed to want to crawl under the sidewalk.

"I love it. A lot." Macy shifted her tote bag higher. "My art skills are limited to coloring inside the lines. I admire talent like this." Macy leaned forward. "Is it for sale?" Not that she had a place to hang such a painting. It was meant for grander things than her apartment.

"It will be, soon as I can do some research on proper art pricing." Janet tapped Leanne on the shoulder. "This one thinks we should give it away. Since she ain't in a hurry to be making her millions, we're gonna stir up some interest. Then, when she has more paintings—" she paused to glare at Leanne and Macy had the feeling this was a common refrain "—we'll have us a show."

Leanne crossed her arms over her chest and squeezed. Since she was petite already, it was like watching her try to disappear.

"I don't want that attention, Miss Janet. You know that." She shook her head. "I've gotta get the cash register set up." She hurried toward the door, but paused. "It was nice to talk to you, Macy." Then she was inside the shop.

Janet's long, despairing sigh floated down the sidewalk. "You know, all my life, I've hustled. Done a million different things, most of them just because I love it, not because it paid money. Woman gets to my age, you think she'd be slowing down. Relaxing."

Her mournful tone struck Macy as funny, but she did her best to keep a straight face. "But…no?"

Janet nodded. "Work part-time at the elementary school like I always have because those kids need me." She pressed both hands to her chest. "Started flipping spaces with my best friend, and you *know* Regina needs me. She does not have my flair for color." She shrugged as if it couldn't be helped. "We've got this little shop which is going to be nothing but fun now that Leanne's in place. Girl arranges stock like she was born with a price tag in her hand."

Macy said, "That's a lot to keep you busy." And whatever it was, was working. Janet vibrated with an energy that was inspiring. If she'd been wondering if her life had reached peak boring, she could take a page from Janet's book.

"And now I've got to fix Leanne." Janet pointed to

the painting. "Can you imagine talent like that and she doesn't want to show it off. I swear, how do I fix this for her without losing my best manager?"

Macy stared hard at the library. She'd wanted to drop her books, not solve all of Sweetwater's problems from the middle of the sidewalk.

But she had a suggestion.

And the fact that she knew the answer meant she had to say it. It was a flaw in her personality she had no interest in changing.

"Maybe the problem is focusing on Leanne," Macy said slowly as she worked it all out in her head. "If you had other local artists on display, that might make it easier for her to handle the idea of a show or valuing her artwork." She studied the crack in the sidewalk as she considered all the options. Janet would have to track down more artists. "You could run an ad in the paper, request portfolios. Offer to sell on commission. I don't know how that works, but…"

"You don't worry your head about that. Regina Blackburn will figure out the details. Woman is murder on contracts." Janet Abernathy squeezed her arm. "I like the way you think, Macy Gentry." Her eyes narrowed. "Know any artists?"

Pleased with the praise and how well her day off was turning out, Macy rocked back and forth, considering the problem.

Then the memory of Martin Kingfisher and his Cherokee double-sided baskets lit like a lightbulb over her head. "As a matter of fact, I might. How do you feel about Cherokee art? I know a local basket maker." Imagining how Martin Kingfisher would fire up any room he landed in made her grin. "And he would dominate your art show in the best way. If you want people to be drawn to your events, to love art and the people who make it, you need to talk to Martin Kingfisher."

Janet leaned back as if she hadn't expected that. "Well. Kingfishers are kind of…" She trailed off as if she couldn't come up with the right words.

"I know and it's ridiculous. Call him. You won't be disappointed." Macy was on a roll. "If you don't believe me, give me an hour and I'll bring back a sample of his work. All it will take is one look and you'll understand he's good at what he does. You'll have to meet him to understand what a special guy he is. I promise, he's an addition you won't regret."

"I like you, Macy. Something about you makes me trust you." Janet grinned. "All right. I'm going to do some measuring, some planning and some asking around. After I talk to Regina. She makes every plot better." Janet absentmindedly patted Macy's shoulder. "Wonder who owns this empty storefront next to us because art needs room to breathe." She chuckled softly. "I sound like I know what I'm talking about, don't I?" Her pleased grin was contagious.

"Janet, if you don't mind," Macy said as she reached into her bag and pulled out a flyer, "we're having an open house out at the ranger station this weekend. Here are the details. I'd love to see you there." Inspired, Macy leaned in to whisper, "I'll introduce you to Martin Kingfisher. How about that?"

Janet studied her face. "I like a fellow woman who sees opportunity and goes for it." She pinched the piece of paper between finger and thumb, and winked. "I'll see you there." Then she marched inside Sweetwater Souvenir.

"Disss-missed. But it was a good morning's work, anyway." Macy was still smiling as she continued down the sidewalk. Encouraged by her early success, Macy stopped inside each storefront and got everyone to agree to hang a poster. Almost every interaction started with a cold shoulder, so she was worried about the crowd size of the open house.

*Do the best you can, Macy. That's all you can do.*

The flyers were up. She'd made her stand. She'd accomplished a lot for her "sick" day. "Time to hit the best spot in town."

"Smiling when she walks in the door," Astrid said from her spot behind the large desk that dominated the center of Sweetwater's library. "Usually I see that smile as you're leaving with your tote bag full of books. Always the sign of a satisfied reader. I guess we managed to find you a hobby after all." She nodded her head so firmly that her wild blond curls shook. The fat orange cat spread out across her desk opened one eye before lazily flicking his tail in disapproval.

"Well," Macy said slowly as she stacked the books she was returning, "not so much. I have solved several problems with one conversation, though. Since I've been on a real losing streak lately, that's nice." She pushed the pile of books forward. "I failed at all of these. Knitting and crocheting take too much concentration and learning. Same for guitar playing…" Macy shook her head sadly. "I actually threw this book across the room."

Astrid's scandalized gasp upset Pippi who jumped up, shot them both an ugly look and headed for a quieter corner.

"I didn't hurt the book." Macy didn't *think* she'd hurt the book, but it was not a good idea to tell the librarian she'd tossed it onto the floor. Librarians had to be sensitive about those things.

"I hope not." Astrid made the tsking noise between her

teeth as she flipped through the *Guitar for Kids* book that had pleased them both so much. "I'll have to rethink my plans for my next suggestion if you're going to punish the books for your own shortcomings." She raised her eyebrows over her glasses and then the corner of her mouth quirked up. "The fact that I'm only sort of joking about that should concern the both of us, but let's move on."

Confused, Macy saluted. "Yes, ma'am. It will never happen again, I solemnly promise." If she ever threw a book again, she would definitely not tell Astrid about it. "You have another suggestion?" Macy checked her watch. It wasn't even noon. Unless Astrid had a fabulous idea, she was going to be in danger of proving Ash right by failing to avoid the Reserve. The not-knowing-what-was-happening was killer.

Astrid looked sheepish and hesitated as she spoke. "I was thinking…" She used both hands to pick up a superthick book with a piece of paper on top. She lifted the paper to show the book cover: a beautiful shot of a fancy camera.

*I will not impatiently demand that she get on with it. I will not.* Macy crossed her arms over her chest.

"I've always wanted to learn this. I mean, photography. Not like professional-grade where I'd go into business kind of photography, but you know…" Astrid's longing gaze landed on the exit. "For fun. Take the camera out and shoot interesting shots. I spend so much time locked up indoors, which I love, do not get me wrong, but photography could be the hobby that gets me out and about. Seeing things."

Macy did not get where this was going. "So, you found a hobby for yourself?" That was nice. That wasn't anything Astrid needed to tell her about, though. She'd come in looking for help, not…this.

Astrid huffed out a frustrated breath. "What I'm saying...badly...is there's a class at the camera shop in Gatlinburg." She waved the piece of paper in front of Macy's face. "I want to take it, but I like to have company when I try new things. Would you like to take it with me?" She waved the paper again. "Eight weeks. One night a week. Gatlinburg. We could eat dinner there and then go to class." Then she dropped the book back down and held out the piece of paper. "Are we going to do this thing or not?"

Macy read the details. The cost of the class? Free.

Except for one little thing: the cost of the camera.

"I know. You were looking for an easy, inexpensive thing that could keep your brain occupied, not an investment," Astrid said. They'd had that long conversation on Saturday when Macy had marched into the library, desperate to find a distraction that would mean Ash was wrong, wrong, wrong about her inability to stay away from the Reserve. "This is not that. But it could be fun. You obviously love hiking." Astrid motioned wildly at her. Macy stared down at her uniform, not sure what the librarian meant, but it was impossible to argue over her love for the Reserve's trails. "Think of all the lovely photos you could take while doing that."

Macy handed her the piece of paper. "You've managed to do the impossible. You've given me the task I needed to make sure I don't go near the Reserve. I guess I'm headed in to Gatlinburg to buy a camera." Pleased more than she could say by Astrid's invitation, Macy sighed happily. "This sounds amazing, Astrid. I can't wait."

Astrid clasped her hands in front of herself like a kid excited for Christmas. "Really? We're on?"

"In January, we're going to take photography classes together." Macy offered her hand to shake. Astrid waved it off and ran around the desk to wrap her arms around Macy in an enthusiastic hug. A hard squeeze had Macy laughing.

"A smile to a laugh. This place is working its magic today." Astrid gave her a hard pat on the shoulder and stepped back. "Something to look forward to after Christmas."

Some of her excitement dimmed. January seemed a long way away.

"There's no reason we have to wait until January to have dinner, though." Macy tried to be casual about the suggestion. At the same time, Leanne Hendrix's face popped into her mind. "We could do a girls' night out." She'd see how it went, then make the suggestion that they include Leanne. Even Christina could come if Astrid was up for it.

Look at her, planning regular dinners with friends. Preparing to spend a large amount of money on a truly frivolous purchase. No angry Gran in her head for a minute or two...

What a difference a day could make.

"Great idea. I was thinking..." Astrid trailed off. "That I should try to get the other single ladies together. Maybe we could set up a thing. With them." Astrid didn't name names, but the choices were so few that Macy believed they had to be thinking of the same people.

"Sounds good." It really did.

"Next time Winter is in, I'll ask her." Astrid nodded. "It's settled."

Macy froze as she flipped through the photography book for beginners. "I was thinking of Christina Braswell and Leanne Hendrix."

Astrid's eyebrows raised. "Five of us. That's awesome." She nodded enthusiastically. "That's a real party right there."

It could be. Astrid was right. Would the other three agree? Picturing forthright Winter Kingfisher seated next to shy Leanne Hendrix didn't give her confidence. Macy could feel the anxious thought settling in and realized it didn't matter. Astrid was committed. And all either of them needed was the first step. They already had that.

"Can't wait." Astrid rubbed her hands together as if she was plotting a great escape. "Let's go to The Branch next Friday. It's not much of a wild night on the town, Sweetwater's only bar that serves just beer and light beer on tap, but it's comfortable. Then we can make plans for the next time. Can you invite Leanne and Christina? Winter's supposed to be coming in to talk to me about the story times she does, but she's got a few things going on. If I don't see her, I'll call her." Then Astrid frowned. "I should check on her, anyway."

Since she'd just spent Friday night at the Kingfishers' plotting the protection of Winter's career, Macy understood completely. "Give it a shot. I'll talk to Christina and Leanne, and even if it's you and me…" Macy shrugged. She would be content. She was already content to have made a plan with Astrid. Just when things had gotten so bleak, it looked like she was making a turn that led to better things. Life was funny that way.

"I got a few new romances in and the crazy thriller everybody's talking about. Nobody knows it's here yet," she added in a singsong. "Want to check it out?"

Macy laughed. "Yes, of course I do."

"Holding books for a day for my favorite customer is pretty much the extent of my power as town librarian. Benefit from it." Astrid produced a book as if out of no-where and pressed it into Macy's hands.

Being called her favorite was nice. It was like being a VIP at the library. Awesome.

Macy handed her library card over and brushed off both shoulders. "Good to know I have such powerful friends."

As she sauntered out of the library, Macy decided that getting away from the ranger station now and then was worth it. She might have ulcers, thanks to her worry about what was happening without her, but she'd managed some good work that day.

On her way back to the car, she stuck her head in to invite Leanne to The Branch. The shock on her face before Janet accepted for her was worth it. Who cared what people said? Macy knew for a fact that people could be wrong, wrong, so very wrong.

Then she settled in her car, pulled her phone out to check for an update from Ash and cursed under her breath when there was no news. "Of course not. He got what he wanted. He's not thinking of me." Determined to do the same, Macy pulled out on Main Street, made a circle through town and hit the road to Gatlinburg.

# CHAPTER ELEVEN

DURING A FUN couple of hours in Gatlinburg, Macy had lunch, scouted future girls'-night-out locations, which were slim, and entered the camera shop where she gritted her teeth through a solid hit to her credit card. Buying a digital SLR camera with enough bells and whistles to make taking a photography class worthwhile wasn't cheap.

It was easy, though.

And before she knew it, Macy was headed back to Sweetwater under the happy haze of good food, plans for the future and some retail therapy. All in all, a successful day.

Then she remembered she still had to go to the grocery store.

"Not even that is going to put a dent in my mood. Not today." She tipped her head up, determined to make the quick stop.

The closer she got to Sweetwater, dread swamped her.

"I hate that place," she muttered as she made the turns necessary to roll into the parking lot.

Cooking would never make her short list of potential hobbies. Yes, she loathed the grocery store, from all of the walking up and down the same aisles to the hassle of dragging all the bags back into her apartment and unpacking them before she could make herself something to eat. It was so inefficient. Also, she lived alone. She might be able to pawn some of her creations off at the ranger station, but most days, the staff there was limited. The volume of leftovers would eventually overwhelm her.

Ash might appreciate it if she experimented with new dishes, but if she tried to bring in a fancy casserole, he'd be out. Not only out, he'd be mad about it. She'd imagined his lack of food bravery to be the result of limited exposure.

That had been before she met his parents. Donna Kingfisher had no doubt put a fancy casserole down on the family table more than once. And Ash would have been the dutiful son and eaten what was in front of him, even if he'd made the rosehip-tea face, too.

"Photography is a much better choice. No grocery store, fewer dirty dishes and it was an incentive to get out into the Reserve more often. Girls' night out is a strong addition, too." And the bonus? She didn't need Ash Kingfisher for either.

Rolling her eyes at how often her thoughts returned to Ash, Macy lifted her phone out of her purse. She'd managed to make it through the entire day without texting him. If she did it now, what could it hurt?

You said I couldn't do it. Want to apologize now or wait until I get into the station in the morning? Macy hesitated before she hit Send. Was it the right tone? She tapped her lips as she tried to come up with something even more gloating. "An emoji. Like a big ol' grinning yellow face." She flipped through the choices before sighing. None of them captured the proper tone. "Not gonna lug themselves home, Macy Elizabeth." She hit Send, shoved her phone back in her purse and slid out of the car.

After her trip down the first aisle was aborted, thanks to a cart with a wonky wheel, Macy picked up her speed with the rest of her shopping. She'd managed to hit all the most important junk food groups and the incredibly important, life-sustaining eggs, cheese and milk aisle. Scrambled eggs were never sexy; they were always easy and fast. Macy quickly counted up the items in her basket and kicked the wheel when she realized she'd missed twenty items or less by four. She trudged over to the longest line and settled in to wait. She heard the ding of an incoming text but before she could pull her phone out of her purse, someone said, "Girl, I did not expect to see you out and about this afternoon." Christina Braswell was in the shorter express line. If anyone could make grocery shopping glamorous, it was Christina. She was wearing the same jeans and T-shirt Macy had seen her in when they'd had lunch together, but under a coat that managed to be both puffy and sleek only on her.

"Can't remember if I've ever seen you out of the uniform. Bet you seem six inches shorter in jeans." Macy knew it was simply an observation, but coming up with an appropriate response was beyond her.

Then she remembered her promise to Astrid. "If you can take the time away from your true love, Astrid and I are having dinner at The Branch next Friday. Want to join us?" Macy tapped her fingernail on the shopping basket, the nerves surprising her. "Leanne already said yes."

Christina whistled loud and long, drawing a few stares. "She agreed to come to The Branch?" She smiled. "I'll have to join you, then, and run interference with Brett. He doesn't want either of us in that place, because of Leanne's sobriety." Macy started to offer a change of venue, but Christina waved her off. "Forget it. In this town, The Branch is the place to go. It has to happen sooner or later, and I'd love to get Leanne out of her apartment."

"Okay. Astrid and I were talking about making it a regular thing." Macy kept her tone light and airy as if it didn't matter much. "Leanne can definitely pick the next place."

"Good idea." Christina left her much better spot and took the place in line behind Macy. "Bit of a day out at the Reserve, wasn't it? I figured everyone was laying low, licking some wounds, and I don't know... Maybe polishing their résumés." She sighed. "Brett refuses to do that, but I keep telling him, if Ash goes, he might be next. The chief ranger will be careful about keeping on anyone loyal to Ash. He's good at his job, but when the guy in charge wants you gone, it can be very hard to stay." She obviously realized where she was because she sent two quick peeks over both shoulders to make sure no one was close enough to hear what she'd said.

Since it was Sweetwater and this was the only grocery store in town, there were at least five heads turned in her direction.

Christina winced and bent closer. "Are you okay?"

Mad at Ash Kingfisher all over again for leaving her out of what had obviously turned into a Big Deal, Macy leaned closer. "Ash insisted I take a sick day. I didn't but I didn't go into the ranger station, either. What did I miss?"

Christina's eyebrows shot up. "Missed all the excitement. Probably for the best."

Before Macy could ask for details, Christina whispered, "They were ambushed. At the press conference."

For the second time that day, Macy's heart lurched into a full gallop, making it hard to breathe. When the cashier yelled, "Next!" Christina urged her to step forward. Macy quickly unloaded her basket and turned back. "The chief ranger was there?" Her horrified whisper carried halfway to the back of the store, but there wasn't much she could do to lower her tone. Was it her fault, the result of her grand speech over banana nut bread? The only real advantage they'd had was surprise. If the chief ranger had been there…

"Not the chief ranger. Whit Callaway. The younger Whit Callaway. Junior. Wonder if he hates being called Junior. We should try to get that trending. The weasel can't be on the up-and-up. Brett was left out of the conversation, but when he described seeing the guy in person, he used the words *fake* and *smarmy* and since Brett is the nicest guy I know…" Christina's eyes were wide as she shook her head slowly. "I heard it was a theatrical display, but only from one side. Whit was outraged at the way the Kingfishers were trying to use the press conference to try to stop the lodge project. Ash and Winter, they were dumbfounded. Brett said he managed to escort Whit inside, but he had no idea how everything turned out. Those reporters waited for Junior to come out and then for Winter to answer questions. Brett said they stayed for hours."

Macy was frozen as she imagined what that must have looked like, how Ash and Winter would have struggled to adjust to Whit's sudden appearance.

None of them were prepared for this kind of drama.

"Your total is $63.67." The cashier was watching her closely, in order to catalog all the details, so she could pass them along to every shopper that came behind Christina. "You can run your credit card now." She dipped her chin down to motion to the card reader.

Impatiently, Macy swiped her card.

"That's all I know," Christina said as she plopped her basket in front of the cashier. Her apologetic grimace before she glanced around at their small, interested audience made it easier for Macy to load up her bags. She'd get the rest of the information directly from Ash. Even if she had to threaten him with fancy casseroles.

"Thanks, Christina." She tried to communicate a whole conversation with her eyes. *I will be into the campground diner tomorrow. There we will exchange phone numbers.* Instead of saying any of that, she raised her hand and headed out of the store as quickly as she could without running. She tossed the groceries into the trunk, slammed it shut and dug around in her purse to yank out her phone. She was already composing the quickest message of her life when she noticed the text.

At first, she thought Ash had answered her.

Then she realized it was from her boss, the big boss, the head of Administrative Services for the Smoky Valley Nature Reserve. She worked for Ash day to day, but Monica Grey had hired her, would fire her if it came to that, and she wanted to talk to Macy.

The instant hard lump in her throat took a minute to clear, so Macy reversed out of her parking spot and did her best to slowly turn into the nearly nonexistent rush hour traffic trickling through Sweetwater. It had been about fifteen minutes since Monica had sent the text. Should she forget the groceries and dinner and head to the small cabin on the Reserve that Ash used and find out what was going on?

Her first instinct was to pick up a sword and rush to Ash's side. Why was Monica calling her?

"No way to know but to call her back, Macy." As soon as she parked in front of her apartment, Macy made the call. She gripped the steering wheel tightly while she waited. Maybe it was too late in the afternoon to catch her. What if she'd left early?

"Monica Grey," she answered smoothly.

"Hey, Monica, it's Macy," Macy added on a strangled cough when she realized how perky she sounded. Nerves did that to her. She overcompensated with cheer.

"Oh, yeah, hey. Ash emailed first thing this morning to tell me you were sick and request Nicole's help. I didn't want to disturb you if you were still feeling terrible, but I need to get you to come into the office tomorrow. Can you do that? If you're still ill, you can head back home afterward, but we need to talk."

Macy waited for more explanation, but silence was her answer.

"I'm planning to be back at my desk in the morning, but I could make the trip to Knoxville if you need to see me. Can we talk about this over the phone instead? If not, is Nicole available to cover a few hours?" Macy asked.

Monica cleared her throat. "Well, that's what we need to talk about. When you come in tomorrow, we're going to discuss your options with the Reserve."

Macy stared hard at the number four on her apartment door as she tried to decipher what that meant.

"Options *instead of* working at the Otter Lake Ranger Station?" Macy asked slowly.

Silence was her answer again, and then Monica sighed. "You have a job at the Reserve, Macy. Don't worry about that, okay? It's just that…" Monica cleared her throat. Was she nervous? "Ranger Kingfisher has recommended that you be moved from the ranger station to another post. He believes Nicole is a better fit at this time, although he has written one of the most glowing recommendations I've ever read. I'd like you to meet with the chief ranger. He's searching for a new assistant. You could fill the spot."

Macy closed her eyes and tried to refocus them on the number four again. Everything was hazy.

"Tomorrow at nine? Does that work, Macy?" Monica asked. Had she been forced to repeat herself? Macy wasn't sure.

Eventually, she managed to agree that the time would work and ended the call.

Getting out of the car was impossible, however. Instead, she leaned her head back against the headrest and stared at the fabric upholstery on the ceiling without seeing it.

Ash Kingfisher had managed to surprise her.

He'd done the one thing she'd never imagined he'd do, and it hurt worse than she could have guessed.

He'd fired her.

## *CHAPTER TWELVE*

WALKING DOWN THE street in Sweetwater had never seemed intimidating to Ash Kingfisher. He'd grown up on Main Street. Smoky Joe's had been there as long as he could remember. Sometimes the scenery changed a fraction; shops like Sweetwater Souvenir moved in. This time, Janet Abernathy and Regina Blackburn had given the storefront a face-lift; some of the other shops lining the busiest street in town had done little but change the name on the door. Since the town had been incorporated around the turn of the nineteenth century, the storefronts were unique and could seem frozen in time.

When he walked into his barbershop, the place he'd had his hair cut ever since his mother had given up on long hair as a statement, time seemed to stop.

The small crowd of regulars there were in the middle of a conversation, but everything halted as soon as the electric doorbell announced his arrival.

His barber, Andy, raised his hand. "All right, Ash?"

After giving the other men in the small room a quick scan, Ash nodded. "You have time for a trim before you close?" Woody Butler was seated in Andy's chair, his eyes locked on Ash in the mirror. The old guy had a good head of hair, but how long could it take to give him the same cut he'd had since Reagan was president?

"All right, Ash." Andy nodded toward the straight-backed bench he kept in the shop window. Saturdays could be busy, so Ash avoided them. Andy's was a gathering place for every old-timer with a few hours to spare.

Monday evenings, half an hour before closing, had always been Ash's time slot. He'd never encountered a crowd like this.

If he'd wanted a place to make his case to Sweetwater's movers and shakers, this wasn't it, but this was a solid link in the town's informal communication network.

All eyes were locked on him; but before Ash could make a thing of that, his old high school principal walked out of the tiny restroom at the back of the shop.

Still, not one of them said a word.

If Ash were a betting man, he'd make a wager that he'd been the subject of conversation before he'd entered. Another option: the Reserve and its troubles. Could be the weather, but they'd have no hesitation to complain about the cold weather, no matter the audience.

He'd spent a fair amount of time in the barbershop since he was a young kid. Weather conversation pretty much followed a pattern. If temperatures were dropping, they'd say it was too cold. And the reverse when temperatures were rising.

This strange silence in the unusually crowded room was a brand-new thing. It made Ash uncomfortable.

"Here. Turn that up." Woody pointed up at the television in the corner of the room. Andy left it muted most of the time, so it was often ignored, but the subtitles along the bottom announced an upcoming segment on the Smoky Valley Nature Reserve. When Bailey Garcia's face filled the frame, Ash had to bite back a moan. It wasn't that he was surprised. She'd asked him for an interview, so he knew she was working on a story.

The chief ranger hadn't fired him. Not yet. He was

going to be spit polished the next time he appeared on camera while representing the Reserve.

Unless this crowd of old codgers chased him away.

"All right, Woody." Andy brushed off his shoulders and removed the cape that was taped together with shiny duct tape in three different places. Nothing changed in Andy's shop, not even things that should be tossed into the garbage.

Woody slowly stood up and stretched, his attention on the television. "Can't miss this story right here. Believe I'll have me a seat. Wife's making meat loaf." His grimace suggested he was in no hurry to get home.

Ash stifled a sigh and slid into the chair while he waited for Andy to make change in the ancient cash register.

Then Andy dropped the cape over his head and started working.

They didn't need to discuss options. His haircut had been the same for years and Andy had been his barber.

The sounds of occasional snipping filled the air before Bailey Garcia came back on screen.

The sight of him standing on the sidewalk in front of the ranger station settled his nerves. It was a report on their press conference. Nothing more.

Every man in the room inched closer to get a better handle on the volume. Even Andy paused as he listened to Bailey's rundown of everything Ash had said. When she held up the packet of information they'd handed out, Woody whistled long and loud. "She's got the smoking gun."

Ash closed his eyes for a minute. Smoking gun? Was there such a thing? Did bureaucratic red tape smoke at all?

Then the segment was over. She didn't announce that

she was working on a follow-up. That was for the best. He hadn't heard from the chief ranger, not even after he'd filed the paperwork needed to transfer Macy away from the ranger station. For some reason, Ash had expected that to lead to…something.

Monica should have protested. Macy should have texted him angrily when she found out. Leland Hall could have called to inform Ash his little ploy wouldn't work and Macy could stay at the ranger station until the Callaways pulled the plug.

So far, nothing.

Ash was thinking so hard that he didn't realize all eyes in the shop had returned to him.

When he did, he cleared his throat and fluffed the cape out over his arms.

"All right," Andy said, his comb pointed at Ash. While he was stalling for time, Ash tried to remember if he'd ever heard Andy say anything other than those two words in that order. Surely he had.

If he waited long enough, would Andy be forced to say something else?

"Diner was dee-serted this morning," Woody drawled from his seat in the window. "Made my favorite waitress Chrissy sad." His eyebrows drew together into a white, bushy line of disapproval. "Y'all up to something out there at the Reserve or not? Scheming to stop forward movement and whatnot."

Ash considered his options. There weren't many. "Nope."

Then he stretched his legs out and waited for Andy to resume cutting. Nobody moved.

If that had worked, he would have celebrated. Instead, he added, "Love that place. Love this town. Grew up here. I won't do anything to hurt either. You better look further afield for your suspects."

Andy returned to cutting Ash's hair without saying a word. Was that settled?

"Suspects of what?" Woody drawled.

Ash stared at the old guys as Andy finished clipping and cleaning up the mess Ash had walked in with. Whatever else Andy did, he had the "lawman special" look down. When he whipped off the cape, Ash stood up and pulled out a ten-dollar bill. He held up a hand as Andy wordlessly offered to make change.

The urge to make a run for it was strong. Instead, he stopped at the door. "I know there's plenty of support in town for a new lodge. The Callaways are pushing hard because a new lodge could draw lots of visitors and money, but it'll destroy The Aerie. That's been my issue all along. That report? Only confirms what I've said from the beginning." Ash tapped the doorknob, anxious to make a good case. "I've never done anything underhanded, though. I'm committed to serving the people of Sweetwater and the mission of the Reserve. The Callaways hold all the cards. Somebody's gotta watch over their shoulders to make sure they aren't cheating us all out of the place we love."

In a nutshell, that was it.

"All right, Ash," Andy said with a firm nod.

Woody's lips flattened. "Them Callaways. Rich gettin' richer at the expense of this town." He shook his head in disgust. "Expect they'll come out smelling like roses, too."

"Please don't turn your back on the Reserve, no matter what comes of the new lodge." Ash hated how the words tasted, but the strong, silent routine wouldn't get him the support he needed in Sweetwater. Battling the Callaways to stop the lodge would be easier with the town behind him just as Winter said it would.

Woody rubbed a hand over his mouth before standing. "I like a man who does the hard thing, Ranger. Expect I'll remember to tell some others who might feel the same." He leaned forward. "I have your word you're on the up-and-up." Then he offered his hand to shake.

The fleeting question about what a crook might say in this situation was gone before Ash could answer it. Didn't matter. "You have it. Kingfishers love the Reserve. Protecting that land comes first. The job is second."

Woody's eyes narrowed. "The job, you say?"

The man's alert interest was more than Ash expected. "Not sure how long there'll be Kingfishers serving at the Smoky Valley Nature Reserve. The Callaway family is still in charge there." Ash remembered Winter's serious face as she pondered the possibility of how to tackle them. "If any of you know the members serving on the board of directors, I'd take it as a…" Ash stopped to clear his throat, the words catching so he had to force them out. "It would be a personal favor if you'd make your support for The Aerie and for me known to them. Been working in the Reserve for more than a decade. I'd like to keep doing it, lodge or not. I never stirred up the governor but convincing the Callaways of that is a no go. I'm going to have to go around them." He paused to watch the old guys consider his request. Then he waved at Andy and stepped back out on the sidewalk.

Grateful for the falling temperatures then, Ash paused to study the storefront of Sweetwater Souvenir. The beautiful painting in the window caught his eye. The landscape featuring the peak of The Aerie trail in bright sunlight was amazing. He was half a second from finding out the price because it belonged in the visitor center when he heard someone call his name.

Before he could turn to see who it was, Sam Blackburn had wrapped his arms around Ash's shoulders in a substantial bear hug. Sam tried to lift him up before grunting and switching to hard, pounding thumps on his back.

"I've missed you, too." Ash stumbled forward on his bad leg before he aimed a jab at Blackburn's abdomen. Hard muscles kept him from doing too much damage. "Firefighting must be giving you a workout."

"More like search-and-rescue equipment, but whatever it is, you'll never have a six-pack like this, Kingfisher." Blackburn held both arms out from his sides.

"It's a good thing I've missed you, you cocky so-and-so." Ash held his hand out and gripped Blackburn's for a hard handshake. "You told me you'd be here tomorrow."

"Avery got out of her last class a day early, so we hit the road. She wanted to come home." Sam waved at Sweetwater Souvenir. Ash could see or almost see Avery with her mother, Janet Abernathy, in the storefront. Christmas greenery made a frame around them and the striking painting.

"We're headed over to The Branch to have a burger." Sam shoved his hands in his jeans. "My mother's busy, she's over in Cherokee doing research on…something. Consignment contracts? I've lost track which scheme they're on. Why don't you join us? Unless you've got a date?"

Ash grinned. "It's contagious, I guess. You fall in love, you think everyone comes down with the virus."

Blackburn shrugged. "It's definitely got an upside."

He pointed broadly toward The Branch and Ash watched Avery give him a thumbs-up in the window. "You don't even need words to communicate. Cute."

Blackburn sighed. "She is awfully cute. Me? Ruggedly handsome, but still attractive in my own way. Let's get inside. I expect this chill is hard on you since you're not used to the cold."

For a split second, Ash wondered if Sam was making a jab about his bad leg. Then he realized he was putting on Colorado superior airs. "You were born and raised here just like me, Blackburn."

Sam nodded slowly. "Uh-huh, but I've had to toughen up."

Ash rolled his eyes, while Blackburn brayed with laughter like a donkey. "Why have I missed you?"

Sam urged him down the street. When they reached The Branch, warmth hit Ash in the face as soon as the door swung open. Neon signs lined the bar, but only small groups of tourists sat at the tables.

"Sam Blackburn, you rascal," Sharon, the owner, bartender and keeper of peace at Sweetwater's only bar, yelled from her spot behind the taps. "Wondered when I'd see you again."

"Four burgers, Sharon, and your coldest root beer." Root beer was Sharon's signature drink. Since she ran the only bar in town, it was an interesting choice, but it was difficult to argue with how it hit the spot. Sam pointed toward a booth in the back. "This will be the quietest table."

Ash limped up the three steps and slid in across from Sam. "Heard you're having some excitement out at the ranger station." Sam leaned back. "Were you going to tell me what was going on or just let me read it in the paper?"

"Texting all that?" Ash shrugged. "Nothing you could do about it, anyway." The urge to tell Sam it was all under control was strong, but Sam had loved the Reserve for a long time, too. Fresh perspective might help him dream up a solution.

"From Colorado, I might not be able to save the day," Sam said as he stretched an arm out along the booth. "But here, I could…" He frowned. "Well, there's got to be something."

Ash ran a hand over his nape, aware of the cool breeze there now that his hair was cut. "I've got my best people on it." Or he'd had his best people. He'd sent his right hand away.

"Best people." Sam studied the ceiling. "I'm sure your sister is on that list. Winter is formidable. But she's marrying a Callaway." He grimaced. "You've been dragged into a mess, haven't you?"

"My mess. Nobody to blame but myself, since I couldn't keep my objections to myself." Ash was surprised at how much Sam Blackburn's opinion mattered. Before the guy had left Tennessee to chase bigger fires, he'd have called himself Sam's mentor. Now? He wanted to make sure nothing bruised Sam's good opinion of him.

"You did what you had to." So there was no doubt in Sam's mind. That was a huge relief to Ash. He'd had his own doubts along the way. "Building a lodge…" Sam shrugged. "I could see how it makes sense, but not there. That's too special, one of the most unique trails we've got." He knocked on the wood table. "Winter going to be okay? Having an engagement wrapped up in the mix can't be easy."

"She'll be okay, but the engagement won't. My mother will celebrate. Winter…" Ash stared hard at the bar. Two root beers were sweating away right there on the edge. He could go get them. "Whatever she decides to do once this all shakes out will be amazing. That's for sure, but ending an engagement will stick with her."

"Seems like saying you'll marry someone's gotta be one of the scariest decisions a person can make. Walking away from it is probably terrifying."

Ash crossed his hands on the table and waited for Sam to expound. When he didn't, Ash drawled. "Do you speak from experience, Sam?" If they'd gotten engaged in Colorado, Ash had missed the update.

Sam coughed. "It's even more complicated when one party is as skittish as can be." He shrugged. "I'll win her over yet, though. But why don't we dig into your love life instead?"

Ash held his hands out. "Open book as always. No true love or otherwise to speak of."

"I can tell there's something else." Sam shook his finger. "But I can wait. Glad Macy is on your team. The two of them together? Her and Winter? You should be able to handle the Callaways, no problem."

Ash nodded. "Well, that's the only play we have left, to outmaneuver them with the board of directors. They don't make up the majority. If we can get the board to shut down the lodge project or at least reconsider the question while also supporting me and Winter in our positions…" It did seem like a pretty big long shot when he named it all in one fell swoop like that.

Sam whistled. "Gotta focus on the finish line, not all the jumps you gotta make along the way." He made a writing motion. "That's pure gold right there. You should write it down."

Ash blinked slowly at Sam and waited for him to get serious again. "If I fail, there goes my job. There goes Winter's job."

Sam leaned forward. "And Macy, too. Maybe Hendrix, since you hired and promoted him, but Macy will get caught, won't she? No way she'd quietly take the Callaways firing you, probably argue herself right out of a job. Unless the politics have changed in the year I've been gone, it's a tricky spot for both of them, too." Sam's face reflected Ash's concerns and it was another confirmation that he'd done the right thing about Macy.

"I've had her transferred. Macy. Hendrix is on his own. There's nowhere else to send him to wait this out, but Macy I can try to help." Ash scrubbed his hands over his face. "It's been a long day. Press conference. Paperwork without Macy's help. And Nicole…" He shook his head. "She's nice. Conscientious, but I can tell I make her nerves kick up. At the end of three months, she'll have an ulcer while I learn to levitate on my way to the door in order to keep from startling her." Of all the knots he'd worked through that day, facing doing the same tomorrow and hereafter without Macy had been depressing.

"Macy was okay with your plan to protect her?" Blackburn asked slowly. Ash could hear his doubt and understood it.

"No. She's not okay. I haven't heard a word from her, but I know she's not okay." Ash winced. "I've almost called her a dozen different times to explain, but she's smart. She'll see through my plan and we'll be okay. As soon as this dies down, I'll get her back, offer her a raise if I have to smooth ruffled feathers, and it'll all be fine. Back to normal. Just the two of us, manning the ranger station."

Sam pursed his lips and didn't answer immediately. Ash finally looked up to see that Sam was busy studying the tabletop.

"You don't think it'll work like that." It was like he and Blackburn had taken up the two voices arguing in his head ever since Whit Callaway had left. One side was certain it would all work out. The other was as determined that he'd made a fatal mistake.

"Macy's like your secret weapon at the ranger station." Sam tapped his fingers on the table. "Now's not the best time to be without your weapon. Is it?"

"No, but…" The answer there on the tip of his tongue revealed too much. Since he'd given Blackburn enough of a hard time when he'd been half a second from letting his girl go, Ash was convinced Sam was biding his time to give it all back to him. Being a smart-aleck grump was nice most days. When it came back around to stare him in the face, it was less positive.

Blackburn's slow grin was the confirmation Ash expected that he'd shown his hand. Sam bent his head closer. "Something you need to tell me? Like, there's some girl trouble thrown in here?"

Ash retreated. There was almost no chance that he could play this off successfully, but he was going to try. "She's a friend. A coworker. A young woman alone in this town and in the whole wide world who depends on this job to be her safety net. I won't let anything happen to that. I've sent the staffing recommendation in to the Administrative Services director and I believe Monica will see and understand that talent and passion like Macy's needs to be utilized better."

"Nice corporate speak there, Ranger. But you don't want her to go. Because you'll miss her. Because you feel…" Sam studied his face.

"Impossible to answer. I'm a boss, kind of. I'd never make a move like that." Ash thought about her holding his hand on the way to his parents' house. It had been an awkward, funny episode, but it had been impossible to ignore how nice it felt coming from Macy Gentry.

"You *were* a boss. Now you're not. Maybe that was

a good decision you made there. You can ask her out."
Sam waggled his eyebrows.

"Ash Kingfisher wants to ask a lady out?" Janet Abernathy drawled from her spot at the end of the table.
"Do tell." She slid a tray on the table with two burgers
and two root beers while Avery, her daughter and Sam's
girlfriend, did the same on the other side. "We got here
just in time."

"Who's the lady?" Avery asked in a singsong. "We're
only here for ten days, but a lot can happen in that amount
of time." She pretended to be pulling strings on a pup-
pet. "Point me at her."

Sam's snort was loud enough that Sharon turned to
check on their table. Avery pounded Sam on the back
and waved her away.

"This lady? Yeah, she won't be persuaded." Sam
chuckled to himself as he took a big bite of his burger.
"And it's exactly what Ash Kingfisher deserves."

Ash was determined not to say another word, but the
weight of Janet's stare and Avery's got to him. "Macy is
too young. She's too..." Alone. Positive. Happy for him.
"She could do better than an unemployed park ranger
with a bum leg. She deserves the chance to find more."

"Plus, she's probably ready to kill him for shoving
her out of the ranger station." Sam sipped his drink and
then waved it at Ash. "When you mess up, you go big."

Was it true? Oh, yeah, but there was no use in hash-
ing out his faults there and then.

"Do I know Macy?" Avery asked as she glanced from
Sam to her mother and back.

"Probably not, she's new to town." Janet wiped her
mouth with her napkin. Ash thought about arguing that
Macy had been there for five years or so. How was that
new? In terms of Sweetwater's residents, it was brand-

new. And defending Macy over a small point like that would show too much concern.

"She's the ranger station's office manager. Was the manager, I guess. Ash transferred her without telling her." Sam's eyebrows were raised. Both Avery and Janet stared at him as if they were certain he'd crossed the line.

Regret had turned the three bites of hamburger he'd taken into a lump in his stomach.

It was too late to undo it now. If he didn't want Sam Blackburn to know how much he thought of Macy, he certainly didn't want the chief ranger or Whit Callaway to find out. Withdrawing his transfer, either before or after Macy reacted, would betray his feelings.

When neither woman had anything to say to that, Ash had to swallow hard to clear his throat. He was gulping his drink and ignoring the pitying looks they shared over his head.

"You know, I've had to learn this lesson myself, so maybe it will help you." Avery leaned closer as jukebox music kicked up in the opposite corner. The Branch never got truly out of hand, but it was the only rowdy entertainment in town. It was good they'd gotten there when they did. They should be finishing up before the dance crowd arrived.

"You can't plan every step, Ash." Avery reached across the table to touch his hand. "Start with the first step. And you can't make it about her. It has to be about you."

Ash looked at Avery and was reminded again of how much steadying she'd needed that night in the hospital. She'd been there for Sam—hurt while fighting a forest fire that'd gone bad—even though it was hard and even though she'd been uncertain what their future could be. Sam had followed his career across the country; Avery had managed to figure out that what she wanted could happen in Colorado, maybe even better than Tennessee.

And she hadn't let her fears stop her.

"So what do we do first about the lodge?" Janet asked. "When we were out at the campground diner last, Regina and I were shocked at how few people were there."

"And I'm sure you know why." Ash was certain Janet wouldn't have missed the gossip in town.

That was Sweetwater. Everyone knew everyone. It was a tourist town, but it was also a small town. The connections were impossible to ignore, and they meant that news spread in an instant.

Janet shrugged. "TV reporter is saying Kingfishers are playing dirty politics to stop the lodge. People in town seem split between those that think the Callaways are pro-Sweetwater at heart and…" She glanced over at Ash. "Well, I'm not sure you have anyone exactly in your corner, but lots of people doubt that you'd intend to harm the Reserve. Kingfishers have been in town a long time. Just because nobody knows you anymore doesn't mean the Kingfisher name doesn't stand for something." She paused, seemingly to replay what she just said. "People are willing to give you the benefit of the doubt because of your last name. That's what I mean." She bit into her burger, obviously satisfied she'd given a nice recap of the gossip in town.

"They don't know him?" Sam asked. "What does that mean?"

"Never in town. Never at the diner." Janet shrugged. "Don't know him."

Ash had heard it from several different people now. At some point, he'd have to accept that it was true.

"After the accident, you sort of crawled into a cave."

Sam watched him. "I dragged you out now and then, but I left."

Before dinner could turn into a mushy intervention, Ash said, "I'm a grown man, Blackburn. I can take care of myself, no dragging needed."

No one agreed with him.

"What happened?" Avery asked and then bent closer. "You don't have to tell me, but I'd like to know."

Ash mangled a few french fries. "I grew up on Otter Lake, and I was certain I was invincible there. I used to be like Blackburn, testing the limits to feel alive, except I got caught. Slipped in a climb without the safety equipment. That's it. We were injured, but nothing tragic happened. It's not a story worth telling." Satisfied he'd covered everything, Ash gulped his root beer.

"Except…" Sam raised an eyebrow. "Your career…"

Ash tipped his head back to stare at the ceiling, dull wood beams overhead. "I made a great law enforcement ranger when I started. When you're really good at something, you never imagine it'll go away. Some parts of it haven't. I can name plants and tell you about the winter feeding habits of the black bear, but I can't…do what I did. Physically. I'm embarrassed because I did something stupid to throw it away and determined to fulfill the post I have now to the best of my ability. I've built new educational panels for the visitor center. I've hired the best talent for all areas of the park. I have studied until I know the place inside and out. And I've stayed out of trouble." Ash cleared his throat, realizing his voice had risen as he spoke. "But I'm still about to lose my job." He took a big mouthful of his burger and chewed angrily until everyone else concentrated on their own dinner.

Then Janet wiped her mouth. "Here's the thing. I'm not sure I have a game plan for the girlfriend. You've fouled that up, unless I miss my guess, and you should try to straighten it out." She tapped him on the shoulder. "Brett Hendrix did it. You can, too. Nobody messed up romance like that boy, and look at him and Christina now." She shook her head. "No, I cannot help with that," she said definitively and unaware of how Avery's lips were twitching. "But I can help you with your image problem. I have two suggestions. First, I hear through the grapevine that your father is an artist. Baskets." She raised an eyebrow and Ash was forced to nod. Even when his father wasn't around, the baskets dominated conversation. "We're going to put some of his baskets in at Sweetwater Souvenir. You can help me get that done, right? Macy told me she'd introduce us at the open house. I'll be there. Regina, too. The lovebirds will be smoochin' it up in front of whatever fancy 'photographic backdrop' it is Macy's advertising. We can get Sweetwater to show up if you'll do the same. In exchange, you get me a deal with your daddy. Macy said he's the key to a successful art showing at my as-yet-unnamed art gallery."

"When did you talk to Macy? She was home sick today." Ash leaned back, ready to be shocked.

"She was up and down Main Street, hawking your open house." Janet tapped the table. "In full Smoky Valley Nature Reserve uniform, I might add. She's a credit, Ash. Unravel your knots, you hear me?"

He wasn't shocked. She'd ignored his orders. That should never surprise him, so Ash inhaled slowly and exhaled. "Getting my father there is no problem. Neither are the baskets. Whatever you cooked up with Macy, she's right." If he texted his father right now, Martin Kingfisher would have the car loaded and parked in front of Sweetwater Souvenir before they made it out the front door of The Branch.

"What was the second part of the plan?" He'd lost track of the conversation. Probably because too many problems were swirling around and he'd somehow landed back at baskets.

"Easy. Operation We Love Kingfishers." Janet's smile was bright. "When I go into Smoky Joe's, I will tell everyone there about the new plans to feature local artists like Martin Kingfisher. I will rave over the family and…" She made the voilà motion with her hands and seemed pretty pleased with herself.

Ash didn't want to lose what little support he'd gained, but he had to know. "That's it?" It couldn't be that simple.

Janet nodded. "If you want to help, ask Macy out on a date. Show her off around town. Kiss her in the campground diner." Janet nodded until Ash followed suit. "Win the town over. Show them who you are. Pretty young woman on your arm is a story everyone loves to tell."

Avery joined in the nodding. "I don't have as much ammunition as my mother, but I could stop in and talk to Astrid. She's a big fan of Winter. I'm sure she would be happy to talk about how wonderful her work at the library has been. The kids eat her stories up." When Sam choked, Avery elbowed him hard in the side. "Not everyone has the talent to keep a child's attention, Sam. Winter has a *talent*."

"Okay, so we've got the library and the schools covered." Janet ticked off the places on her fingers. She was a volunteer secretary at the schools; since parents relied on the Reserve for entertainment, especially in the summer, reaching them could be a big help. "Local businesses will be your biggest targets. Odella over at the coffee shop. There's the hardware store."

"My barber's on board. He only knows two words, but it's nice to count on him," Ash muttered.

"What you need is something big, Ash." Avery propped her elbows on the table. "A love story...like my mom said."

If he hadn't shot himself in the foot with the only woman he'd be interested in spinning a love story with, fake or otherwise, Ash might be looking forward to that.

"I'll talk to Macy, but to be safe, you better come up with a plan B." Ash watched everyone at the table agree with him and wished for a little less ready capitulation.

"You were a good friend to me, Ash Kingfisher," Avery stated. "So I'm going to tell you something my mother used to spout to me." She glanced around the table. "Mountains move one rock at a time. Slow and steady, Ash, just don't give up. As long as you're moving, you're still in the game."

Sam's kiss caught Avery's attention, and Janet's amused sigh barely registered as Ash considered Avery's advice. He wouldn't give up on Macy, not until she made it clear he had to move on. Convincing her could be akin to wearing down a mountain.

But the suggestion of moving a mountain made him think.

What if the new lodge at Otter Lake was no longer a yes or no proposition? The location of the proposed site was the biggest problem.

The Aerie was the most beautiful spot in the Reserve, but that would disappear when the lodge was built on top. If he could convince the Callaways that a lodge in the shadow of The Aerie, one built in the clearing around the old weather station, was the best of both worlds, everyone could win. A lightning strike had ignited a wildfire there almost a year ago. The grasses had almost recovered but the forests still showed the scars.

What if they could cover those scars with something beautiful, a lodge that would draw people to the Reserve for the beautiful views of The Aerie and Otter Lake? Construction on the gentler slope would be easier, faster, less expensive. The Reserve would still lose some habitat, but it had already been damaged by fire. With the lodge on site, restoration of the forests would immediately jump up the priority list within the Reserve.

It all made sense. Yes, it would mean delays, but the end would be an addition to the work of the Reserve, not destruction.

This was the answer.

Convincing the right people to ask the right question was the first step.

# CHAPTER THIRTEEN

MACY FORCED HERSELF to slow down as she made the turn into the district office. If Monica Grey had seen the speedometer on Macy's trip to Knoxville, she might have had some concern about Macy's judgment.

She'd carefully ironed the uniform so that the chief ranger would find no complaint there.

And she'd forced herself to put down her phone every time she'd picked it up to text or call Ash Kingfisher.

It wasn't that she couldn't see through his plan. If the chief ranger was fooled by this transfer, Macy would be shocked. Still, she needed the ammunition of however this conversation went down before she marched into the ranger station and informed Ash that she'd made a few of her own decisions.

"Get your head in the moment, Macy Elizabeth." Her grandmother would have been unimpressed by Macy's sleepless night. To her, one job was as good as another. The important part was having a job.

Breaking the pattern of letting her grandmother's joyless ghost stop her from doing what she wanted had started with a crazy camera purchase for a frivolous hobby. Today, she was going to expand that tiny crack by demanding Monica Grey override Ash Kingfisher.

Macy was ready to demand her spot in the visitor center. She'd built it herself.

If Ash didn't want to work with her, he could just… transfer himself out.

His glowing recommendation showed she'd done nothing wrong, and he was not the most popular employee in the Reserve. She might be able to pull this off.

All night long, she'd battled back and forth, taking different sides of the argument, and…

This was all she could live with. She'd back Ash Kingfisher in any battle that came, but he'd need to apologize for putting her through this meeting.

And he would.

As she pushed open the door to the district office, Macy tried to remember the last time she'd been inside. It had been a few years. In the beginning, she'd been a floater like Nicole, working part-time where she was needed. It had been great to see all the different kinds of work being done to protect Tennessee's natural beauty at each reserve, but Otter Lake had stolen her heart the first day she'd turned up at the ranger station.

Was it because Ash Kingfisher had been there, even grumpier than he was now because his wounds were fresh and the disappointment had settled into his bones? Macy had never been able to turn her back on wounded animals.

Or people, either, for that matter.

Ash had needed her then. That had been some of the draw to the ranger station. Clutter had threatened to take over his desk, and the desk in the lobby had been a wasteland of empty boxes and a ringing phone. Carving out her space had been a challenge and she'd loved every minute.

Teasing him, poking him, making him mad…she'd had to learn her way. Maybe she wasn't done learning yet.

"Macy, it's good to see you in person. Monica's running late but she's almost here." Kayla stood from behind the desk. Instead of the mannish Reserve uniform, Kayla might have been a clone of Winter Kingfisher in her dark suit coat and skirt. She had the same Reserve pin, and Macy realized with a flash that working in Knoxville would change more than her commute.

No one would think she fit here. Ash's last-ditch effort had no chance of succeeding.

"Is Winter in today?" Macy asked before she thought it all the way through. The chance to abuse Ash to a friend was attractive. His sister might not be open to it, though, even if Macy offered to buy lunch.

Better to wait until they had a few girls' nights under their belts.

Kayla frowned as she clicked away on her computer. "I don't have her out of the office today, but with the news…" She shrugged and then put her hand to her ear. "District office, this is Kayla." She listened and clicked some more. "The chief ranger is in a meeting right now, but I'll be happy to take a message. Of course, Mr. Callaway. I'll let him know." Her eyes flicked toward Macy, but Kayla smoothly touched the earpiece to end the call. Macy was doing her best to see the note Kayla scribbled, but she'd never been good at reading upside down.

As a door swung open, Macy jerked back quickly.

"Miss Gentry, why don't you come in? Monica's caught in traffic, but she'll be here any moment." The chief ranger stood in the doorway, his broad shoulders nearly blocking the opening completely.

Nerves threatened to swamp Macy then. Maybe it was the uniform that heightened her anxiety. Or the way Leland Hall watched her, the careful stare of a police officer hard to meet head-on.

Or it might be the anger she felt about Ash's situation. Whatever it was, Macy's temperature rose ten degrees and she was pretty sure flop sweat was imminent. The only way to handle that was...

She held her hand out. "I'd be happy to, Chief Ranger." He shook her hand and turned to step into his office. "Kayla, could you bring us a couple of bottles of water?"

Had he noticed the sweat on her brow?

Kayla brought in the water and then stepped back outside. Macy could hear her speaking and crossed her fingers in the hope that she was actually talking to a live person like Monica Grey, instead of into her earpiece.

"I was surprised when I got the transfer paperwork from Ash yesterday." Hall leaned back in his chair and studied her. "What happened?"

Because she'd been asking herself that ever since Monica's phone call, Macy wasn't sure she had a good answer. Still, Ash had his reasons, namely protecting her, so she'd support his play. "I know that Ash has spoken highly of Nicole in the past." She glanced around the chief ranger's office as if she were sizing it up. Instead, she wanted clues on the future of the lodge project or Ash's job. Leland Hall's desk was clear. There were no files, no binders, no ragged newspapers, no pens with bite marks or fish-shaped coffee mugs. Just bare, smooth, expensive-looking wood.

If she'd been on the fence about an opportunity to move to the district office before she got here, one look at his desk would have decided her.

"Sorry I'm late. Stalled school bus." Monica Grey walked in, her pantsuit wrinkled but still sharp. "I hope you're telling her about the opportunity we're hoping to create here in Knoxville, Ranger."

Monica handed Macy a piece of paper with a job description. "Executive assistant to the chief ranger." She raised her eyebrows. "You would handle scheduling and communications, along with the other offices here, of course."

"You called me in to talk about a promotion?" Macy asked as she slowly read over the short list of duties. "Or not. Is this a promotion?" The details were pretty thin, although she did some of her best work with the least established procedures.

"It's a brand-new position, Macy," Monica said, the cheer in her voice less than convincing. "Ranger Hall and I have been discussing his need for more help here in the office so that he can spend more time in the Reserve." She shrugged. "This is coming together at exactly the right time. I've discussed my plans for this position with Ash. I expect he knew as soon as he heard me say I was looking that you'd be the natural candidate. You basically set up the visitor center at the ranger station with very little direction. This could be the next step up for you. What do you think?"

Macy studied Monica's face. There was not a bit of hesitation in her eyes. Monica believed what she was saying and honestly wanted Macy to have an opportunity to do more.

Then why couldn't she shake the feeling that this was a test of some kind?

The way Leland Hall watched her had something to do with the uneasy feeling, no doubt. If she'd had to guess, his weighing stare was the outward sign of an inward measurement he was taking.

And if he was testing her, it was only fair that Macy do a little feeling out herself.

"Well, I know I could do this." She leaned back and crossed her legs. "But tell me why I'd want to." Then she braced herself and added, "Leland." Monica's shift in her seat at Macy's use of the ranger's first name confirmed one of Macy's suspicions. Leland Hall took himself too seriously.

For her first week at Otter Lake, Macy had trotted out a "Ranger Kingfisher" now and then until Ash had put a stop to it. He'd said, *We're coworkers and that's a mouthful. Stick with* Ash, *Macy.* He'd always treated her like an equal.

The way Kayla delivered water bottles and Monica cleared her throat nervously in the sudden, tense silence convinced Macy that this district office operated on a much more formal level.

She'd never be happy with that. If she had to come into this office every day, she'd be a nervous mess by the end of the second month.

The chief ranger leaned slowly forward and braced his elbows on the desk. "Do you like working at the Reserve, Macy?" He might as well have been a lawyer in a courtroom. She was tempted to say "leading the witness," but the atmosphere was already tense enough.

"I do." Macy mirrored his body language. "But it's important to me that I trust my boss and believe that he's committed to the mission of the Reserve. Because why else do this?" She shrugged. That's what it came down to.

Hall said, "Every review you've had here has been glowing, and then this..." He snapped. "What changed between you and Ranger Kingfisher? Something we ought to know here in Knoxville?"

Was he asking if there was something between them? Implying that it had gone wrong? That was more proof how little he understood Ash.

"You mean other than an honorable man being targeted as a scapegoat to satisfy the Callaways?" Macy asked. As she watched the chief ranger's eyebrows rise, Macy understood that she'd stumbled around and hit a land mine. Ash had told them over dinner how Hall had encouraged him to get the study on The Aerie, how little he'd supported the lodge. Had he seen a chance to stop the project without taking any of the risk?

Hall's eyes narrowed but he smiled. She didn't trust that expression any more than she trusted him.

"I see Ash has been filling your ears."

Macy blinked. "With what, Leland? What could he have told me?"

Monica cleared her throat. "We've gotten off track. We're talking about a new job, not the news stories circulating. Those will go away, leaving us with the Reserve and the work still to be done."

Macy nodded, certain Monica was trying to help her keep her job. She should let this go, but when it came right down to it, she didn't want to work in the district office. The job might be all right, but this was no Otter Lake.

"The news stories will die down. Monica's right." The chief ranger pointed at Macy. "But there's no guarantee that everyone will keep their jobs. You should think about it, Macy. I have enough respect for Ash to know his faith in you has been well-placed. He doesn't exaggerate the truth. But to keep your career on track, you should step away from Ash now."

The cold shiver that hit Macy was impossible to ignore. Hall might as well have said outright that Ash would be gone soon.

How could that be? The Callaways would never find another ranger as well equipped to run the Otter Lake Ranger Station as Ash Kingfisher.

The only reasonable explanation was discouraging.

"I understand that, but there's no reason for me to leave Otter Lake. I enjoy running the visitor center. I appreciate your interest in me, but I'd like to stay where I am." Macy shook her head. "I'm not sure I have a case, but if I'm terminated or forced to change positions, I'll have my lawyer contact you." Macy stood slowly, doing her best to hide the nervous shaking in her hands. Blowing up her easy escape was dumb, so dumb, but it was the only way to go.

Leland Hall studied his hands. "You'd follow Ash anywhere, I guess. And now I see that when he goes, you should, too."

He stood up and motioned toward the door. "Be careful on your drive back to Sweetwater and get a copy of the letter Ash wrote for you to take with you on interviews." His expressionless face meant she could see nothing of what he thought, but her own panic was going to escape pretty soon. "Wonder if the next anonymous tip that hits the news ought to be about a relationship between the head ranger and his secretary. Workplace romance is a tricky line, but between a manager and a subordinate, with the potential for harassment... It's a bad look for Ash." Leland propped his hands on his hips. "Ask Ash if he'd like to plan a press conference on that."

Too angry to answer, Macy skirted around Monica's chair and yanked the door open. She was in a full march by the time she made it to the exit, but Monica was able to stop her from sailing right through and out into the parking lot. "Macy, wait."

Since Monica had always been fair to her, this morning's debacle excepted, Macy paused. Her heart thumped hard and loud in her chest, but she was almost certain no actual steam was escaping from her ears.

That must be why it felt like her head was a second away from exploding.

"I'm sorry. I have no idea what's going on here, but

that wasn't a job interview." They moved outside where Monica paced up and down in front of her. The two of them had all the pavement covered.

"Your boss is not a nice guy. He threatened Ash and me, and he's lucky I'm wearing the uniform that Ash holds in such high regard. Otherwise, I might have to soak out bloodstains." Macy spit every word through clenched jaws and realized she was making fists with both hands. Should she tell Monica she didn't mean anything she was saying? Surely she understood blowing off steam.

"Listen, you wouldn't be the first person I've met who wanted to pop Leland Hall in the nose, but there are better ways to get even," Monica said as she squeezed Macy's shoulder. "And he's not my boss."

Macy tried to concentrate on what Monica was saying. "I don't get it."

"I report directly to the board of directors. So does the chief ranger. We have different areas of supervision, but in essentials, we are at the same level. The chief ranger is in charge of land management and security for the Reserve. All the other areas, including visitor experience, belong to me." Monica sighed. "That means nobody is firing you unless I allow it and there's no chance I'm going to lose your talent, experience and commitment to the goals of the Reserve. Plus, if it ever comes down to it, I wouldn't mind having you go to bat for me."

Macy bent her head as she tried to decipher what that meant. Was she going to have a paycheck to cover the rent or not?

"You should prepare yourself for Ash to go, Macy." She held up a hand to stall Macy's protest. "I've been here for a long time, almost two decades. And I believe you'd be wise to keep your distance from Ash. There is one other position open. The fire chief is looking for an office manager to take over the security documentation and accreditation procedures. When the Reserve business expands with the lodge the Callaways are planning—" she sighed "—and it's only a matter of time now, the state requirements for fire safety and prevention will grow. The chief needs someone to organize extra crews, payroll and scheduling."

Macy stared at the road ahead. It all sounded…intimidating. That was the first word that came to mind, but she refused to say it out loud. Her grandmother had insisted that a person could do anything they set their minds to. The key was to act like she knew what she was doing.

Fake it until she made it.

She'd done the same thing to build her spot at the ranger station. She could do this with the fire team. She already knew the chief and respected him.

"What do you think?" Monica asked softly. "I understand if it's too far from what you want to do. Too far from Ash." She grimaced at Macy's shock. "Oh, whatever. He's a great guy. Kind of grim and in definite need of a laugh or two, but you gotta admire the man who'll do the right thing even when it's difficult."

Macy wasn't sure how to answer any of the questions she heard in Monica's words.

"Meet with the chief. What could that hurt?" Monica said. "If you don't think it'll work, I'll write you a recommendation myself and make some calls around Knoxville to see what kind of openings turn up. And if you're set on staying in the visitor center, I'll back you. We may lose, but I will stand with you."

Struck by how kind Monica was being, Macy forced a smile. She was used to plotting and planning to force things to work out. Monica was ready to give her what she hadn't quite asked for.

"Okay, I'll do that." Macy nodded slowly. "And I'll take you up on your offer if this doesn't work."

"No reason to believe it won't, Macy." Monica's reassuring voice lifted Macy's spirits a bit. "The fire chief is a cuddly kitten compared to Leland Hall and you had that guy on the ropes. Ash never knew what hit him, did he?"

There was no way to answer that properly, but it was nice to smile.

"If there's something between you and Ash—" Monica held up both hands "—not that I'm saying there is, but if there is, this could be the best thing that ever happened to you. Distance should make it easier to see what you two have." She shrugged. "And that's all I have to say about that."

"No warnings about relationships with coworkers?" Macy asked as her pulse settled and it became easier to breathe. Ash had pushed her away on the ride home from his parents because of his position. If that relationship was gone, there would be nothing holding them back.

Not if he, too, wanted to see where it would lead.

"Go see the fire chief. Let me know where to send your paperwork when you make the move." Monica motioned over her shoulder with her thumb. "Send me any extra strength you have as I go back in and deal with the chief ranger. The guy does not like losing and you handed him his hat." Her lips were twitching as she stepped back inside.

Macy got behind the steering wheel and wondered exactly what she was going to do with herself next. Her need for a job weighed heavily with her urge to see Ash, to talk to Ash, to yell at Ash and to make him apologize for pushing her away.

Of the list of things she had to do, getting the fire chief to give her a job seemed the easiest. Her grandmother had taught her to knock the easiest things off the to-do list first. That gave her some momentum as she ran up against the more challenging tasks.

And getting Ash to understand his error and correct it was going to take some thinking.

She'd make sure the rent was covered. Then she'd tackle forcing Ash Kingfisher to fall in love with her.

Her trip back to Sweetwater was almost leisurely. What a difference having a plan made. She could almost believe her grandmother would have been pleased with the way she was working things out, not because her grandmother would have ever countenanced needing a man for anything, but at least Macy had her priorities straight.

"Cover the bills, then do what you want," Macy muttered as she drove up to the fire station. Passing the campground diner, Macy was pleased and relieved to see a solid line of cars filling the front row of the parking lot. "Maybe what I said yesterday mattered." The shot of confidence came at the right time.

She was not too far away from planting her flag at the ranger station and refusing to move. Sweetwater might not have been the home she was born to, but it was home.

And Ash Kingfisher better get his head in the game.

When she slowed to park in front of the large building that housed the fire engines and all the equipment the team used to fight fires and to set prescribed fire needed for the protection of the habitat in the Reserve, a line of guys wandered out from one of the open bays.

"An audience. Wonderful." That hadn't been a part of the equation when she'd been plotting how this would go.

Not that it mattered. She could adjust. "Morning, boys." Macy shut her car door.

Rodriguez bowed low. "Macy. My lovely. Have you come to give your backdrop an inspection?"

The thing about working with a lot of handsome, flirty men was that it never got old. Rodriguez was in love with Sheila, the comanager of the hardware store. He was just having fun, so Macy played along and waggled her eyebrows. "Show me what you got."

He clapped his hands and then cupped his mouth to yell, "Cho! We need water!" In a well-organized scramble, the guys surrounded the backdrop she could see edged around the corner of the firehouse. When she turned the corner, her mouth dropped open. "You built me a mountain." When she imagined how kids would love the display, Macy jumped up and down. "This is awesome."

"You haven't seen the half of it," the fire chief said from the shady bay opening. Macy clasped her hands together, anxious for it all, and when water trickled down in a perfect miniature model of Yanu Falls, she gasped. "Who did this? I need to know because we are going to build wonderful things together."

Every man in the crew pointed at a new guy, someone she hadn't met yet, so Macy marched over, her hand extended. "You're a genius."

His grin was subdued but the guy shook her hand. "Ronald Cho. Call me RJ."

Macy patted his shoulder. "RJ. You're a good man to know." The rest of the crew hustled to turn the water off and Macy clasped her hands together as she imagined how people would talk about her open house for... Who knows how long this impression would last but it would.

"You coming to talk to me?" McKesson drawled.

"Monica Grey tells me I have my first interview for the administrator position at one." He lifted his arm and studied his bare wrist. "I expect that's about now."

Glad she'd done enough role-playing that the detour didn't knock her completely off guard, Macy nodded. "Chief, I'm going to need you to give me that job." She pointed inside the firehouse. "Show me your office."

McKesson blinked slowly before turning. "Follow me."

That was a good sign. She'd butted heads with so many rangers. How nice would it be to work for a boss that didn't need extensive training before she got to work. If Phil McKesson was prepared to listen to her right off the bat, they could go far and fast.

His office was cluttered enough that she felt right at home. A little trash pickup, some filing and a stern recycling policy would whip the place into shape.

"How do we do this, Gentry?" The chief's voice was gruff, but if she wasn't mistaken there was a slight sparkle in his blue eyes. "I already know you. If you want a job here, I'll make one for you. I'd trust you to drive the fire truck if you wanted to."

Macy snorted. "You don't mean that, Chief. Wouldn't be safe." She wagged her finger. "And that's what we're going to do together, standardize safety procedures, meet and exceed requirements to improve the firehouse's rating to keep pace with the lodge expansion, and generally have this place running like the fine machine it is." Macy leaned back in her chair, satisfied with her opening argument.

McKesson sighed. "I can't argue with that, but I've got one concern."

"What?" Macy asked as she scooted to perch on the

edge of her seat. Was there something she hadn't antici-
pated?

"I like Ash Kingfisher. Losing you will not make him
happy, and no one will be able to run that visitor center
the way you do or handle Ash as well. I don't want to
make an enemy of the head ranger." He made a steeple
with his fingers and tapped his lips. "I also don't want
Monica Grey mad at me. Not quite sure how to thread
this needle."

Relieved, Macy smiled. "Ash signed transfer paperwork. Monica gave me a choice, so if you don't want me
here…" Macy wrinkled her nose. "Well, we both know
that's not going to happen."

The low rumble of his laugh was nice. It didn't shake
up her insides how Ash's rare laugh did, but she could
imagine fitting in well with Phil McKesson's setup.
"Gotta warn you. My relationship with Ash is about to
change."

"Oh?"

"Not sure to what, but we're either going to fall in
love or…" Macy shrugged a shoulder. "Why even open
the door to another option. He's going to love me." She
blinked innocently at him. "I've decided."

McKesson cleared his throat. "I imagine you're right.
Kingfisher's always struck me as a smart man."

Macy nodded. "I'll report tomorrow. Eight o'clock."
She waved vaguely around the office. "You have trash
bags, right?"

When his lips shifted into a flat line, Macy knew it
was time to go. He'd thank her for it later. "Much obliged,
Chief. I'm looking forward to being here."

"I'll get plenty of rest tonight, so I can keep up."

When she marched back to her car, Macy felt as if ten

pounds had slid right off her shoulders. This was going to work. Next up: the ranger station and bringing Ash Kingfisher to his senses.

## CHAPTER FOURTEEN

WHEN ASH HUNG up the phone after Leland Hall told him to clean out his desk that afternoon and his cabin on the Reserve by the end of the next week, he knew he should feel worse about losing the job he'd loved for a decade.

Maybe because it was only the latest development, not the final word, but he was less upset than he'd expected. Before the chief ranger's call, he'd talked to his sister. She'd been so excited he'd had to ask her to repeat herself twice, and he still wasn't sure what she meant when she said she had a "secret weapon" in the battle with the Callaways to win over the board of directors. She was smart. She was happy. He was content to leave it in her hands.

The Callaways had called a meeting in Nashville on Friday. The board of directors wanted Ash there. He'd have maps to distribute and the bullet points of his suggestion for the new site of the lodge on the Reserve.

The view from The Aerie would have been spectacular. He hoped his new location could wow.

"Nicole, have we got any empty boxes?" Ash called through the open doorway. Her footsteps were immediate and fast, and she appeared holding a cardboard box.

"Like this, Ranger?" She held it out like a sacrifice.

"That's perfect." Ash did his best to gently take it from her, but neither of them had a handle on it and the box tumbled to the floor. Ash forced himself to stop and let her scurry to pick it up. "The chair is fine, Nicole. You can put it right there. Thank you."

She was smiling and nodding as she left, so Ash did the same. "All right. My last day and we're really starting to gel here."

He made a slow circle between the desk and the table behind it, ready to grab all his personal items and put them in the box. Most of the souvenirs he'd picked up were about Smoky Valley Nature Reserve. Programs they'd planned. Trophies presented to the Reserve for participation in restoration projects. He pulled some photos down off the ragged bulletin board. He'd show them to Sam and they could reminisce about old times. The fish mug Macy had given him on the first birthday he'd celebrated at the ranger station went in the box and he picked up his phone to text her.

Then he realized he wasn't sure what his reception would be.

Transferring her without her okay had been a dumb move. A man should apologize for that level of stupidity in person. He turned the phone over and over in his hand before shoving it in his pocket.

The rumble in his stomach reminded him that it was lunchtime.

For the first time in so long, he didn't want to sit there at his desk. Frozen dinners for lunch were terrible, and there was no reason to sacrifice his time today. It would be his last. Whatever didn't get done would still be there when…

Ash didn't want to picture another ranger behind the desk, being slowly buried under paperwork. That was how he'd imagined he'd die, a fateful flow of recycling and monthly reports meeting on his desk, covering his head, suffocating him.

Without Macy to drag him out, it would no doubt be fatal.

"Nicole, I'm going to head down to the diner for lunch." He stuck his head out of his office to check on her. "You okay for an hour with the phones?"

She had the phone to one ear as she stared up at the map of the Reserve. On his way past, she held up her thumb and returned to giving directions over the phone. Her laugh was smooth. She still sounded more like a junior high kid than a veteran of the Reserve, but she was good with directions over the phone and her answer about a good trail for kids was spot-on. She held up a binder and turned the page and Ash realized Macy had done everything she could to make sure whoever sat behind the desk of the visitor center could represent the Reserve professionally. She'd set Nicole up for success without ever knowing this day was coming.

That was who she was. Organized. Prepared. The kind of person who made everyone around her look better, feel better.

Add to that Macy's outlook on every day, her inability to back down, the mischief in her eyes and the excitement she sparked whenever she stepped into a room, and Ash was filled with regret.

Going on without her, even if he managed to salvage his position, would hurt.

He'd sent her in to make Leland Hall look good.

Dumb, dumb move.

The rumble in his stomach churned again, and Ash realized there was little he could do to go back. He'd finish this day and then...

He paused by the SUV the Reserve had provided. He hadn't owned a personal car in years.

Ash shook his head and slid into the driver's seat.

"This isn't the end, Kingfisher. Not yet. Don't run out and sign up for car payments until you reach the final decision." Ash started the engine and backed out of the spot. "Since there's nothing else you can do about the job, get the rest of your life in order. Move the mountain one rock at a time."

He studied the parking lots as he drove to the campground. They didn't have a lot of traffic like they had in the spring, but the numbers looked good for a sunny December day. Had his speech to the boys in the barbershop changed some minds?

Or Sam Blackburn had flashed a smile or two and used his charm on the ladies in town.

Either way, the Reserve marina had some traffic and the parking lot of the diner showed business was steady, not crazy busy, but holding. That was good. The upturn in numbers in revenue could be evidence for the board of directors that Sweetwater believed Ash.

Would that be enough to sway any of them to vote to keep him instead of pleasing members of one of the wealthiest families in the state?

"Can't hurt." Ash pulled into a spot near the door of the diner. "Three good things, Kingfisher. Let's keep the positivity flowing." He relaxed in his seat. "No frozen lasagna for lunch. Whatever the special is will beat that microwave meal to bits." He reached over to grab the ranger hat on the seat beside him and then smiled. "If this is really it, no more hats." He wished he could text Macy. She might be the only person he knew who'd get the humor. Then he realized that he'd done the one thing he had to do to feel perfectly ready to find out if Macy wanted to try something more than friendship. She'd owe him nothing now.

"If I can get around her irritation and rage, I can talk

her into a date." Ash wasn't sure that counted as a third good thing, but the way his spirit responded to the open door suggested it was.

"Get some lunch. Hunger is making you stupid." Ash slid out of the SUV, determined to act like he knew what he was doing.

Then he opened the door to the diner and stepped inside, and every head swiveled his direction while conversation died. Ash paused in front of the cash register, ready to pretend he'd come in to order something to go. He'd pick the quickest thing, something like coffee, and beat a hasty retreat.

"Kingfisher, I saved yer spot." Woody Butler called from the line of seats at the counter. "They's serving meat loaf sandwiches today. If you won't tell my wife I *do* like meat loaf, just not hers, I'll ask Chrissy to make you up a plate."

Since no one in the diner had looked away, Ash had no real options. He dipped his head and then said, "Good call, Woody. It's been years since I had a good meat loaf sandwich." He did his best to walk slowly over to the stool, meeting stares as he went. When Janet Abernathy and Regina Blackburn waved hands from a booth in the back corner, Ash relaxed a bit. He had friends in the room. No matter what happened, he could enjoy his lunch still.

"What'll you have to drink, Ranger?" Christina asked from behind the counter. "Tea?"

Ash nodded. "Please."

Christina slid a glass in front of him. "Monroe'll have your sandwich right up." Then she leaned against the counter and watched him.

Ash darted a glance up at her and then over at Woody. With both of them staring, it was impossible to pretend he wasn't the subject of everyone's curiosity. "Looks like the head ranger position will be open for a bit." He sipped his tea. "The chief ranger tells me today's my last day." Ash cleared his throat and then said a little more loudly. "But we'll go before the board of directors to make the final decision. They owe me that much."

Woody clapped a hand on his back. "Sure thing they do, them Callaways."

Christina delivered his lunch plate to him, the smell of the warm meat loaf reminding him he was starving, no matter how many people were cataloging the details of his visit.

"Mayo?" Christina asked and then slid some packets toward him.

Ash slathered the bread, took a bite and washed it all down with half a glass of tea.

And he felt better.

"As far as I know, Brett's okay." He met Christina's stare. "Leland didn't mention him, so I'm hoping that he won't be foolish enough to try to get rid of an experienced officer with a spotless record."

Christina shrugged. "Other than you, you mean." Her eyes were serious as she watched him. "You know no matter what happens, Brett would stand with you. No sense in worrying yourself over it."

"Macy would have, too," Janet said from his right side. Ash didn't sigh loudly but he wanted to. He'd managed five minutes without worrying over Macy's transfer.

"Now, now, Ash, I didn't come to lecture." She smiled brightly. "I came to remind you of your promise to have your daddy at the open house." She clapped a hand on his shoulder. "You haven't forgotten, have you? I'm going to have a little flyer of my own to hand out there for my art show. Macy dropped one of them baskets by this morning, and I want him. In my show. You hear me?"

"Yes, ma'am." Ash's meek tone surprised him, but Janet accepted it as her due.

She turned to address the room. "Those Kingfishers. If you've been in this town long enough, you know that's a family with roots deep in Sweetwater. I'm not sure how I feel about the Reserve going on without a Kingfisher in charge of Otter Lake." Janet tapped a hot pink nail against her cheek. "What do y'all think of that?"

Ash finished his sandwich and then drank another half a glass of tea that had been mysteriously refilled.

"Them Callaways," Woody muttered, and it was enough of an answer that several people in the room nodded along with him, their frowns an indication that they also disapproved.

"I hope you'll come out to the open house on Saturday." Ash faced the crowd, aware that he had to say something. Letting everyone else do the heavy lifting to sway the town of Sweetwater was not his method of doing things. "Macy Gentry has planned a full display of information about the winter programs at the Reserve. There will be something fun for all ages and anyone who wants to follow a ranger out to check on the otter habitat will get the chance." Ash propped his hands on his hips. "I'm looking forward to enjoying the evening as a spectator myself. I might even get to see the otters instead of signing reports about them."

He'd thought it was a pretty good line. The fact that it got no response was a downer.

Then he realized everyone was looking over his shoulder, so he turned, half-expecting to see either Leland Hall or Whit Callaway behind him.

Macy was paused at the end of the counter, her arms

tangled in a tight knot over her chest and her narrow glare locked on him.

If Ash had ever wondered whether Macy got madder than he'd seen her at the ranger station, he had his answer.

"Um, hi." The long whistle behind him confirmed Ash's immediate certainty that he had no idea what to say and nothing that came out would be right.

"Glad you're looking forward to the open house that I nagged for weeks to get you to approve." She took a step closer. "If only there was some way you could communicate that to me, a sort of device that has buttons on it. You could push one and it would connect to mine and one of us could speak into it while the other listened. Hmm... what would you call that? Never mind. You wouldn't use it. You didn't use it to tell me you were firing me."

Ash opened his mouth to protest and to suggest they step outside to hash this out.

Then he remembered Janet saying Sweetwater didn't know him. They hadn't heard much from him since the accident and why should they? He hadn't done much except keep his head down and work.

Now he was caught in a spectacle that would spread like fire on dry ground cover.

And Macy deserved to say everything bubbling up. He wanted to clear the air. Here was his chance.

"I wouldn't even know that you had been fired if I hadn't stopped in to the ranger station to tell you exactly what I thought of this high-handed—" she motioned wildly "—firing of me!" She clapped both hands to her chest. "Can you even imagine?"

Ash grimaced, determined to stay quiet.

She was on a roll, a beautiful, strong, beautiful, fiery roll.

"Well, guess what, Ash?" She marched a step closer

and squared off with him. "I don't work for you anymore." She tipped her head up. "That weasel in Knoxville? I don't work for him, either."

Ash would die before he grinned at her in that second mainly because her wrath would make death the better option, but he was relieved. She could do wonders in the district office, but he wanted her closer.

"Phil McKesson. He's agreed to give me a job." She stared hard into his eyes. "I work for the fire chief now, Head Ranger. You aren't my boss anymore."

The urge to wrap his arms around her and...

What was he going to do? Celebrate. He could congratulate her. She'd made a good decision.

When she blinked slowly, he understood that he was running out of time.

Her voice was softer when she said, "I know you did it to help me, Ash, and I appreciate it. I never once thought you were anything other than a hero, even when I wanted to kill you with my mind." She was fighting a smile. That was a good thing, wasn't it? "I don't work for you anymore," she repeated.

His smile was impossible to stop, and he said, "That means, when I offer you my hand, you're going to hold it. Oh, wait, you did that already." Her lips curved before she returned to a narrow glare. "I can ask you out to dinner and no one's gonna suggest I'm a bad guy, abusing my power." He ran his hand down the silky smooth skin of her forearm. "We can drink rosehip tea and dance in my parents' kitchen even when the world is not falling apart."

Macy seemed to remember that they had an audience as she glanced over her shoulder.

Ash admired her gumption so much in that instant. Neither one of them played to crowds, but she'd transformed a bad thing, something that could have hurt them both if she'd let it, into another brick in the foundation he needed in Sweetwater.

"Fine. You don't need me for anything. We both knew that all along, Macy Gentry." Ash shrugged. "Where does that leave us?"

Macy held both hands up. "That leaves us right here." She put her hand on his chest, the warmth a sweet reminder of their dark drive down the mountain to his parents' house. "You can either kiss me right here, Ash Kingfisher, or you can get out of my face."

Ash tipped his head back to study the ceiling, the laughter caught in his chest happy and crazy and so weird and new and awesome that he wanted to remember it always.

Then he slipped his hand over her cheek to cup her nape, determined that this first kiss would satisfy both Macy and their audience. When he bent closer, the sparkle in her eyes captured him and everyone else fell away. He brushed his lips to hers, caught her sigh and then repeated the motion until she rested lightly against his chest.

He would have stayed right here, Macy in his arms, her lips pressed against his, while magnolias floated around them except...

Woody Butler cleared his throat. "Reckon they're dating?"

The silence of the diner was broken when Christina Braswell muttered, "Oh, Woody, you've got the romantic sensitivity of a groundhog."

Chuckles spread throughout the diner and eventually Macy eased back from him.

"I'm going to miss seeing you at the visitor center," Ash said while he clasped her hand in his, "but I sure am glad we can do that now."

"We could have done it before and easier," Macy said, "but this is going to work out fine. Everybody, make sure you tell someone else by the end of the day. Ash Kingfisher is goofy in love. Macy Gentry said the chief ranger is a weasel. And the ranger station open house is the place to be this Saturday." Macy nodded and then turned to Ash. "Now what?"

He brought their entwined hands to his lips and kissed. "Want to help me clean out my desk? Then let's go climb The Aerie. I've got some free time. Maybe we could find a camera. I need some shots of the road to the old weather station."

Macy frowned as she considered that. "I know someone with a fancy camera." Then she shrugged. "She hasn't taken a class to learn to use it yet, but how hard could it be? Let's get climbing."

Before he could ask what that was about, Christina was waving his bill. "On the house, lovebirds. Hit the trail already." Her grin was contagious.

Once they were outside, he was reminded of his depleted prospects thanks to the Reserve's SUV. "A man with no job, no place to live, no car to drive…" Somehow he'd become a worse bet than he'd been as her boss.

Macy squeezed his hand. "Forget that. Today, we're climbing. Tomorrow, we'll get back to saving the Reserve."

Ash studied her face. "Quite a change of heart from Gran's 'all work and no play' philosophy."

Macy nodded. "Yeah. And it's working out for me."

Ash knew he was grinning because it felt weird, and yet, right. "It's working for me, too."

Macy marched around to the passenger side and he wrestled the handle out of her hand to swing the door open. Her bemused smile was nice. Ash had a feeling that everything was going to work out. No matter what happened with his job or the lodge or Winter's engagement, finding three good things would never be difficult with Macy in his arms.

## CHAPTER FIFTEEN

IF ANYONE HAD told him making a presentation in front of his sister, the Callaway family and the Reserve's board of directors would mean the difference in having a job and hitting the unemployment line, Ash might have considered taking his chances with the latter.

"Last time I saw you look like that, you were getting ready to hold a press conference." Winter poked him in the chest with his hat. "Are you going to put this on?"

Remembering the immediate shot of confidence it had given him at the press conference, Ash settled the hat on his head. "Are you sure you can't handle the presentation?"

"I handled getting us the invitation. I did the hard part. You bring home the win," Winter said through a fake smile. "If you knew what I had to promise to get Caleb Callaway to show…"

"Ranger Kingfisher, I understand you'd like the opportunity to state your case." Whitney Callaway, Senior, the head of the Callaway family, sat at the end of the table. The business-class hotel's furnishings were drab, but his expensive suit shone in the setting. That was a suit meant for high-rises and mahogany desks. Ash was glad for the uniform. "Is this going to be an admission of guilt, or what?"

"I haven't come to plead my innocence, sir." Ash cleared his throat, aware of the catch that was going to become a crack in his voice. "I have a new lodge proposal I'd like to show you."

Whit Callaway, Junior, sighed. "Because of your extensive engineering, construction and park planning experience, I guess." His suit was almost as nice as his father's. That made the contrast to Caleb Callaway's plaid button-down stark.

If Caleb Callaway was Winter's secret weapon, why did he appear to be bored beyond belief?

"The number one objection to the lodge is the location. The Aerie is precious habitat for several bird species, including the bald eagle." Ash clicked the little remote in his hand, watched the photos speed by and cursed under his breath as he slowly went backward. "Construction here would not only destroy those ecosystems but even more land would be cleared to build the necessary roads. I don't have to tell you the extent of the impact such a difficult build would cause." *Because it was all in the report that made you mad enough to fire me.*

*Move on, Ash.*

"Sweetwater is in favor of a lodge on Otter Lake." Ash advanced the slideshow to the picture he and Macy had taken when they'd climbed The Aerie. "What if, instead of a lodge built looking down on the valley, the Reserve had a lodge with the most perfect view of the peak, as well as access to Otter Lake from the land surrounding the old weather station? A fire cleared acres there earlier this year. The road is already partially built, and the land is nearly flat, one of the few places in the Reserve where we can say that." Ash pointed at the wide, open area showing minimal recovery from the fire. "It's almost like this place was built for a resort with five-star views." Ash carefully set the remote down. "I don't have the skill to draw that place or to build it, but I can certainly imagine a lodge there."

Ash stopped speaking, but his brain quickly sifted through all the bits and pieces to make sure he'd covered everything he needed to say.

"Why would we take the advice of a man who has aided the governor, a man who has shown no concern for Tennessee lands before, not until I started beating him in the polls," Whit Callaway snapped. "This change of plans will lead to a delay. We needed to get the project moving yesterday."

"You've already got a delay. This moves us forward." Winter's impatience was obvious.

Caleb Callaway stretched in his seat. "It's not often the universe hands you a neat solution to all your problems, is it, Kingfisher?" Ash shook his head but Caleb Callaway was watching Winter. What had she promised him?

Whitney Callaway drummed his fingers on the table. "Wish you'd come to us with this in the beginning, Kingfisher. You played dirty first. How are we supposed to let that go?"

Ash wanted to argue, but what good would it do? He'd already said he wasn't the source.

"Listen," Caleb said, "does anyone want to waste their time arguing that this isn't a good solution and better location than the original one?" He blinked slowly at his brother and then stared at each person seated around the table. "Let me hear it if you like the idea of tearing up The Aerie."

Missy Andrews, owner of a small chain of grocery stores in East Tennessee, said, "Wouldn't it be worth it to do another environmental impact study and have an architect review the new site?"

Whit crossed his arms over his chest. "Fine. We're

still getting rid of the Kingfishers." He held up his hand. "All in favor?"

When no one joined him, Ash wanted to inhale and exhale loudly in relief.

Caleb turned to catch Winter's stare. Ash thought she was yelling at him silently, but he couldn't decipher the words. "One more thing before we vote on Ash Kingfisher's proposal and employment." Caleb drawled the last word. "I was the one who involved Richard Duncan. Sent him the environmental impact study because I knew he'd in turn stir up enough fuss to slow the project down. That much media coverage for his campaign? How could he not?" He shrugged as if he was saying, "Now what?"

Whit leaned back in his chair and propped one hand on the arm. "Underhanded. Want to tell me why? You haven't shown interest in the Reserve in years. How did you even know about the report in the first place?"

"I hate board meetings. That doesn't mean I don't care about the Reserve. The rush to get this built made no sense. Fitting the election timeline? Dumb idea. My company, Summit Builders, works projects like this, too. I have friends who do these environmental impact studies all the time. It's not a big crowd. Once I got a look at it, I knew I had to do something." Caleb studied his brother and then glanced at Winter. "It was the right thing to do. That used to be a Callaway point of pride."

Whit Callaway, Senior, waited for anyone else to add something and then grunted. "Whit concentrates on the election. Caleb gets involved in the business and I get my lodge, a moneymaker of an idea." He paused to think. "And there ain't no way around it, Ash Kingfisher keeps his job as head of the Otter Lake Ranger Station."

No one shouted in celebration, but Ash could hear the party in his head.

He realized no one had said anything about Winter. She glared at him, which he took as a warning not to push his luck then and there to make sure her job was safe.

"Guess that's settled. Kingfishers win the day," Caleb Callaway drawled.

"I'M GOING TO need you in that costume in the next five minutes, Rodriguez," Macy said as she checked off one of the last remaining items on her to-do list. "If anyone actually does show up, they'll be arriving soon and I do not want to have to explain why there are no otters in this first-rate model of Otter Lake."

"But the head is so heavy and so big," Rodriguez whined. "It's going to mess up my hair." He ran a hand over his closely cropped curls. Macy had learned his hair and the buzz cuts several of Phil McKesson's crew preferred were more about safety than fashion. Fighting fire was no place for flowing locks.

"I'm thinking the otter isn't the only thing with a big head." Macy raised both eyebrows at Rodriguez to make sure he caught her drift. "Seems I remember you campaigning for this job, something about how your girlfriend would never forget it."

"That was before I put the head on." Rodriguez held it up. "Thing must weigh twenty pounds." Macy could hear her time slipping away, so she spun around, cupped one hand to her mouth and shouted, "Cho! Ronald James Cho. Report to the photo background." She craned her neck until Cho split through the crowd of rangers gathered around to see how his waterfall worked.

"You shouted." He propped his hands on his hips, the twitch of his lips the only sign that he was ready to laugh at her.

Macy waved her clipboard. "I don't have time to wrangle this man into his otter costume. You do it." Over his shoulder she could see the trays of cookies Christina was carrying. Was she going to put them out now? It was too early, much better to wait until the crowd arrived.

As she walked away, Macy shouted over her shoulder, "Next year, we're going to need you to engineer a lighter head for Rodriguez, Cho." She barely hesitated as she realized how that sounded and then decided she'd fix that after she straightened out the food and drinks.

As soon as she stopped in front of the table, Christina said, "No notes. I don't want any notes on how we're doing this. It's hot chocolate and cookies, Macy." The hard expression in her eyes convinced Macy to move on. "You and I are destined to be friends. Don't ruin it by starting a fight over snacks, you hear?"

Brett Hendrix waved a walkie-talkie at her and motioned her over to the fire engine. "We had three groups leave from the Yanu trailhead thirty minutes ago. I expect them to be back in the parking area in the next half hour or so."

"And then they'll come here." Macy nodded firmly.

"Or else," Brett muttered grimly.

Macy blinked. "Are you making fun of me?"

He immediately shook his head. "No. No way. I'm too scared of your ruthless leadership to make fun of you." He held up both hands. "These three days of working with the firefighters have made you mean."

She started waving her clipboard at him.

"I'm joking." Brett muttered, "A little."

Macy nodded and checked off food and drinks on her to-do list. There was only one item left. "Where are the Kingfishers?"

Brett hesitated and then said, "They'll be here."

Macy hoped so. What would she do if this open house,

the one she'd wanted to be a boost to the ranger station and a kind of gift for Ash, failed? If Sweetwater picked up the boycott for some reason, she'd never get a shot at doing this again.

"I've come to defend you." Christina slid under Brett's arm. "Is she trying to organize you?"

Macy lowered her clipboard and studied the rosy sky. The firefighters were arranging two campfires in the fire pits near the overlook. From here, she could see Phil McKesson standing behind the s'mores table. His arms were crossed, but he was surveying the ranger station, ready to hand out skewers and marshmallows as needed.

The law enforcement rangers were pacing slowly next to the Reserve SUV parked on the other side of the lot, the lights along the top lit but not flashing yet.

The campground diner's table was ready. The guys from the marina had set up a fishing game where kids could catch plastic fish and exchange them for candy.

Every area of the Reserve had shown up for her; what if Sweetwater didn't?

"Should I be able to hear my heart pounding in my ears?" Macy asked herself as she stepped away from Brett and Christina.

She'd be stronger if Ash were here. She'd have to pretend that poor attendance was nothing but a bump in the road for his sake. Without him, would she be able to pull on armor and pretend that everything was fine?

It was fine. Win or lose at the open house, she had a great new job. Ash and Winter had no doubt conquered the board of directors, but she hadn't heard from either yet. Two days he'd been gone. That was one day more than she was comfortable with. In the end, where Ash worked was less important than how soon she could kiss him hello. The success of this event wouldn't stop the sunrise or sunset or anything about the big picture.

"Three good things." Macy concentrated on the crowd around her. "I have friends I didn't know I had." Brett and Christina, the fire crew, Chief McKesson... They'd all shown up when she'd asked. "Desserts. We've got cookies, s'mores and hot chocolate. The world is pretty all right."

Then she realized the third good thing.

Her last-minute flash of brilliance was arranged close to the sidewalk in front of the ranger station.

"Hold this. Don't lose it." Macy smacked her clipboard on Brett's chest and headed over to make sure Leanne Hendrix was okay. The way she fidgeted in her chair worried Macy. Would she bail before the party even got started?

"Are you all ready to paint some faces?" Macy asked in the perkiest voice she could imagine.

Leanne straightened all her paints and cleared her throat. "Last chance, Macy. You should rethink this. No parent in Sweetwater is going to want the town's original wild child painting their kids' faces." She glanced nervously over her shoulder to where her children, Parker and Riley, were charming the fire chief into the night's first s'mores. "Face painting is easy. You could do it. *Anyone* could do it."

Stung at Leanne equating her talent with just any person's, Macy paused.

"I could have done every single thing in this open house myself, Leanne. I could. But that doesn't mean I can do it the best or that I could do it all at the same time." Macy plopped down in the folding chair opposite her. "I get it. You aren't sure *you* can do it." Reverse psychology worked nine times out of ten on Macy. Her grandmother had perfected it. Was Leanne susceptible? "Make me your first living canvas." So she was going to spend the rest of the night with a butterfly painted across her face. It was fine. It matched all the butterflies in her stomach.

"He'll be here." Leanne shook her head as she evaluated her brushes. "Whoever you're looking for, he'll be here."

Macy tipped her chin up. "I don't know what you're talking about. I have to make sure everything's in place and—"

Leanne closed Macy's mouth by tilting her head back with one hand under her chin.

The tickle of the brush was so quick that Macy only managed two thoughts.

What kind of animal was Leanne painting?

Did face painters only do butterflies?

That had been her plan because she wasn't sure she could manage much else.

It didn't matter. Leanne smiled as she worked, so some of the jitters must have faded away in the short time she was painting. Riley Hendrix appeared and studied Leanne's work. "Dope, Mom."

Macy noted Leanne's amused expression. "Kids don't really say that anymore, do they?" Leanne asked.

"Have a dope marshmallow, Mom," Parker yelled as he raced across the parking lot. "Chief wouldn't let me keep the sharp stick, but he gave me a spare graham cracker." Parker spun in a circle and then shouted, "Paint me like a snake. I want to be a snake!" He bent down to hover next to Leanne as if he'd wait right there until she was done as the first car in a short line of traffic pulled into the parking lot.

"Looks like you're going to have a party after all." Leanne smiled at Macy. "And you were nervous."

Caught off guard by her own laugh, Macy clapped both hands to her chest. "Nervous? Me? No."

"Uh-huh." Leanne motioned with her head. "Out of my chair. My next customer is ready."

Macy was ready to march over to meet the family of four that had climbed out of the first SUV, but a man-size otter with an enormous head skipped over to intercept them and guide them to the fire engine.

"I should have warned him not to steer every visitor toward the fire team's displays." The law enforcement rangers would be peeved; since they had handcuffs, it wouldn't do to annoy them. Things could get out of hand. Macy shook her head as she watched the second family arrive and head over to the hot chocolate table. Christina was pointing here and there at all the activities and Brett stepped up with a sweeping motion toward the ranger station.

That was the point of the whole event, to show off the new educational panels Ash had imagined, commissioned and managed the installation of.

"And he's not even here to see it." Macy pulled her phone out of her pocket, glad she'd insisted on auxiliary lighting for the parking lot. The sun was setting, the better to show off the bonfire and to encourage people to step inside the ranger station, but the temperature was also dropping. This party needed to get rolling and soon.

"Checking to see how soon you can leave your own party?" Ash asked from behind her.

More relieved than she wanted him to know, Macy turned slowly. "You were pushing it, Kingfisher. I have most of the Reserve's resources at my fingertips, including fire engines and cop cars with sirens and flashing lights." Macy stepped close enough to feel the heat of his skin. "I missed you."

He cupped her cheek. "Not nearly as much as I missed you." He glanced left and right to check the crowd. "I want to kiss you."

Macy tipped up to press her lips to his and smiled at his laugh. "I don't have the patience to wait tonight."

"Yeah, you never have been good at waiting." Ash ran his thumb over her cheek. "I like it."

Macy frowned. "You were going to be here to help me set up." She wished she had her clipboard. She could show him all the fun he'd missed out on.

"I had a couple of unexpected stops to make." Ash pointed over to the ranger station. His mother and father were talking with Janet Abernathy. "My dad insisted we bring some baskets."

Macy laughed. "He and Janet are already negotiating the art show, then."

Ash pursed his lips. "If by 'negotiating' you mean my father asking how many Janet wants and my mother trying to double the number, yes."

Macy patted herself on the shoulder. "I'm a genius. You make sure both your parents know that I arranged that meeting."

Ash studied her face. "Oh, they know, but why does it matter that you get the credit?"

"I'm hoping to be invited back to dinner." Macy's smile grew into a huge grin as Ash reached down to tangle their fingers together. "Think you could make that happen?"

"Probably, as long as you're prepared to drink my portion of rosehip tea as well as your own."

"Did you learn to negotiate from your mother or your father?" Macy wasn't sure she was getting the better end of the bargain or not. Twice the health but also twice the tea.

Ash laughed, the low, rough sound a caress that started a warm glow in Macy's chest.

Then she frowned. "You're a civilian, right? What's with the uniform?"

Then she realized what that meant. "You got your job back?" Ash clamped a hand over her mouth and she realized how loudly she'd said it.

"Winter found us an unexpected ace in the hole. Caleb Callaway admitted he was the one who leaked the report, not me," Ash said as he wrapped his arm around Macy's waist. "Looks like I'll be back running the Otter Lake Ranger Station. Do you think that will be good news or bad news to Sweetwater?"

Macy studied the milling crowd that had grown while she and Ash talked. Cars were lining the road now, and every booth and table had a small crowd. It was all working out exactly as she wanted.

Then she realized Ash was watching her. "What?"

"I asked if my being reinstated would be well received by Sweetwater."

Before she could answer him, Woody Butler clapped him hard on the shoulder. "Ash Kingfisher, good to see you here. Need me some cookies." Then he was moving on through the crowd, making a straight line for the campground diner's table.

Macy stared up at Ash. "Seems like good news."

"Are you going to come back and manage the visitor center?" Ash asked. "I only hire the best."

This close to him, it was difficult to imagine working anywhere better than beside Ash. Then she remembered how many fights they'd manage to have in an eight-hour day before they switched gears to...whatever they might become.

Between that image and the list of things she'd get to

tackle with the firefighters, it was easy enough to say, "No, I have a good job. I will work with Nicole, though. You'll see how awesome she is with visitors." Convincing her not to jump when Ash grumbled would only take a bit of time. Macy had needed that herself.

Ash nodded. "Fine. We'll have lunch together in the diner, then. And dinner in town."

"I can scramble eggs. I would be willing to do that for you." Macy touched his chest, hoping he was getting the message that the domestic arts were not her strong suit.

"I like eggs." Ash shifted closer. "This is a good plan."

"We're out of marshmallows, Gentry. There is a situation at the s'mores table." Phil McKesson shifted his pants higher and motioned over his shoulder as if she might not know where that was. Then he narrowed his eyes. "You aren't trying to hire away my administrator, are you, Head Ranger?" He squared up as if he were either preparing to take bad news on the chin or to throw the first punch.

"Nope. She's happy where she is, Chief. I will be picking her up for lunch, though." Ash glanced at her out of the corner of his eye. "Maybe dropping her off for work, too."

Macy rolled her eyes. "Go inside the break room. I put four more bags of marshmallows in the bottom right cabinet." She shrugged. "I was afraid no one would show." Then she checked her phone again. "Six o'clock. I better make an announcement so we get people inside to see the new panels." A dark car slowed on the road as she tugged Ash closer to the photo booth the firefighters had built. The backdrop would serve as a small stage.

While she waited for the crowd's attention, she searched the crowd for RJ. He held up the box and stepped closer so that he could troubleshoot any problems.

She'd evaluated and discarded several ideas to get the crowd's attention. She'd even asked the guys at the fire-house to hit the siren. When they'd tried it on the run-through, she'd decided splitting headaches were not the takeaway she wanted the people of Sweetwater to leave the ranger station with.

The easiest way to do this? The showstopper.

She pointed at Brett, who hit the power strip providing electricity to the lights closest to the backdrop. The sudden darkness caused people to stop. Then Cho hit the magic button, lights twinkled inside the miniature waterfall and water trickled down to form a pool.

The oohs and aahs were satisfying. This was the magical moment she'd dreamed of for their first open house.

Weeks of hard work paid off right there in that moment, as Ash watched from his space at the back of the crowd, a small smile curving his lips.

"Hello, everyone! Can I please have your attention." Macy held up her arms until the crowd focused on her. "Welcome to the Otter Lake Ranger Station's first open house. I'm hoping this will become a seasonal event because there is always important work happening at the Smoky Valley Nature Reserve. The men and women who serve here are committed to protecting the lands within the boundaries, preserving plant and animal species, and making this a place you'll bring your families to for generations. Some of you already have." Macy had rehearsed what she wanted to say, and she was carefully not meeting anyone's eyes but Ash's. Seeing the crowd would mean awkwardness like her morning speech at Smoky Joe's.

But the couple that had gotten out of the dark sedan threw her off her rhythm. When people in the crowd started to shift restlessly, she cleared her throat. "We want you to enjoy all the activities we've put together, but before you go, please stop in to see the new educational displays developed by Head Ranger Ash Kingfisher. Winter is a busy time here at the Reserve. Step inside to find out what the rangers are doing now."

Before she could wave her hands and shoo people back to…whatever, Winter Kingfisher was cutting through the crowd, Whit Callaway being towed behind.

Apparently, the show was not quite over.

## CHAPTER SIXTEEN

ASH WATCHED HIS sister lead Callaway up next to Macy and wondered how this was all going to play out. When he'd dropped his sister off at their parents' house, she'd been gripping her cell phone so hard he was afraid she'd break her hand. He'd believed the demise of the Kingfisher-Callaway engagement to be imminent.

But here they were.

If Callaway tried to steal the credit for either Macy's hard work or the fire crew's engineering, he'd have a chance to use his fists yet.

Ash maneuvered through the crowd to stand closer. If he needed to get to Macy or Winter fast, he could from that position.

This close, he could read confusion on Whit's face.

Whatever Winter was up to, she was the only one in on the plan. He scanned the crowd. Everyone was intrigued. The people of Sweetwater understood that something interesting was about to happen. He turned back and glimpsed a tall guy in a baseball cap at the back of the crowd. From here, it was hard to be certain, but if it was who he thought it was...

Caleb Callaway had crashed the open house.

Ash couldn't remember a single occasion Caleb attended events on the Reserve. When Ash had demanded answers from Winter about what she and Caleb Callaway had talked about inside his office, the conversation that had convinced him to step up and take responsibility for releasing the environmental impact study to the governor, she'd given him a deadpan expression and changed the subject. Whatever was between her and Caleb, neither one was acting like Ash expected.

"Sweetwater, before you head back out to the party," Winter said as she smiled warmly at the crowd, "I'd like to take care of some business. You might be wondering who will be leading the discussion of the panels inside." She pointed at Ash. "Head Ranger Ash Kingfisher will be in charge tonight and moving forward. The Callaways have reinstated Ash." Winter sighed happily at the murmurs that swept the crowd. "Yes, Sweetwater will continue to have a direct line to the leadership of the Smoky Valley Nature Reserve, someone who's grown up here. You will be able to count on Ash Kingfisher to stand up for Otter Lake and the people who love it."

She patted Whit on the back and said, "And you'll all be happy to know that the lodge project will be moving forward. Thanks to Ash Kingfisher, the board of directors has approved an investigation into a new building site, one near the old weather station. The Callaways are committed to doing this the right way, with a complete environmental impact study first." She nodded at the applause that swept through the crowd. Whit visibly relaxed. He must have been as surprised to hear the positive reaction for the Callaway family as Ash was. Did that mean the engagement was saved? "A project of this stature will have a long timeline, but by the end of next week, you should be able to contact Monica Grey who will be acting as the public outreach officer until a new one can be hired."

"There's no need to quit, Winter," Whit said as he turned to step between her and the crowd. "I want you by my side as I campaign, but you are too good at your job to leave. I get that." He wrapped his hands around her arms. "Everything can be like it was."

Ash was half a second from jumping up next to his sister when Winter gently urged Whit back to her side. She kept his hand in hers and Ash had no idea where she was going with this. When his parents stepped up beside him, he turned to ask his father with a glance what he should do. His dad shrugged. "She's in control. Better let her lead, son."

He would, but he'd be ready to defend his little sister as soon as she gave him the go-ahead.

"Macy, do you see my parents?" Winter asked and then nodded as Macy pointed them out. "Right. Mom." Winter waited until their mother waved her hand to acknowledge she was listening. "I don't know if a miniature model of Yanu counts, but I promised I would take Whit up Yanu, you remember?"

"Yes," his mother drawled, as confused as the rest of them. "I'll allow that it counts as a hike to the top." Then she crossed her arms over her chest. "Are you going to kiss him?"

Realization dawned as Whit turned to Winter, a confused frown on his face.

Winter promptly gave Whit a hard shove into the pool of water. "No, Mom, I decided to push him off." The gasps of the crowd died as Whit struggled to sit up soaking wet.

"You know, I think that pool recirculates right to the top," his father said slowly, the tone of wonder amusing Ash. He wanted Macy next to him badly in that minute. This was a story they would tell their kids. Once again, he was so proud of his sister.

"Don't believe it'll wash the skeeves off that one." His

mother's grim tone was too much. Ash's chuckles drew attention. When his father joined in, more than one of their neighbors gave them worried frowns.

"I can't marry a man who'd come after my family. I can't vote for a man who will chase money, and not at the expense of this place that I love. I can't stay on at the Reserve or go through with a wedding, but it'll all work out. One last thing before I go," Winter said as she scanned the crowd. "Is the *Sweetwater Sentinel* here?" She nodded as she pointed at a man with a camera in front of his face. "Good. The governor is going to defeat Whit Callaway in the upcoming gubernatorial election, and I'm going to help. I hope I can count on Sweetwater's votes. And I'd like to introduce the man who made sure Richard Duncan got a copy of the environmental impact study. This man is not Ash Kingfisher." Then she pointed at the guy in the baseball cap who was hauling Whit Callaway out of the recirculating pool.

When Caleb Callaway lifted his cap, the number of excited murmurs that swept through the crowd matched the flare of tension in the crowd. Woody Butler asked, "Who now?"

Ash wanted to chuckle again as he heard the answer whispered, repeated and finally shouted until Woody held up a hand to signal he understood. "Got it. Carry on."

Caleb cleared his throat. "Yeah, I…" He yanked hard on his collar. "Construction at The Aerie would have been a mistake, but the Callaways are going to correct that. Thanks to Ash Kingfisher." He shoved his hands in his pockets. "Thank you."

Then he disappeared into the shadowy parking lot. Ash watched him go, dumbfounded that the lazy, laidback guy from the board meeting could be even worse in front of a crowd than he was. The whole night had turned out to be a revelation.

When Whit Callaway jumped down with a loud splat, several people muttered. Woody was angry when he snapped, "Them Callaways." But Whit had nothing to say as he marched off.

Macy stepped back to the center of the backdrop.

"Well, you came for an exciting update on what is happening here at the Smoky Valley Nature Reserve." She nodded slowly. "You got more than you bargained for." She pursed her lips, her eyes darting here and there in the crowd while she visibly searched for the right thing to say, and Ash couldn't stand it anymore. She was dying up there and all that had to happen was one final "go see the ranger station."

When he was next to her, he said, "To make sure no one leaves here dissatisfied, I'd like to say thank you for coming. I'm happy to be back. Macy Gentry deserves so much credit for putting this together. You can expect more in the future. We're going to get married someday. Tours of the educational panels inside will start in two minutes." Then before Macy could say or do anything else, he pressed his lips to hers. The cheers of their friends, family and neighbors were nice, but nothing mattered more than her understanding that they were in this, whatever it became, together.

When the kiss ended, Ash realized that as long as they were front and center on the miniature Yanu Falls and in each other's arms, most of Sweetwater was prepared to stand around and watch them.

"Follow me." Ash helped Macy down and led her to the overlook. It wasn't the highest trail or the prettiest view or even the easiest climb, but it was quiet.

"Was I hallucinating?" Macy asked, panting a little

as she hurried to keep up. "Did you say we're going to get married?"

"My parents did when they met on Yanu. It's a lucky spot." Ash held her hands and they came to a stop.

In the faint light of the parking lot below, he could see the urge to argue crossing her face. When she didn't, Ash felt as if he'd hit the lottery. She understood their connection as well as he did. They had a chance to go all the way.

"You're supposed to be giving tours in the ranger station," Macy said as she inched closer to him. "Maybe you should kiss me and get to work."

"Good advice." Ash lightly touched her cheek. "I want to name three good things before I go."

"Okay." Macy slipped her hand into his. "I get to hold your hand whenever I want."

Excellent start. Ash immediately felt taller, stronger, better. She had that effect on him.

"Let's see. Number two. You have the tiniest, cutest bear painted on your cheek." Ash smiled at her shock.

"Leanne painted a bear. That's awesome." Macy fidgeted in place. Her very next stop would be a mirror. "The next time we do this, remind me to put a mirror at her table. I wish I had my clipboard."

Her aggravated tone was familiar. Ash usually heard it aimed at him, but it was sweet in this situation.

"Nothing but good luck for us." Ash didn't need a bear as a sign. The change he'd been fearing had been nothing but positive. He wished his *enisi* was around so he could prove messengers just had messages.

"Right." Macy put her arms around him. "And number three?"

Ash peered at the darkening sky. The stars were faint but they were there. Tomorrow he'd be able to get up and come to work in the place he loved. Buckeye Cove and Yanu Falls and all the places he loved were still home.

And Macy would be there, working alongside him to protect their home.

Ash studied her face. Feelings. He was no good at admitting them even when he was having them. "I'm not sure I need three things anymore. I love you, have for longer than I can remember. We needed a little shake-up to get here, but as long as I have you, life is exactly as it should be."

"Ash Kingfisher, you do have a way with words. I love you, too, even when you're wrong and bossy. We butt heads, for sure, but here, standing next to you is where I want to be."

As always, she had to have the last word. Why did he think that was cute? Life with her would be unpredictable, exciting.

Macy's smile was beautiful. Holding her in his arms was the only luck he'd ever need.

\* \* \* \* \*

# COMING SOON!

We really hope you enjoyed reading this book. If you're looking for more romance, be sure to head to the shops when new books are available on

## Thursday 21$^{st}$ February

To see which titles are coming soon, please visit

**millsandboon.co.uk/nextmonth**

MILLS & BOON

# MILLS & BOON

## Coming next month

### CARRYING THE GREEK TYCOON'S BABY
Jennifer Faye

"I'm pregnant."

Xander stumbled back as though Lea's words had physically slugged him in the chest. The back of his knees hit the edge of the bed. He slumped down onto the mattress. Maybe he'd heard her incorrectly.

"Could you say that again?"

"Xander, I'm pregnant. And you're the father."

That's what he thought she'd said.

But this can't be true. Could it?

Xander knew all too well that it was quite possible. They'd spent that not-so-long-ago weekend in bed...and there was the time on the floor...in the living room—

He halted his rambling memories. He didn't normally let loose like that. In fact, he'd never had a weekend like that one. It was unforgettable. And apparently in more than one way.

The silence dragged on. He should say something. Anything. But what? He'd never been in this position before.

He needed time to think because right now all that was going around in his mind was that he was going to be a father. He wondered if this was what shock felt like.

"I...I need a little time to absorb this," he said. "We'll talk soon."

He wasn't even sure if he said goodbye before disconnecting the call. He had no idea how long he laid there staring into space before an incoming text jarred him back to reality.

I'm going to be a father.

The profound words echoed in his mind.

How could this be? Well, of course he knew how it happened. It was a weekend that he would never forget, much as he had tried. Lea's stunning image was imprinted upon his mind.

Still, he never thought he'd hear that he was going to be a father. A father. His heart was racing and his palms were damp.

His mind slipped back to the time he'd spent on Infinity Island. He never thought that it would change his life. But it had. And now he had to figure out a plan. He was known for thinking on his toes, but this was different. This was a baby. His baby.

And he had to do whatever was best for the child.

But what was that?

Continue reading
**CARRYING THE GREEK TYCOON'S BABY**
Jennifer Faye

*Available next month*
www.millsandboon.co.uk

# LET'S TALK
## *Romance*

For exclusive extracts, competitions
and special offers, find us online:

 facebook.com/millsandboon

🐦 @MillsandBoon

📷 @MillsandBoonUK

**Get in touch on 01413 063232**

For all the latest titles coming soon, visit
**millsandboon.co.uk/nextmonth**